Vicious Grace

"A chilling novel. . . . I couldn't put it down."
—*Fantasy Literature*

"Darkly creepy plus brimming with raw emotions. . . . *Vicious Grace* takes urban fantasy to a new level."

—*Single Titles*

Darker Angels

"An urban fantasy packed with intense emotions, cleverly original escapades, and an engaging group of characters."

—*Single Titles*

"Written with such tension that the book nearly vibrates in your hand. I read it in less than twenty-four hours, barely pausing to work, eat, or sleep."
—*Reading the Leaves*

"A fascinating and entertaining thriller."
—*Genre Go Round Reviews*

"A wild tale in a surreal world that is our own, just with elements we never see. . . . A fabulous read."
—*Night Owl Reviews*

"A dark urban fantasy series that could easily become addictive."

—*Pop Syndicate*

Unclean Spirits

"Smooth prose and zippy action sequences."

"Between the novel's energetic pacing, Jayné's undeniable charm, and the intriguing concept behind the riders, *Unclean Spirits* is a solid entry in the urban fantasy genre."

"Pure entertainment. . . . Jayné is strong, sexy, and smart, but she isn't too much of any of these; she is far more real and vulnerable than your average heroine."

"You won't find the same old supernatural capers in *Unclean Spirits*. It builds its own mythology, its own shadowy, intriguing world."

graveyard child

BOOK FIVE OF

THE BLACK SUN'S DAUGHTER

M. L. N. Hanover

POCKET BOOKS

New York London Toronto Sydney New Delhi

Pocket Books
A Division of Simon & Schuster, Inc.
1230 Avenue of the Americas
New York, NY 10020

This book is a work of fiction. Names, characters, places, and incidents either are products of the author's imagination or are used fictitiously. Any resemblance to actual events or locales or persons, living or dead, is entirely coincidental.

First Pocket Books paperback edition May 2013

POCKET and colophon are registered trademarks of Simon & Schuster, Inc.

For information about special discounts for bulk purchases, please contact Simon & Schuster Special Sales at 1-866-506-1949 or business@simonandschuster.com.

The Simon & Schuster Speakers Bureau can bring authors to your live event. For more information or to book an event contact the Simon & Schuster Speakers Bureau at 1-866-248-3049 or visit our website at www.simonspeakers.com.

Manufactured in the United States of America

10   9   8   7   6   5   4   3   2   1

ISBN 978-1-4516-7808-6
ISBN 978-1-4516-7815-4 (ebook)

To Rosemary Woodhouse

graveyard child

prologue

If he had shouted, it would have been better.

"You don't look fat," he said, the words almost uninflected. "You look pregnant."

He stood in the bedroom doorway, leaning against the frame. The beautiful boy she'd met back in Florida was gone, and this ghost was in his place. The dark hair looked dry now. Dusty. The darkness under his eyes seemed permanent. Carla looked down at her belly, sick with shame not only on her own behalf but for what she had done to Jay. If she hadn't given in, they would still be flirting together, going off to Disney for the day with the young singles group or driving to Daytona Beach with her cousins. He was a man. It had been her job to be modest. To make sure things didn't go too far.

She'd failed.

"I just thought . . ." she began, and then the tears started and she choked a little.

"Sweetie, the reason the one with ruffles has all those ruffles? It's in order to make you look like you're just fat. The people who make wedding dresses aren't stupid. They know how to hide what needs to get hidden," he said. He sighed. "And so do I, right?"

She sat on the bed, the springs creaking under her weight. Hers and the baby's.

"I always imagined the day I got married, you know? The dress I'd wear. How pretty I'd look. Kind of stupid, eh?"

It was four thirty, and the winter sun spilled through the window, ruddy and dim. She could feel the cold radiating from the window. It never got this cold in Florida. Jay stayed where he was long enough that she was afraid he'd walk away. When he stepped toward her, she felt relief and dread. Relief because he was going to sit beside her and take her hand. Dread because she saw in the way he held himself that he didn't want to. The bed creaked more, the mattress pressing them closer to each other. He took her hand.

"This isn't what you wanted," he said. "It's not what I wanted either. We're solidly in plan B territory. But it won't be like this forever. I can get back. And you can help me. It's going to be okay."

"I love you, Jaybird," she said.

"You're a beautiful girl, Carla mine," he said. He stroked her cheek and she leaned into his touch. He kissed her just like she knew he would, and for a few seconds they were who they'd been before. Two young Christians deeply in love. He pressed his forehead against her temple. His smile was so close, she could barely see it, but she knew it was there. It made everything better. Not right, but better. His hand slipped onto her breast.

"When exactly do you have to meet your dad and Pastor Michael?" Carla asked.

"An hour."

"You think maybe you ought to . . ."

He pressed back against her. The bed protested.

"Jay," she said. "The baby."

He sighed, nodded, stood.

"It's just that, with your family coming in, I don't think we'll have much private time for a while."

"You can wait until after the wedding," she said, and the words were sharper than she'd meant them to be. Harder. And worse, she didn't regret them.

She stayed in the bedroom watching the light die in the west while Jay washed his hands, found the car keys, and ate a container of strawberry yoghurt standing in front of the old, green refrigerator. The sound of traffic from the street was like an echo from another world. He didn't say good-bye when he left. The front door only opened and then closed. She watched him get in the car, the dome light on him like a halo for a moment, and then darkness. The engine roared and squeaked. A belt was slipping. Jay didn't know how to fix that kind of thing, so he just put up with it. The headlights came on, and the father of her child, her soon-to-be husband—the man she would wake up beside for the rest of her life—pulled out into the street. He either gunned the engine out of anger or just to keep the old car from stalling. She didn't know which.

With him gone, she watched the neighbor's Christmas lights glow. Christmas day was gone, and they'd probably stay up until after New Year's. She tried to take some joy in them, then turned on the TV just for noise. She didn't care what was on. She texted her best friend from Orlando, but she didn't get an answer. She screwed around online, playing stupid games on Facebook and trying not to think. They wouldn't come in until the day before the wedding. Her parents. Her sister. Her brothers, except Carlos, because he'd just started a new job and couldn't get the time off to go to Wichita to watch his slut little sister's shotgun wedding. She clicked on a link and a grinning cartoon goat popped up asking her to confirm her in-app purchase and she hit Cancel, pushed at her eyes with the back of her hand, and clicked over to the fashion news. It was just the baby making her emotional. Everything would get better when the wedding was over. And better than that when she gave birth and she could hold her son.

She wished they could have stayed in Orlando. It killed Jay to go back to his family and ask for help, but there weren't a lot of jobs in Florida right now, and the money Carla made as a paralegal would just about cover the day care she'd need in order to work. If they were here, Jay's parents could help out, and not just with babysitting. His dad went to church with the landlord of the new apartment. The place was ragged and worn and it smelled like old ant poison, but it was cheap. Cheaper than it would have been for someone else. Jay had other friends. Connections. He'd grown up here. It was his town. If they couldn't make it here, they couldn't make it anywhere. He had laughed a little when he said that, but she could hear the distance in it.

It had been so sweet when it started. Jay was a gentle man. Kind and strong and funny. And he'd looked pretty damn good in his swim trunks. They met through the church. He'd just moved away from his family for the first time, and the joy he took in being on his own shone in him like a lamp. He hadn't been wild. He didn't go out drinking or anything like that. But there was a sense of freedom about him. Of possibility. That had probably been better than the swim trunks. It had all seemed so easy at the time. One thing had just led to another, and then there they'd been, naked and sweating on top of the nubbly orange bedspread, and her praying right then that she'd get away with it. Other girls did. She could too.

Only she couldn't.

The baby shifted uneasily, pressing against her from the inside. Hunger gnawed at her, but she knew how it would go. She'd stand at the refrigerator, wanting steak or liver and onions—she'd always hated liver and onions, but not now—and there would only be noodles and lunch meat. Leftover casserole that Jay's mother had left for them. She'd stand there with the cold air pushing at her just like the December chill from the windows until she gave up and ate something. Anything. Then, about thirty minutes later on, she'd puke and go to sleep.

Might as well cut out the middle part.

She turned off the computer and the TV and went into the empty bedroom. Her body felt too heavy. Not like she was fat, but like someone had turned gravity up too high. She wondered what was taking Jay so long. It had to be nine, nine thirty by now. The city outside her window was black as midnight.

The little glowing alarm clock by the bed said it was six forty-five. The night had hardly even begun.

Carla kicked off her shoes, pulled back the covers, and clambered into the bed. She'd have to get up later. She'd have to eat and shower and brush her teeth and put on a nightgown. For right now, pressing her head into the dust-smelling pillow with her clothes still on—her dress that didn't make her look fat, just pregnant—felt like the best and only thing to do. She was pretty sure she wouldn't fall asleep. Or if she did, not deeply. She dreamed she was in her old place in Orlando, looking out a bathroom window that wasn't there in the real world. Someone was outside it, looking in. A man with a round, bald head and a bright smile. In the dream, she knew she should have been scared of him, but he looked so nice.

The baby squirmed and shuddered like he was having nightmares of his own. At first, Carla thought that was what had woken her. Then the voice came again.

"Carla? It's okay, but you need to wake up now."

It was a man's voice. Not a man she knew. And it was inside the apartment. Her heart started pounding.

"Who's there?" she said, trying to keep the fear out of her voice.

"It's all right," the man said. "I'm here to help you."

"Get the fuck out of here," she said. "I'll scream. I've got a knife."

"You don't," the voice said. "And if I'd wanted to

hurt you, I wouldn't be telling you that I'm here. But please wake up. I have to talk to you, and we don't have very much time."

Carla kicked off the covers, and they slid down to the carpet with a hiss. She should have been cold. The room was cold. The dress clung to her, tacky with sleep sweat. She walked forward slowly. She could run for the front door. Or get her cell phone and call the cops. Call Jay.

The man was sitting at the kitchen table. His pants and sweater were black, his pale fingers laced together before him. His head was shaved to the scalp. For a moment, it seemed that his paper-pale skin was covered in black tattoos. The marks were on his fingers, the backs of his hands, his throat, his ears, his eyelids. Even his lips were striped with black. The marks and symbols made her think of letters in alphabets she didn't know or mathematical notations. She had the sense that if she looked in the whites of his eyes, there would be symbols written by the blood vessels. Then as quickly as it had come, the impression was gone, and he was only a pleasantly smiling stranger in her house. The kitchen was dark except for the overhead light, and it made him seem like he was on a stage.

His smile was rueful.

"Hey," he said. "I know you've only got my word to go on, but I actually don't usually sneak into other people's houses like this. Most of the time I've got pretty decent manners. If you want to get a knife or something, I'm perfectly comfortable with that. Or I could make you some tea."

"What the fuck are you?"

"Short form? One of the good guys."

"How did you get in here?"

"Magic," the man said, his voice losing its apologetic tone. "I got in here using magic. Because I need to talk to you. I need to warn you. You're in danger. And more to the point, your baby's in danger."

Carla put a hand to her belly. As if in response, her boy kicked. A little thump in the middle of her palm.

"Not from me," the man said, raising his hands, palms out. "I want the cycle broken. That's what I'm here for. To stop it before it starts again. Surprisingly thankless job, actually, but the benefits package is decent and . . ." He let out a long sigh. "Honestly, Carla, I'm usually a lot less verbose than this. It's something I do when I'm nervous, and I'm really nervous right now."

"Why?"

"Something really bad is coming," he said, trim fingernails scratching absently at the back of his other hand. "Something big and powerful that's killed some of my friends. It's like a demon, and now I'm pretty sure it's after your baby. And I'm scared that you might not believe me."

Carla stood silent for a long moment. It was

madness, and she knew it. If the man in her kitchen wasn't crazy, then he was obviously some kind of satanist. But he didn't sound like that when he talked, and everything he said seemed to fit with some growing but still unspoken suspicion of her own. She shouldn't talk to him. She should tell him to leave or start screaming or something.

"What is it?" she asked, her voice hardly above a whisper.

"I don't know what your fiancé has told you about his family. About his sister," the man said. "How much do you know about Jayné Heller?"

CHAPTER ONE

When my uncle Eric Heller died, he left me a lot of money—like small-nation kind of money—and what I thought at the time was an ongoing fight against demons and unclean spirits. When I got in fights, I was impossible to stop, and spells and magic that tried to find me failed. I figured that he'd put some sort of protective spell on me.

I hadn't had a clue.

Since then, I have been thrown nearly off a skyscraper by a demon-possessed wizard. I've snuck through the depths of a hospital haunted by the kind of spirit that brings on genocides. I've watched a friend collapse from internal bleeding after a bunch of mind-controlled people tried to kick him to death. I've felt my own body being controlled by something that wasn't in any way me, and I've been locked in a basement by a bunch of priests who were willing to sacrifice me to save me.

The most frightening thing I've ever done was tell my dad I was going to a secular university.

Getting everything in place had been a long complex of deceit and intrigue. I'd used my babysitting money to rent a post office box and filled out applications for three dozen colleges that didn't have the word *bible* in their names. I'd taken the tax returns that my parents had given me and made copies to send to all the financial aid departments without their knowing. For months, I'd snuck the paperwork into the house and hidden it under my mattress, taking the letters out at night with my bedroom door locked. I looked over all the pamphlets with beautiful pictures of campuses and descriptions of college life like a starving woman paging through cookbooks.

The first acceptance letter I got felt like a bomb going off in my rib cage, but I had to pretend nothing was going on. I sat at dinner that night, glowing on the inside and trying not to smile. My brothers, Jay and Curtis, were blissfully oblivious, but I could tell my parents suspected something was up. Probably they thought it was a boy.

I cobbled together a high-interest student loan that didn't need a cosigner, a work-study position, and a couple small scholarships based on an essay I'd written as a junior in high school. And I had enough money left to buy a one-way plane ticket to Phoenix. I was going to be a Sun Devil, and every day I got out of my bed, fought for my turn in the bathroom, went to church with my family, and bowed my head in prayer felt like a little more of a lie.

I didn't know the word *compartmentalization* at the time, but if you'd looked in the dictionary, I'd have been the picture next to it. I was Jayné the good little girl weighing her options with her parents and not entirely sure she wanted to go to college at all, and I was also Jayné who was already committed and getting ready to leave. My plane left on Thursday morning at ten a.m. I told my father Tuesday night after dinner.

I remember all of it. My father's face went red, my mother's white. There was a tremor in his voice while he explained to me that I was forbidden to go. He used that word. *Forbidden*. Jay took Curt to the TV room and they pretended to watch *The Simpsons*, but I knew they were listening. I sat at the dining room table with my hands pressed flat on my thighs and my heart doing triple time. The lump in my throat was so solid I was pretty sure I was going to vomit. And quietly, confidently, implacably, I defied my father. I was going. I was old enough to make my own choices, and I'd made them. I was sure if he prayed hard enough, he'd see that it had to be this way. All the things I'd practiced saying quietly in the bathroom mirror.

My dad? Yeah, he *detonated*. Shouting, slapping his open hand against the table so hard the centerpiece jumped.

I'd heard the phrase *twisted in rage* before, one place or another, but this was when I really understood it. And my mother stood in the doorway, her hands fluttering in front of her like birds in a cage. He called me things he'd never called me before: stupid, naive, a selfish bitch, and I'm pretty sure *wannabe whore* figured in there someplace. I called him a monster and a mind-fucking control freak. Our mutual hatred and anger peeled the paint.

He told me to get my cheap ass up to my room and not to come back down until I'd seen sense. I remember that part very well.

I stomped up the stairs, slammed my bedroom door closed, and left by the window. Two days later, I was in Dallas/Fort Worth Airport, weeping over my one suitcase. And a week after that, I was a Sun Devil. We hadn't spoken since. The only one I'd ever touched base with at all before last week was my little brother, Curt, and then I hadn't gone into great detail. *Dropped out of college, got a huge fortune when Uncle Eric died. Oh, and did you know he was an international demon hunter? Or that he was an even bigger asshole than Dad? Or that I have a spirit living inside me called the Black Sun, and it gives me superpowers sometimes? How's high school been for you?* Didn't see going there.

And yet, there was exactly where I was going. Back home to where it all began, or if it hadn't begun there, at least someone might know some of what had happened. Might be able to explain some of the confusion that my life had become since Uncle Eric died.

The snow had been coming down since we crossed the New Mexico border into Oklahoma. It was all hard round balls like bits of Styrofoam that tapped against the windshield and flew away again before they had the chance to melt. China Forbes crooned from the speakers about falling stars falling forever, and Chogyi Jake snored gently in the passenger's seat. I imagined Ex behind me, staring moodily out the window, and Ozzie curled up with her nose tucked under her tail; but since I couldn't see them, that said more about my state of mind than theirs. Gray clouds pressed the sky low enough it felt like a ceiling. I could feel the highway getting slick under the tires just by the way the steering wheel vibrated.

"I think the dog needs to go out," Ex said.

Chogyi Jake grunted, yawned, and leaned forward, blinking into the gray.

"Seriously?" I said.

"Well, I'm not positive," Ex said. "She's just got that look on her face."

"What look?"

"That the-backseat's-fine-with-me-if-it's-fine-with-you look?"

"Okay, message received," I said.

"We could use some lunch too," Ex said.

"Next stop coming up," I said, willing my voice to be cheerful.

Ten miles on, a service station huddled at a high-way exit like a luckless hitchhiker. Along with gas pumps and the kind of bathrooms you have to go outside to get to, it boasted a little sandwich shop. Ozzie got to her feet as I pulled in, her wagging tail making a rhythmic thumping against the seat. Ex had apparently been right. It was kind of cute. I hadn't pegged him for a dog person.

"I'll take her for a walk," Ex said as I killed the engine. "You can order for me."

"Meatball sandwich, no cheese?" Chogyi Jake asked, though he didn't have to. We'd all been working together for years now, tracking down rid-ers. They were the spiritual parasites—*riders* was the generic term—that snuck in from the Pleroma or Next Door or whatever we called it and took up residence in the bodies of men and women. Bodies like mine. They were responsible for vampires and werewolves and lamias and a whole taxonomy of things that made the world weirder and more dangerous. Once upon a time, I'd thought we fought against them, but that had turned out to be a little simplistic.

We'd traveled across the world together, the three of us, and—once upon a time—Aubrey. Only Aubrey was back together with his once and future wife, Kim, in Chicago, rebuilding the life that my uncle Eric had destroyed for them. And so it was just the three of us heading back to my family to try to figure out what Eric had done to mine.

Well, the three of us and my dog.

"Large iced tea," Ex said, opening the SUV's rear door. The blast of cold air pressed against the back of my neck for a second before the door closed again with a crash. I reached around for the leather backpack that I still used instead of a purse. Chogyi Jake stretched, squinting out into the snow. I felt another passing urge to apologize to him for ditching him back in New Mexico, but it would have been about the millionth time I'd done it, and I figured after about six hundred thousand it might start getting annoying.

"You good?" I asked.

"I try," he said, smiling gently.

I smiled back. "Smart ass."

The service station was small and tacky. Christmas tinsel still hung on the edges of the counter, and a bin of clip-on reindeer horns squatted by the bathrooms with a hand-drawn sign saying 50% Off. We ordered at the counter along the eastern wall, then sat at a chipped Formica table and watched the semis roll by on the highway. The horizon was lost, sky and earth fading into a uniform nothingness. I ate two bites of my sandwich and pushed the rest away.

"Do you know what you want to ask them?" Chogyi Jake asked. He had a way of stepping gently into the middle of deep conversations we hadn't had yet. Since I'd called my mother a week before and arranged for this sudden, probably unpleasant reunion, he hadn't asked me why or what I hoped to gain by it. We could skip all that. I leaned forward and shook my head.

"I keep thinking I should start with the riders. I mean, if they don't even know that riders exist, everything else I want to know starts sounding pretty sketchy. Or with Eric. Or with whether Mom really had an affair."

"Why do you want to know about that?"

I plucked a potato chip out of his bag.

"You don't think it's important?"

"It might be," Chogyi Jake said. "Or it might not. But I wondered why you would begin with that."

"It's not her," I said. "It's not like her. I mean, I can't imagine that she'd ever do that."

"Are you thinking then that it must have been the product of magic," he asked, "or that you might not understand your mother as well as you believed?"

Outside, Ex and Ozzie trotted back toward the SUV. I'd seen dogs smile before, and she trotted along at his side, looking up at him, a black Lab with a graying muzzle and fewer problems than anyone else in the car.

"I was thinking magic," I said. "You're telling me it's not?"

"I have no way of knowing. But I see how it would be difficult . . . maybe impossible . . . to look into one part of this without looking into all of it."

"I love you. I do. But I don't even know what the hell that means."

He laughed and I grinned. Ex opened the SUV door and Ozzie hunkered down, thought about it, and then jumped, clambering up to the seat. The lousy little radio at the back of the station went from commercials to an old Lady Gaga tune without changing tempo.

"I mean," he said, choosing each word as he said it, "that we're going in hopes of understanding what Eric's plan was. How you came to have a rider in you, why he left you his accumulated wealth, what his greater purpose was. All that."

"Right," I said.

"It may not be possible to address that without addressing other issues. Who you are to your family. Who you have become. What your relationship is to them."

"Boy, am I not seeing that," I said.

Chogyi held up a finger. In someone else, it would have been condescending. In him, it just meant he needed a second to think.

"If your mother's infidelity wasn't related to Eric or the Black Sun or anything that's happened in the last few years, does that make it unimportant to you?"

And so maybe then I did understand. I'd been away for a long time. I wasn't the girl who'd snuck out the window. I wasn't even the girl that girl had changed into. I had to be five or six incarnations down from that by now, and each new version of me had taken me a little further from who I'd been. Yes, I wanted to know about Eric and my father and my mother. I wanted to know why Dad had forbidden us from talking to my uncle. I wanted to know why my uncle had helped me hide the tattoo I'd woken up with after my epic sixteenth-birthday lost weekend. I wanted to put it all in place. But I also wanted to see what happened when I walked back in the door, and that didn't necessarily have anything to do with ghosties or ghoulies or long-legged beasties.

Which was what made it scary.

Ex pushed into the station, brushing corn snow out of his long, pale hair. I more than half expected the guy behind the counter to give him the hairy eye, but instead he lifted his chin to Ex and said, "Peace be wit'cha."

"And also with you," Ex answered, and headed over to our dingy little table. "Snow's getting thicker."

"Think we'll have a problem getting through?"

He sat across from me, scowling.

"Don't think so," he said. "The new car looks pretty weather ready. And we're on a major highway. It's not like we're going between Taos and Questa again, and you handled that just fine."

"Yeah," I said, surprised by the prick of regret. Some part of me had been hoping the roads might close. We might all be forced off into some Bates Motel–looking dive where I could put off the trip for a few days. Until after New Year's. Possibly forever. Forever would be good. Ex took a bite from his sandwich and nodded toward mine.

"Not hungry?"

"Guess not," I said.

"Get it wrapped up, then," he said. "You might want it later."

"Don't worry about it," I said. Ex could be weirdly paternalistic, but as long as I was the one signing his paychecks, I didn't mind. Not too much. I found myself secretly pleased that we hadn't fallen into bed together before. It was going to be hard enough introducing them to my parents as it was. *Mom. Dad. These are my friends. They're both men, and we go everywhere unchaperoned. The nice one's the ex–heroin addict, and the grumpy one used to be a Catholic priest.* Never mind. I might as well have slept with him.

I couldn't help it. I laughed. Ex's scowl deepened, and he shot a glance at Chogyi Jake.

"Just thinking," I said. "It took me years to get away from Wichita, and it's a ten-hour drive back."

"Life's strange that way," Ex agreed.

Ozzie looked out from the SUV, her dark eyes nervous and her breath fogging the windshield.

WE WERE only a few days past the winter solstice, so darkness came on early. Ex took his turn driving, and I took the backseat with Ozzie, letting my head rest against the metal of the doorframe. Ex got to change the music, so we were listening to some old jazz numbers he liked, and I closed my eyes for a minute. Just to rest them.

In the dream, I was in the desert. It was the same place I'd been a thousand times before, though now the bare landscape had scars and scorch marks. She was with me, the other Jayné. Most of my life, I hadn't known what she was, only that sometimes I would dream that there were two of me. Now I could see the lines in her skin where the plates of the mask met. Her eyes were still like mine, though. Her hands were folded in her lap, and mine were too and they were the same hands. Far above us, two suns burned in the limitless sky. One of them pressed down heat and light, but the other, paler one radiated purification.

You will outgrow me, one of us said, but I didn't know which, and the thought left me sad and elated. I had the sense that this was what going away from home was supposed to be like. Sorrowful and exciting, terrifying and grand. *You will outgrow me, and so we should be ready.*

"Jayné?"

I opened my eyes, disoriented for a moment. We were on a two-lane road. Not the highway.

"Jayné," Ex said again, "what's the place we're staying?"

"Best Western," I said. "They take pets."

"And it's on Fifty-Third."

"Yes," I said, leaning forward. "What's the matter?"

"I can't find it," he said, "and there's nothing *here.* Seriously, I think someone stole your city."

I blinked. We'd outrun the clouds and the snow, and dark fields opened on either side of us, unfolding forever. It was unreal because it was familiar.

"That up ahead on the right?" Chogyi Jake said, his voice uncertain.

"No, that's Heights. It's a high school. You went the wrong way off I-35. You have to turn around. It's right by the exit there."

"Thank God for the native guide," Ex said, pulling over to the shoulder and waiting for an oncoming truck to pass. I leaned back. I'd known a kid who went to Heights. Jimmy Masterson. He'd had a high forehead, he'd asked a friend of mine to homecoming, and he hadn't even crossed my mind in years. Ozzie chuffed as Ex made the turn. I put my hand on the dog's side.

"Well, Toto," I said. "We're in Kansas."

CHAPTER TWO

In the morning I took Ozzie for a walk in the freezing brown of December, the leash in one hand and a cup of coffee in the other. The steam from the coffee was like my breath. The chill left my face feeling tight and expressionless. I wasn't looking forward to the day. Ozzie did her best to ignore the leash, pulling me along when there was something interesting to sniff at, and standing like a rock when I was trying to move her along. I couldn't complain about it too much. She'd lived a long time without anyone telling her what to do, and in her place I probably would have done the same.

When I got back to the hotel, Ex and Chogyi Jake were at the Country Kitchen. Ex was on his way through a plate of bacon and eggs with a cup of acid-smelling coffee. Chogyi Jake was eating yoghurt and drinking tea. I plopped down beside Ex and caught the waiter's eye. He nodded that he'd bring me a menu in just a second. It was a lot of information in a small gesture, and I wondered if it was a local idiom, or something I'd been seeing and doing all across the world. It was so small, so automatic, that I couldn't remember.

"Where's Ozzie?" Ex asked.

"I put her in the room."

"Not the car?"

"Cold," I said. "Besides, Mom doesn't like dogs in the house. They shed."

The waiter swung by, dropping off the promised menu. It took only a couple seconds to realize I didn't want anything. I folded my hands on the table and quietly willed the guys to finish. A vague nausea floated at the back of my throat, and the smell of bacon wasn't helping.

"So what's the plan?" Ex asked.

"Go home," I said. "Talk. See what we can find out about Eric. Jay's going to be doing some wedding preparations still, and I'm hoping that we can use that to put people at ease."

"You sure you want us horning in?"

"I don't see an option. Besides, they're going to be pretty damn curious about all of us. Won't be hard to start conversations."

"I think what Ex is asking is whether this is a private moment, or if you want us there with you?" Chogyi Jake said, then ate the last of his yoghurt. I coughed out something close to a laugh.

"Are you kidding? I can't do this alone."

"Just thought we should check," Ex said. He sounded a little petulant. I had the momentary urge to put my hand on his, to reassure him. I'd spent weeks traveling with him, just the two of us together. I didn't know if the distance I felt in him now was from being back with other people or if he was still grieving for Father Chapin, his old mentor who'd died in my arms less than a month before. Or if he still thought of me as an innocent woman possessed by a demonic force from which he had to save me. Whatever it was, I didn't put my hand on his, and if he noticed, I couldn't tell.

The waiter came, and I settled the bill. Twenty minutes later I was turning the SUV down the familiar streets, my breath shallow and my brain spinning. There was Mr. and Mrs. Mogen's place, but the old green truck he'd driven had been re-placed by a red Impala. A younger man's car. I wondered what had happened. We passed Carol McKee's house, where I'd gone for Wednesday Bible study from the time I was twelve until I was sixteen. I was driving down two different streets; the one I saw with single-story houses with no fences to divide the yards, one-car garages built back when cars must have been about a foot thinner, and then I was also going down my street where I'd always been. Where I belonged.

There's a way things are supposed to be, and it's how it was the first time. A city was supposed to be like this. I'd been to Denver, Chicago, New York, New Orleans. I'd traveled through the winter desert of northern New Mexico. I hadn't thought about the ways they were exotic for me. Now, for the first time, I could see. They were strange and rich and uncanny because they weren't Wichita. Until I saw it all, I didn't know how much I'd missed it, and after about three minutes I wanted to get the hell away.

I turned right, went two more blocks, then left. The houses got a little closer in. More had another story, or half story. And then there it was. A green house with blue trim, a small covered porch with a swing, tight-mowed buffalo grass. The tree I'd climbed in the summers to get away from Jay and Curt. Over on the side, the window I'd gone out of. Home. The driveway had a white Nissan I didn't recognize, and my dad's truck was on the street. There were about half a dozen other cars parked by the curbs too, so I had to go down three houses before I found a space big enough to swing the SUV up to the low curb.

"Are you all right?" Ex asked.

"Right as rain," I said. "Spiffy."

"Because you're looking a little pale."

I killed the engine and sat for a few seconds, listening to the car click as it cooled.

"This is usually where you put in some inappropriate humor," Ex said. I couldn't tell if he was making fun of me or being gentle. Maybe both.

"Why didn't the chicken cross the road?" I said.

"I'll bite."

"Because it was too chicken," I said, and opened my door. "Everyone out. Let's get our travesty on."

I stood on the doorstep for ten or fifteen seconds. It felt like forever. The house was smaller than I remembered it. Like going back to a grade school classroom. Like walking into a recurring dream. I pressed the doorbell.

It wasn't a breath before my mother opened the door. The smells of pinesap and woodsmoke mixed with the generic soap she always bought wafted over me. She looked older, her hair more white than not, her skin thinner. She looked like an older version of my mother. Not the same woman.

"Well," she said through a tight little smile. "I suppose you should come in. Cold out there."

"Thank you," I said, but not in much more than a whisper. I ducked my head as I stepped in, like I was sixteen and late for curfew. I hated that I was doing it, and I could no more stop than I could fly through the air like a sparrow. "This is . . . Jake. And Ex. They're my friends. They've been helping me."

Mom nodded to them both as they stepped into the atrium.

"It's a pleasure to meet you both," she said. "Can I take your coats for you?"

As Ex and Chogyi Jake made their mixed chorus of yeses and thank you ma'ams, it hit me just how lost I was. I'd come here to grill this nice, polite, brittle brick of a woman about screwing around on her husband over two decades ago. I didn't have any idea how I'd even start a conversation like that. *So I heard from this psychic kid in New Orleans that you were knocking boots with someone besides Dad. How'd that happen?* My God, the woman had barely been able to tell me how tampons worked. This was a mistake. I shouldn't have come.

"Who is it?" Jay called from the kitchen.

My mother's eyes locked on mine; hers were the same brown as the woman I saw in the mirror every morning. She didn't turn her head when she shouted back.

"It's your sister."

I stepped into the living room. The Christmas tree was still up and bright with tinsel, even if all the strands of colored lights were dark. Jay stepped into the doorway from the kitchen at the same time a long-limbed, lanky boy with a ghost of a mustache came around the corner from the dining room. Jay's alarm and astonishment looking at me couldn't have been more than mine on looking at my baby brother, Curtis.

"Jayné?" he said, and the voice was deeper, but it was him.

"Hey," I said, and put up my arms. We hugged like it meant something, and for the first time in a long time I felt my anxiety ratchet down a notch. I might be wasting my time looking for answers. My parents might think I was the Whore of Babylon. But I'd gotten to hug my little brother, so no matter what, the trip couldn't be a total loss. And then I felt Jay's arms around us both. We stood there for a few seconds, the three of us, like old veterans who'd shared the same foxhole.

"Jaybird?"

The brown-skinned woman in the kitchen doorway was maybe two years older than me, with a round, pretty face and a baby bump. Jay stepped to the woman's side, his hand on her shoulder.

"Jayné, this is Carla. Carla, this is my sister, Jayné."

The woman seemed hesitant about taking my hand, but my brother damn near crushed me.

"You came for the wedding," she said.

"I . . . ah. Did," I said. "I came for the wedding."

I introduced Chogyi Jake and Ex all around. They were greeted with the friendly confusion that came from being at a family gathering without being family. Normally in situations like this I called them my employees, which was technically true and made people look at me differently, but I knew the next question would be what I employed them for. I didn't know yet how I wanted to bring in the whole demon-hunting thing, but I was pretty sure that wasn't it.

They'd been sitting in the kitchen, all except for Curtis, who had his laptop open on the dining room table with three flavors of social media connecting him, I figured, to other bored teenagers trapped at home for the holidays. The things that jumped out at me were the changes: the old white fridge that I'd stuck notes and kid art on had been replaced by a brushed-steel model. The chairs around the kitchen table had new pads on the seats. Looking down the three steps into the TV room, they'd invested in a massive flat-screen on the back wall. The couch was the same one I'd napped on. The table had the scratch where I'd failed to successfully carve a jack-o'-lantern.

"Can I get you and your friends something to drink?" Mom asked as we filed in.

"That would be great," I said.

"Just water," Ex said, with a smile.

"Ex," Carla said. Her smile seemed forced, and

her gaze kept cutting back to me. "That's an interesting name." The way she said it made it a question. Ex smiled.

"Short for Xavier," he said. "Some friends made it into a nickname, and it stuck. Not the worst thing they've called me."

"How interesting," my mother said. "I hope you'll be coming to the wedding too?"

"We wouldn't want to intrude," Chogyi Jake said.

"Of course not," she said in a way that could have meant *You wouldn't be intruding* or *Of course you wouldn't want that* with equal facility. Chogyi Jake's smile was warm and open as always. What I knew of his life pretty much precluded caring much about whether my mother approved of him, but he wasn't going to be rude about any of it. He was good that way. Still, I felt the warring urges to sweep my friends away from her impeccably polite disapproval or to stand up for them. I hadn't been in the house five minutes, and I had already reverted to eighteen.

"Where've you been?" Curtis asked, curiosity and enthusiasm blinding him to every uncomfortable nuance and subtext.

"Santa Fe," I said. "And parts of northern New Mexico, but we spent Christmas in Santa Fe."

"You have friends there?" Beside him, Carla was checking something on her cell phone.

"Sort of," I said.

"Well, you know the wedding's the third," Curtis said, flopping onto a kitchen chair. "A bunch of Carla's family's coming in. They're having it at the *church*."

The way he said it made it seem impressive, like that wasn't the normal place for a wedding. And then I imagined Pastor Michael with his carefully combed hair and constant chummy grin welcoming a pregnant girl up to the altar, and it got a little impressive for me too.

"It's good to see you," Jay said. "We've been worried."

"No reason to be," I said. "Sorry I've been scarce."

Jay smiled.

"It's just good to see you again. I'm glad you came for this."

Mom finished serving water to Chogyi Jake and Ex, and turned to me.

"Well? Sit down, sit down. No point us all standing around like straws. How's college treating you, dear? Have you picked a major?"

Ex's eyebrows rose. His glance at me said *You really have been out of touch, haven't you?*

"Is . . . is Dad . . . ?"

"He's in the garage," Mom said, nodding toward the door at the side of the TV room. As if I might have forgotten how to get there. "He's working in there."

"I'm just . . ." I said. "I'll be right back."

The garage was his space. The side wall was covered in Peg-Board, with the outlines of his tools to mark where each of them should hang. A few nuggets of cat litter crunched under my feet, escapees from the pile he kept under the car to soak up dripping engine oil. He sat at his workbench, his back to me. The directional lamp lit his hands, the white sleeves rolled halfway up his forearms. He was organizing a can of mixed screws, plucking them into piles by thickness, dividing them into Phillips and flathead. It was like watching a kid playing jacks. The kind of thing people always meant to do but never got around to. Unless there was something else that they particularly didn't want to do.

"So," I said. "I guess you knew I was coming."

"Your mother said so," he replied. His voice was low. In another man I would have called it sullen, but this was my father, so all I could really hear was disapproval. "You here to borrow money?"

"I don't need money," I said, chuckling. Nothing I had bought—houses, cars, tickets to Europe, stays in expensive hotels—could even make a dent in the fortune Eric had left me.

He turned to face me. I'd been prepared for a lot of things. Anger, dismissal, the empty coldness that came when he withheld his affections as punishment. There was more than that in him. There was hatred. And also sorrow.

"Well," he said. "I guess that answers that, then, doesn't it?" He turned his back to me, his fingers shifting the little bits of metal. The scraping sound was like claws against stone.

"I don't know," I said. "Look, I understand that you're angry with me. And I understand why. But I need to ask you some questions."

"Why would I be angry with you? What you do with your own's got nothing to do with me. You just leave me and my family out of it."

It felt like a slap. I actually had to fight to catch my breath.

"Your family?" I said. "They're yours, are they?"

"They are," he said.

"And I'm not."

"Not anymore," he said. "Not like you are. You made your choices. I made mine."

It was like being hollowed. If he'd turned and struck me, I'd have rung like a bell. There was that much nothing in me. I didn't know what to say. I didn't know how to say it. When I did speak, I almost expected it to be her—my rider—taking control, but the voice was all me.

"Jesus *fucking* Christ," I said, pulling the obscenity out in slow, deliberate syllables. His shoulders bunched, but he didn't turn back. Didn't rise to the bait. I was crying now, the tears actually stung. "I mean, goddamn it."

"I won't have that kind of language in my house," he said. His voice sounded thick. Whether it was rage or tears of his own, I didn't know and it didn't matter.

"Yeah, because language is what's important to you. Saying the right words. Actually being a good man? Actually treating me with respect or listening to me or even being in the house to say hello to me when I show up would be wildly un-Christlike. No, hiding in your garage so that I have to come back out here, and then treating me like shit, and telling me I'm not your family anymore—that's *way* better than cursing."

I had my hand halfway to his shoulder. I'd intended to shake him, or turn him around to face me, or something. I don't know what. The invisible wave hit me like the shock of a bomb without the explosion.

Chi. Raw will. Magic. Whatever you wanted to call it, I'd felt it enough times to recognize it. Someone—or something—had just released a lot of power. Too much power to have come from a human.

Inside the house, glass shattered and my mother screamed.

Dad pulled a drawer open and took out a pistol. The barrel gleamed in the light, clean and freshly oiled. His glance at me was fear and vicious anger. Whatever was in there, whatever had happened, he was going to head in like he could handle it.

He was going to get himself killed.

"No. Stay back," I said, jumping for the door. "I'll take care of this."

"Fuck *you*," my father said.

CHAPTER THREE

My father and I bolted out into the TV room practically together. The air stank of heated iron, and my mother wasn't the only one screaming. The first thing I saw was Carla squatting on the kitchen floor, her hand to her belly and her eyes wide. Ex stood in front of her, his hands in fists. The television and the kitchen windows were shattered, and three people were standing by the kitchen table. Two were holding pump shotguns, one at Curtis, one at Chogyi Jake. The third was turning to look at me.

Every square inch of the intruders' skin was marked with ink. The first time I'd seen anything like this, I'd been in an apartment in Denver, talking with a vampire. Back then I hadn't known what any of the markings meant. After three years of studying, I recognized some. The swirling cross of the Mark of Enki. The angled, cruel letters of the Goetic alphabet. They were wizards. They were the same wizards who had killed my uncle, who had hidden the viciously evil *haugsvarmr* under Grace Memorial Hospital.

The Invisible College was standing in my parents' kitchen.

The one without the gun lifted his hands and shouted, and the sound was more than sound. It carried the weight of will. The ragged, meat-tearing noise of it staggered my father back into me, and I put my hand between his shoulder blades to steady him. The wizard's jaw unhinged, and his mouth gaped wider than a normal human's could have. I acted without thought, and I didn't act alone. I felt my body breathing in, taking the power of the wizard's tainted shout into my lungs, pulling his power out of the air. It wasn't something a human could do, but the Black Sun was with me, guiding me.

"No," I said, softly and with enough power that the house shuddered with it. The unarmed man closed his too-wide mouth and smiled like he'd won something. He glanced down at Carla, but she didn't see it. She was staring at me.

The report of my father's gun was deafening, but it was only sound. Without the power of will behind it, it was empty as an echo. The unarmed man's hand flickered, plucking the bullet from the air. Carla shrieked and put her hands up over her ears. My father fired twice more. The man batted the bullets away, his face twisted in concentration. His eyes fixed on me.

He was young. His shaved head left him looking thin and oddly fragile despite the tattoos and the intense power burning off him. I had the brief image of a boy trying to hold on to a fire hose. His will arced out, invisible and unmistakable as a pressure change, and with an almost physical click I was in the familiar space just behind my own eyes.

I was being ridden.

My body went still as a stone, and I could see the wizard's eyes narrow. He'd sensed the change. My father was shouting, holding the gun in front of himself like a cross. I squatted a little, lowering my center of gravity, and kicked gently at the back of his knee, taking him out of the fight without actually hurting him. As he went down, the rider in me moved past him. The other two—the ones with the shotguns—were an older man with brown skin and a dusting of white hair and a thin, pale woman with eyes the color of gas flame. I remembered the first time the Invisible College had attacked me, Midian Clark walking among the conquered firing bullets into their heads. One of them had been a woman who could have been this woman's twin.

My body didn't hesitate. With one hand on the rail to steady me, I swung up the three steps from the TV room to the kitchen. The shattered glass glittered on the floor. The older man started to turn his shotgun away from Chogyi Jake and toward me. In the corner of my vision, my father hunched behind his overstuffed chair as if it would give him cover. My left hand slapped the shotgun barrel up, not grabbing it but striking hard enough to make the man stagger back. I kicked three times at his left knee. He fired the shotgun as he fell, shattering the overhead lights, but Chogyi Jake was on him, controlling both the shotgun and the fall.

"Surrender!" the young man shouted, his will pressing against me like a storm wind. Behind him the woman shifted, her shotgun tracking away from Ex and Carla. The Black Sun kicked past the young man, slamming my foot into the kitchen table. It slid across the room, breaking against the woman's hip. I saw the tabletop scar from my jack-o'-lantern carving snap in half.

I stepped in, driving my elbow up toward the young man's throat, but he was at least as fast as I was. I felt his counterstrike in my stomach without seeing where it came from. My breath left me, and it was my turn to stagger. My feet slipped on the glass and I dropped to my knees. I caught a glimpse of my mother and Curtis huddled under the dining room table. Good, I thought, stay there.

The young man stood above me, his hands out before him. His eyes had turned a uniform bloody red. The rider paused, resting on my fingertips and the balls of my feet. Distantly, I could feel her uncertainty. He turned his palms toward me with a word I didn't recognize, and an invisible sledgehammer hit me in the chest.

I heard Ex calling my name, but it seemed to come from a long way away. Carla was screaming too. I wondered where Jay was. Getting help, I hoped. Calling the police. By the time they came, it would all be over, one way or the other, but at least he wasn't in the room. It was one less person I needed to protect. Time seemed to be moving strangely. Slowly but discontinuously. I was falling to the floor, my heart a bloom of pain, and then I was on my knees again. I felt the rider's will gathering in my right hand, and I tried to add my own to it. When I hit the wizard, the blow lifted him off his feet and threw him against the counter. His head hit the cabinet, splintering it. Half a dozen coffee mugs skittered down around him like snow, shattering on the floor. I leaped, but he was already elsewhere.

"You cannot defeat us!" he shouted, but it wasn't true. His strength was fading. A feral grin pulled at my lips. He was already growing weaker. The Black Sun and I? We were just warming up.

I surged across the debris-strewn kitchen, hammering at him with my fists and my will. I felt him shifting from assault to defense, and I leaned into it. The blue-eyed woman staggered to her feet, and I spared enough attention to kick the shotgun out of her hands and send her back into the living room. I felt a little explosion behind me, and the older man Chogyi Jake had been fighting ran past me, unarmed and limping, for the front door. The rider glanced back. Chogyi Jake was on one knee in the dining room, blood running from his nose and mouth. He had the shotgun in his hand. Behind him, Mom was curled against the far wall, her face pale. I didn't know where Curtis had gone. I could only hope he wasn't chasing after them.

The unarmed wizard's eyes had lost their bloody look and gone for a soft brown.

"What do you want from me?" the Black Sun asked. The power in her words reached into the man, pulled at him. He choked a little, trying not to speak, then bit down on his tongue hard enough that blood pinked his teeth.

"Jayné!" Ex shouted. "Behind you."

I turned.

In the TV room, my father had found his feet. He stood at the end of the couch, holding the pistol with both hands. The barrel shifted from the wizard to me, then back again, as if he wasn't sure who was the real threat. Fear boiled off him like steam. He was a middle-aged man with a paunchy belly and jowls that were starting to sag. Redness like a rash crawled up his sternum toward his neck. This was the man I'd feared so much. This was the man who'd dominated my life so deeply that I'd fled my home and my friends—a whole life—just so I could say I'd done something of my own.

And now he was going to shoot me.

"Gary!" my mother shouted, her voice low and rough. "You put that down!"

I could count on one hand the number of times my mother had used Dad's given name. He shifted the gun toward the boy again, then back toward me. I waited for the muzzle flash, horrified. He lowered the gun. As I turned back toward the wizard, he drove his forehead into the bridge of my nose. I heard the cartilage break more than felt it. He opened his mouth and shouted wordlessly.

The Oath of the Abyss was the common name of a terrible spell. The rough guess I'd been given was that each time someone used it, it dropped their life span by about a year. I'd seen it done twice, both times by Aubrey. From a normal human, it was enough to rock back a rider. Now, from the wizard and whatever spirit was riding his body, it was like getting a hurricane full in my face. The Black Sun staggered, and I felt it lose control of my muscles for a moment. We were both standing there, trying to keep my feet. The overheated iron scent broke, and the kitchen only smelled like the cold breeze through the broken windows. The young wizard sagged, his gaze unfocused and lost.

"Stop him," I tried to say, but my face felt like a rubber mask, and it sounded more like *Ob em*. The wizard turned, hobbling for the front door, and I went after him as best I could. The ground seemed to be shifting more or less in time with my heartbeat. When I got to the front yard, the older man was gone and the sound of a motorcycle blatting away was already fading. The blue-eyed woman was on another motorcycle, and she started it as I staggered down the front steps. The young wizard threw himself across the back of the bike, his arms going around the woman, his head collapsing against her like a puppet with its strings cut. The motor screamed out, and they started moving.

Ex's hand on my elbow was the only thing that kept me from collapsing on the lawn. A red mark around his left eye was deepening toward blue. When it was done blooming, it would be a black eye as profound as any I'd seen. Chogyi Jake came out of the house, shotgun still resting comfortably in his arm. His chin and neck were a single slick of blood.

"Have to go after them," I said. "Where's the keys?"

"We can't catch them," Ex said.

"They were here," I said. "They attacked my family."

"They're on motorcycles. We're in an SUV. Even if there was a chance we could catch up with them, which there's not, none of us are fit to drive. We're more likely to run into a light post."

I sank down to the dead brown grass and let the chill of the air sink into my skin. My body was trembling uncontrollably with shock and the aftermath of the fight. Carefully, I probed my ribs and was pleasantly surprised not to feel the sharp pain that would have meant I'd broken them. Again. I let my head sag down onto my knees while Ex rubbed his hand against my back. The contact comforted.

"How bad?" I asked.

"I don't think anyone's hurt."

I looked over at Chogyi Jake. He was wiping the blood off his face with the back of one hand. My nose felt wide and hot and solid with blood.

"Not badly hurt," Ex said. "And anyway, it's just us."

Just us. Just me and him and Chogyi Jake. Not my family. Not civilians.

"Should put the guns away before the police get here."

"Good point. I'll get them into the trunk. We

might be able to find something useful from them."

I nodded. Exhaustion pulled me toward the ground. My breath was bright white plumes. I listened to Chogyi Jake and Ex talking. The sound of the SUV's door opening and closing. There still weren't any sirens. Not yet. I tried to stand up and staggered. The hand that steadied me was Jay's. His expression was closed. I wouldn't have been surprised by anything—shock, anger, even excitement—but he only put his arm around me and helped me back into the house. The front door was hanging from its top hinge, the lower two having been ripped out of the frame. I didn't know when that had happened. In the living room, the Christmas tree seemed out of place and vaguely obscene, like a jaunty hat on a corpse. Mom was in the kitchen, sweeping up glass like it was just another mess, and her job was to clear it all away before anyone saw. The furnace was roaring, trying to cope with the icy air flowing in through the shattered windows. Jay angled me toward the good sofa and sat down with me.

"That was dramatic," he said.

"Yeah. Sorry about that."

"You know what it was about?"

"No. Yes," I said. "I'm not sure."

He nodded. When I'd left, he'd already been living in an apartment with three other young men from church. He'd put on about twenty pounds and added the beginnings of wrinkles around his eyes and mouth. I'd missed a lot of the changes in his life, and he'd missed out on mine. Chogyi Jake came out of the kitchen with a dish towel full of ice and handed it to me. I pressed it against my injured nose and almost yelped from the pain.

"I think it's broken," Jay said.

"It is," I said.

"So is this what you've been doing all the time you were gone?"

"More of it than you'd expect, actually," I said, smiling weakly.

"Who were those freaks?"

"It's a long story," I said, "and I don't actually know most of it. They're . . . part of what I came home to find out about."

He smiled, and for just a second I could see the boy he'd been.

"So you didn't *just* come for the wedding," he said.

I grinned. It made my nose hurt.

"Sorry," I said.

Carla and Curtis came into the room. Two of the knuckles on his left hand were skinned raw, but other than that they looked okay. Physically, anyway. Carla's eyes were wide, and her right hand was on her belly. She stepped toward us, hesitated, and almost collapsed beside Jay, her head on his lap. I thought there was more than confusion in her eyes. Fear. Sorrow. Love. She wouldn't look at me. I couldn't blame her. She'd been getting ready for her wedding, not an armed assault. I didn't know enough about shock and miscarriage, but even if she'd only watched her fiancé's family get gunned down in front of her, I had to figure it wouldn't be good for the baby.

My blood reddened the ice pack, and the throbbing pain slowed and widened until it felt like my whole face was beating in time with my heart. My mother came and collected Jay and Carla, shepherding them back into the kitchen. She didn't meet my eyes either, and I didn't rise to follow them. Curtis popped his head around the corner for a second, but he didn't stay either. I coughed, and a blood clot that felt about the size of a dime came down from my sinuses. I spat it into the dish towel and then sat there, miserable, listening to the low sound of voices and the scratching of broomstraw against glass. I heard sirens in the distance, getting closer. We needed to get together and make sure our stories all matched. We needed to make sure the police had a version of events that would let them write the whole thing off and not get involved.

Chogyi Jake came back out of the kitchen with a fresh towel of ice, and we traded. He was mostly cleaned up, but his upper lip was a little swollen. At least it wasn't bleeding anymore.

"This could have gone better," I said, and he smiled, because it was funny and it also wasn't.

"It wasn't the conflict I'd anticipated," he agreed.

My father stepped and put a hand on Chogyi Jake's shoulder.

"I'm going to ask you to wait outside, sir," he said.

Chogyi Jake smiled but didn't move. He'd offered to hurt people for me before, and I knew he was entirely willing to stand his ground in my father's house if I wanted him to. I caught his gaze and nodded. It was all right. I mean, what the hell? It wasn't like he was going to shoot me. I chuckled a little at the thought, and Dad scowled at me.

"Of course," Chogyi Jake said, as if it hadn't been my decision. His step was careful as he walked out the shattered front door, and I wondered how extensive his injuries really were.

"Police are going to want to talk with you," my father said.

"Yup."

"It's all right with me if they want to talk with you here. But once you're done, I want you and your boyfriends out of my home. Forever, you understand? You don't have a place here. This is *my* house, and *my* family. Any business you have, you can take up with me. And you haven't got any business with me."

I looked up at him, a sneer plucking at my lips.

In the story, the prodigal son is the one who gets the fatted calf. I didn't know what I'd hoped or expected from him or any of them, but the truth was the trip had failed before the enemy wizards attacked. It had failed the second my father and I had started breathing the same air. *You haven't got any business with me.*

"Fine," I said.

CHAPTER FOUR

The police came in the form of two very nice men who looked over the house with calm, practiced eyes. The way they held themselves and the tone of their voices as they interviewed us implied that they'd seen worse. My guess was they were just relieved it wasn't a domestic violence case. There wasn't much blood, and no one was demanding that anybody be arrested. I thought it was funny how little it took to make it count as a good day for them. They spent most of the time talking to my dad and Chogyi Jake. Dad because it was his house, and he was the head of the family. Chogyi Jake—I guessed—because he was a man, he was older. If they seemed a little suspicious of him; it was probably more the epicanthic folds than anything else.

All the time they were there, I was prepared to lawyer up. Too many questions or just a few of the wrong ones and we could stop talking, call my lawyer, and get a legal defense team in place that could drown the locals in paperwork until they left us alone. It never came to that, and I was more than a little relieved. Flying under the radar was the way I liked it. Just less hassle.

The story was straightforward: Three tattooed people broke in, held the family at gunpoint, broke things, and ran off when my father started shooting at them. Technically, it was all true. By the time they got to me, I had to give them my name and address. I have about seventy houses, condominiums, and apartments scattered around the world, so I gave them the place in Santa Fe we'd just come from because I remembered the address. When they left, I did too.

It should have been more dramatic. This was it. My failed homecoming in its depths. I left like I'd be back for dinner. No hugs, no farewells. Just me and Ex and Chogyi Jake heading out to the car and turning out into midafternoon traffic. The sun was already sinking toward the horizon. They were quiet.

Ex's black eye was getting lovely. I still couldn't really breathe through my nose. Chogyi Jake's swollen lip was starting to go down a little.

I drove with my mind scattered. Part of me was scanning the streets for the Invisible College, and I kept drawing my will up through my spine and into my eyes, ready to peer through the magical disguises that they could use. Part of me was being buffeted by memories that came from driving down streets I hadn't been on in years. And below them both, there I was, shifting in the solitary part of my mind. I had gone home, where I'd dreaded going. I'd gone there for answers, and I'd gotten nothing. I didn't know one new thing about Eric or about my mother or how my family fit in with riders and vampires and body thieves. My own father had come inches from shooting me.

What I felt, there in that private corner of my mind, was a deep relief. I didn't know what it was or what it meant, but I'd gone home, everything had gone pear-shaped, and the sick pressure that had been on me since I'd made that first phone call home was gone. Maybe it was because things couldn't get much worse. Maybe it was because I felt like magical attacks and gun-toting wizards put the conflict back on my home turf. Or maybe it was just that I'd gone to that house, been with those people, and it hadn't turned me back into the girl I'd been before I left.

I pulled into the parking space beside the hotel, turned off the engine, and sat for a moment with my hands on the faux leather steering wheel.

"You know," Ex said, "we should really put together some kind of contingency plan where someone feeds the dog if we all get killed."

"Would be kind of rude to just leave her locked in the hotel room," I said. "I'll see what I can do."

Ozzie met us at the door to my room, jumping a little on her front legs. Her tail wagged so hard it pulled her a little off balance. I scratched her ears while Chogyi Jake got a towel from my bathroom and a bucket of ice. Ex grabbed the leash, and Ozzie danced in anticipation as he fixed it to her collar.

"Be careful out there," I said.

"I'll keep my eyes open," Ex said, and then, before I could go on, "I'm not only doing this for the dog. If I see anything off, I'll let you know."

The door closed behind them and I let myself fall back on the bed. It wasn't the best place we'd been. Not even the best place recently. The truth was that with the money Eric had left me, I could have bought a house and had it furnished and not particularly noticed the expense.

"I think those two hit it off pretty well," Chogyi Jake said.

"Yeah, it's funny," I said. "I would have picked Ex more as a cat guy."

"He has a soft spot for loyalty," Chogyi Jake said. "Do you want to reset your nose here or go to a hospital?"

I looked up at him with an expression that was supposed to say *Really? You have to ask?* My history with hospitals hadn't been good. His either. He smiled and handed me a towel.

"Blow out as much as you can."

Sighing, I sat up and did my best. He'd been right to go with the towel. Kleenex wouldn't have been up to the task. I plopped back down on the bed and he sat next to me, his thumbs on either side of my nose. It sounded like some ripping cardboard, and the pain was intense but brief. He handed me a washcloth filled with ice and three Advil. I sat back. It was easier to breathe, so I took that as a good sign. I took my cell phone out of my backpack. Twenty seconds and three rings later, my lawyer was on the other end.

"Jayné, dear," she said. "What can I do for you?"

"Well, I need a couple things," I said. "Do you remember that report I had you put together on Randolph Coin?"

"Of course, dear."

"I think a few of his friends and associates are in Wichita, and I need to find out what we can about them."

"I'll have something put together. Anything else?"

"Is there a way to set up a trust so that if

something happens to me, my dog still gets taken care of?"

"Nothing easier. Would you want to put my phone number on her tags?"

There were times I loved my lawyer. There were a lot of times, in fact. As far as I could tell, nothing fazed her. If I'd asked her to ship me quicklime and a shovel, she'd have asked if I wanted a defense lawyer along with them. On one hand, it meant never having to explain anything. On the other, I had to wonder whether she'd have been the same for Eric.

My guess was yes.

"That would be great. I'll do that. And also I need to send some money to my family. Just a couple thousand to cover some repairs."

"What address should I send it to?" she asked.

I told her, and we spent about a minute exchanging pleasantries: The new car and phone were great, the research grant had gone through, they'd had word from the property manager in New Orleans that the house there needed a new roof. It struck me as we were speaking just how innocuous the conversation sounded and how much it left out. The new car and phone were there because I'd been on the run from a band of compromised exorcists. The research grant was going to my old boyfriend's girlfriend to help clear my conscience for the years her career had suffered because of Eric's professional and personal destruction of her. The property manager in New Orleans was an ex–FBI agent who'd been possessed by a rider and killed at least a dozen people including her own parents, and the man taking care of her was a wanted serial killer who had been victimized by the same rider. If anyone had been listening to the conversation, it would have sounded like nothing. It *was* nothing, until you scratched it, and then all the deep weirdness shone through.

I dropped the call as Ex and Ozzie came back in. He had a duffel bag over his shoulder that had been empty when it was in the car. It was loaded down now, probably with shotguns. The dog's tail was still wagging, and I had the impression that it hadn't stopped at any point in between. She scrambled up onto the bed and curled up with a look that said *What? I'm small.*

"Anything?" I asked.

"Nothing I could see," Ex said. "Nothing out there's under a glamour. No surveillance that I can see either. It would have been difficult if the city were denser, but there's hardly anything out here to hide behind."

"There's a small blessing."

Ex smiled.

"More like faint praise," he said, sitting on the cheap black desk chair that seemed to come in all hotel rooms and propping his feet on the other bed. "So what's plan B?"

"Don't know. Things didn't go too well with my dad."

"I know," Ex said.

"I mean before that. We were in the garage, and—"

"Yeah, the sound carried pretty well," Ex said. "We didn't hear all the words, but the tone of voice was clear."

"Oh," I said. "Well, that's embarrassing."

"The big question is what the Invisible College was doing there," Ex said, unzipping the duffel bag and taking out one of the guns. "If they came because they knew we were coming. If they've been staking out your home turf since Denver."

He racked the gun, ejecting a brass-and-blue-plastic shell. Chogyi Jake picked it up, frowning, and pulled a tiny Leatherman out of his pocket.

"Yeah," I said. "I was under the impression that we'd broken them back in Denver. Didn't killing their grand pooh-bah break all their spells?"

"All the ones that were tied to the rider that had taken Coin's body," Ex said. "And we kicked the ant-hill. But enough time may have passed that they got their boy band back together."

"A new Randolph Coin," I said. Then I shook my head. "That wasn't what this guy seemed like to me. He was young."

"The body was young," Chogyi Jake said, stepping into the bathroom. "The thing inside it may have been quite old. And possibly quite powerful."

"That's what I mean, though," I said. "He didn't seem . . . powerful. Or maybe powerful but not so-phisticated. I mean, he used the frigging Oath of the Abyss."

"Maybe he's got a thing for shotguns," Ex said, racking and ejecting another round and another until the gun was empty and half a dozen blue shells rolled on the spare bed. "All power, no subtlety."

My phone buzzed. A text message from Curtis: ru OK? What the f was that?

"I suspect he was one of the younger leaders within the College," Chogyi Jake said. "Someone with ties and experience, but still subordinate to Coin."

I thumbed a message back to Curt: I'm fine. Don't worry. I'll be in touch.

It was weak, but I didn't know what else to tell him. This didn't seem like the moment to go into the whole issue of spiritual parasites and secret societies. Partly because he might think the whole thing was exciting, and the last thing I wanted was my little brother poking his hands into the hornet's nest. The less involved he was—the less involved all of them were—the better it would be for everybody.

"We knew that Coin was involved in holding the *haugsvarmr* under Grace Memorial," Ex said, "be-cause killing Coin was what let that damned thing call for help."

"Which is why Eric was in Denver in the first place," I said. "To get rid of Coin and find the thing under Grace and . . ."

"Yeah," Ex said, switching to the second weapon. "That's the question, isn't it? And what? Make some kind of deal with it. It got its freedom and Eric got fill-in-the-blank."

"We've already figured that Eric wasn't exactly one of the good guys," I said. "The Invisible College was working against him. They might be on the side of the angels, right?"

"I think there's room in all this for more than two sides," Ex said. "Eric was a sociopath and a rapist, but that doesn't mean Coin wasn't at least as bad or worse. The Pleroma is full of these things, and that they all fight among each other doesn't mean that half of them are angels and half are demons. They're—"

He broke off, looked away, and started ejecting shells from the second gun. I knew what he was going to say and why he'd stopped. *They're all demons.* The words were as clear as if he'd spoken them. To Ex, all riders were demonic, and all of them needed to be stopped. Even the one in me. That it had saved my life and his a dozen times over didn't matter to him. In his world, I was still someone to be saved, and she—it—was what I needed saving from. I folded my hands across my knees and looked away. I'd made my deal with the Black Sun, and it hadn't done anything yet that made me think it wasn't my ally. And still, I wasn't a hundred percent sure Ex was wrong.

"Well, we can't leave," I said. "Not the way things stand now. And we can't go to my folks and start asking questions."

"So what does that leave us?" Ex asked as he started to break down the shotguns.

Ozzie yawned, stretched, and started to snore wetly. I poked her with my toe, but she ignored me. Outside the window, the traffic from the highway made a low, constant hum. Tires against asphalt. The moon was just shy of full, spilling cold, blue light across the parking lot.

"I think we should try to make contact with my mother outside of the house. No one's going to go against Dad in his own home. Not if he's laying down the law like this. But if we can get her when she's out shopping or coming home from church or something, maybe I can talk to her."

"What about your brothers?" Chogyi called. "They seemed quite approachable."

"Probably are, but they're also the least likely to know anything. Jay's not that much older than me, and he's got his fiancée and her family and the wedding thing to worry about. Curt's younger and probably knows even less than I did."

"Does your mother attend church by herself?" Chogyi Jake asked.

"Sometimes," I said. "But even if her schedule's the same as it was when I was living there, this wedding thing's going to throw it off. Plus which, my dad's going to be on high alert. Plus which, Carla and all her family are going to be around."

"So follow her around," Ex said, "and hope for a chance."

"And hope no one else is following her around in order to take a crack at us when we start doing it."

"Sounds like our usual kind of plan," Ex said, smiling grimly.

My phone buzzed again. Curtis. Who were those guys? Were they in a gang or something?

"Hmm," Ex said, frowning down at the disassembled steel.

"Anything interesting?"

"Nope. The serial numbers are still on them, though."

"Can we trace them? See who they were sold to or something?"

Ex smiled like I'd made a joke.

"This is America," he said. "There's no Carfax for guns. About the best we can hope for is that they were stolen. And then all we'll really know is who they were stolen from."

"Is there any juju on them?"

"Not that I can see," Ex said. "Maybe on the shells, though."

"No," Chogyi Jake said, stepping back into the room. His hand was out flat, carrying something gently. "No magic. But look at this."

It wasn't quite a powder. More like tiny pale stones flecked with bits of red and black color. I frowned and put my fingers out to touch it. It didn't burn or feel cold. I didn't get the weird flesh-crawling feel I sometimes did around magically charged items. It just felt like it looked. Innocuous.

"Rock salt?" Ex said.

"I think so," Chogyi Jake said. "It dissolves the way I'd expect it to. I haven't quite brought myself to taste it, but—"

"We should check the other shells," Ex said. It took us about half an hour to slit the plastic open on all of them. Before we were done, Ozzie had woken enough to become interested in what we were doing and then get bored by it again. All of the shells were the same. Black powder and mundane salt. Ex went back to the disassembled guns, lifting each piece to his eyes and shifting it so that the light played across the surfaces.

"There's no rust," he said. "I can't believe they've used salt rounds in these guns. At least, not on a regular basis."

"Why use them at all?" I asked.

"Because you didn't want to hurt anybody," Chogyi Jake said.

"That's what I was thinking," I said. "So if they weren't looking to hurt anybody, what *were* they doing?"

For what seemed like forever, none of us spoke. When Ex broke the silence, his voice was soft.

"Curiouser and curiouser."

CHAPTER FIVE

I was at a coffee shop in Phoenix a few years back when I heard that my uncle was dead. The man on the other end of the line was very gentle, very solicitous. All I knew then was that Uncle Eric—the one relative who'd always been on my side, swooping in whenever I was in trouble—had been killed. After we hung up, I sat still for half an hour, trying to figure out how I felt. Stunned, horrified, sad. I had the impulse to call home and talk to my parents, but even then I knew it wouldn't be welcome. Dad had forbidden us all to speak to Eric with more or less the same fervor he'd used to forbid me to go to ASU.

I didn't call. Instead, I'd packed up the thin membrane of my own failed life and flown out to Denver, expecting to execute his will and hide out from my collegiate failures for a couple weeks.

Back then, I printed up all the directions to things off MapQuest. When Ex tracked me, he had to sneak a GPS tracker into my backpack. Now, planning out our next approach to my mother, it was all Google Maps and Street View, and I'd had the GPS trackers pulled out of my phone and car. Actually, so that Ex couldn't find me when I didn't want to get found. Some things time changes quickly.

Some things stay the same.

The morning after I talked to my lawyer, the report was delivered by special courier. The carefully anonymous pages had become familiar over the years. I lay on the bed in my sweats and a T-shirt, scratching Ozzie with the heel of my right foot, and went over the pages. The Invisible College had fallen apart after their leader died, but in recent months about half a dozen much smaller, much less organized groups had started to re-form from the ruins of the old one, usually with some central figure taking the role that Randolph Coin had occupied. In Montreal, it was a woman named Idéa Smith who might or might not have been the blue-eyed

woman with the shotgun. In Mexico City, Eduardo
Martinez, who was apparently immune to having a
decent picture taken. In Los Angeles . . .

"Bingo," I said. Ozzie shifted her ears forward.

Jonathan Rhodes had turned twenty-eight in
May, putting him about one presidential election
ahead of me. He'd been inducted into the Invisible
College ten years before. Before that, he'd been a
musician. He'd studied economics and literature
at Tulane for three semesters before he fell in with
members of the College. The pictures of him were
unmistakable. He had the kind of boyish face that
would still look young when he was sixty. Even with
a full head of brownish hair and none of the tattoos
that covered him now, I recognized the man who'd
broken my nose.

The report went on to detail what the three new
leaders had been doing, more or less, in the years
since their own superior died. I skimmed most of
it. The important thing for me was what they were
doing now, apart from kicking in my family's doors
and windows. The answer wasn't particularly satis-
fying. Since the end of summer, they'd been absent.
Vanished. Gone underground like they were hiding
from something. There wasn't a solid date when
they'd vanished, but it looked to me like it had gone
down right about the same time I'd been in Chicago.
I wanted there to be a connection between the two,
and maybe there was one. I just didn't see it.

I got to the last page of the report. A list of out-standing questions that the investigator was looking into now—recent whereabouts, funding sources, activity on the Internet—with the promise that more information would be provided as soon as the questions had reliable answers. Given that I'd only asked for the report the night before, I was impressed they'd managed this much.

I tossed the report on my pillow and got up. My body suffered a kind of all-over soreness that I hadn't felt before. Each individual muscle seemed to ache just a little bit, so there wasn't anything I could do, any motion I could make, that didn't bug me at least a little bit. My face still throbbed if I stood up or sat down too quickly, and the girl in the mirror looked pretty rough. Blood had pooled under both my eyes, and the bridge of my nose had a little shift that it hadn't had before. I washed my face gently. Probably I should have gone to a doctor. If it was important to me later, I could have a plastic surgeon rebreak everything and put it back together. Probably it wouldn't be worth the trouble. I told myself the new nose added character, took a quick shower, and got some clothes on. Ozzie was standing by her food bowl and wagging her tail at me when I got out. She was almost finished with her breakfast when Ex's soft knock came at the door.

"I think it's your boyfriend," I whispered into her soft ears, then opened the door. Chogyi Jake was with him, and they'd brought pancakes. Ex also had a pair of massive 1960s sunglasses with lenses that stretched down past my cheekbones and covered my shiners. My friends were the best people ever. They took turns reading the report while I ate.

"We have their guns," I said when they were both finished. "I was thinking maybe we could use that to make some kind of connection back to them. Figure out where they are?"

"Would be better if we had something with blood on it," Ex said.

"And even then," Chogyi Jake said, "the Invisible College can be difficult to track."

"That's why I was thinking magic. I know they can cast glamours and look different. I thought if we could use my rider, maybe—"

"They're also hard to locate that way," Ex said.

"Kind of the way I am?"

"Like that," he agreed.

"Well, piss. Back to the first plan, then? At least Mom won't be that hard to find."

PLAINS IMMANUEL Fellowship was in an A-frame building with buff-colored brick on the first story and white clapboard above that where the chapel ceiling rose up. Looking at the five low stone steps that led to its doors was like hearing a familiar voice speaking my name. Everything about the building was clear in my mind—the

fluorescent-backlit stained glass in the hall outside
the pastor's office, the blond wood of the pews, the
damp smell of the children's classroom in the basement. All of it was clear. The building itself seemed
like a person. Like another member of my family. Part of me wanted to go in just to be there. To
breathe that air again and see if it really was all just
the way I remembered, or if by changing myself I'd
changed it too.

There was a new sign out by the road, also done
in brick and almost the same color as the building.
It had a section of white with black movable letters.
Today, they spelled out FEAR THE LORD, AND
YOU'LL HAVE NOTHING TO FEAR. Every time I
read the words, I was torn between amusement and
anger.

Ex and I sat in the SUV across the road, watching. Chogyi Jake was out in the cold wind, huddled
into a flight jacket with a stocking cap pulled down
over his ears, making his tour of the building's pe-
rimeter. Looking for the enemy. When he was done,
he'd get back in the rental car we'd hired so that we
could have more than one option in case of an attack. I'd popped for the full insurance on the rental.
I'd gotten a coffee from a Scooter's Coffee & Yogurt.
Ex had too. My mother had gone in the church
about an hour ago. I'd turned off the music when
we got there because I had the idea that it wasn't the
sort of thing that went with shadowing someone.

Between the heater, the engine, and the wind, there could have been a George Thorogood concert going on inside and I wouldn't have known it, but I didn't turn my Pink Martini back on.

The doors opened, and I leaned forward, my hands on the steering wheel. A man in a gray suit came out and trotted to the parking lot. I sat back while he revved his engine and pulled out into traffic. I didn't know what exactly Mom was doing at church, but I didn't think there were services at this time in the morning. Something to do with the wedding, I guessed. Or else something to do with me.

"Are you all right?" Ex asked.

He looked good. He'd put a glamour on himself. It was one of the cantrips Eric had taught him, back when they'd worked together. Back before any of us had known what Eric was. As a result, his own wounds and bruises were invisible, as if they'd healed overnight. He looked like a perfect version of himself unless I really focused on him, and then all the damage became clear. Not a bad metaphor for the rest of him either.

"I'm . . . I don't know. I'm fine. You guys keep asking that. Do I look like I'm about to start sprouting tentacles or something?"

"You're quiet," he said.

"And I'm usually loud?"

His smile was sly, and it made him look better.

"You're not usually quiet."

The church door opened, and this time it was my mother walking out. She wore a simple blue dress that looked too slight for the weather, a thin coat, and a wool scarf that fluttered behind her like it had someplace else it wanted to be. I scooped up my phone and called Chogyi Jake.

"I see her," he said instead of hello. "Going back to the car."

"All right," I said. "Any sign of the bad guys?"

"Nothing."

"Okay. I'll follow her. You follow me."

I had essentially no experience tailing someone. It was the kind of skill set I'd heard about on TV and movies, but I wasn't sure how to go about it. We had two cars, so I had a vague idea that I should stay behind Mom for a while, then turn off and let Chogyi Jake take my place, then switch off again a few blocks later. Either it was a good plan, or my mother had other things on her mind. Even though I was in a lumbering black apartment of a car, she didn't seem to notice me, or it, or much of anything. She went to the dry cleaner's and the bank. I drove with one eye on her, and one on the rearview. I expected to see a buzzing fleet of rider-infested wizards bearing down on me and howling for blood at any minute. That it kept not happening only made it seem more likely that it would.

When she turned into the parking lot of the Save-A-Lot, I got on the phone to Chogyi Jake.

"Okay, this is it," I said.

"Are you sure?"

"I have to get her before she gets the groceries. I don't know if she'll talk to me, but if she's got something in the car that might spoil, I can promise she won't. I could be offering her a million dollars, and she'd blow me off until she got the frozen dinners home."

"If you say so," Chogyi Jake said. "I'll set up on the corner. If I call—"

"I'll get out of there fast," I said, and dropped the connection. The SUV jogged a little as I made the turn into the lot a couple degrees too wide.

"Will you be able to?" Ex said as he slid a fresh magazine into his pistol. I was impressed again how much hunting demons felt like committing crime.

"Able to do what?"

"Get out of there fast. She's your mother. It's kind of a primal relationship."

"I'm the thing putting her in danger. If I leave, that makes her safer. Right?"

"That's my assumption," Ex said as I pulled up to the sidewalk in front of the store. My mother was just getting out of her car maybe thirty feet away. "Just wanted to make sure we were thinking the same thing."

I popped open the driver's door and slid down to the pavement. Ex slid across behind me, closed the door, and drove away. Chogyi Jake's rental—a white

Sebring—was in position at the edge of the lot. I had to fight the urge to wave at him.

I stood on the curb, my hands pushed deep in my pockets. I didn't have a gun, mostly because experience had proven that I was considerably behind Zatoichi when it came to hitting my targets. And besides that, when the fights actually started, it wasn't me running the body. A green truck cruised between us. The guy at the wheel looked like he was about twelve. When Mom saw me, she broke stride a little, the hesitation nothing more than an extra half step. So she hadn't seen me following her. The wind bit at my cheeks and lips, and my heart was beating fast. I held myself still, looking out from behind the massive sunglasses. Her expression went from fear to anger to sorrow so quickly, it was hard to parse. She walked up to me, stopping maybe five feet away. Her body was turned, and it took me a second to realize why. She was protecting her purse like I was going to steal it. Like one kind of threat was all threats.

"I can't talk to you," she said.

"Meaning Dad won't let you," I said. It wasn't what I'd meant to say. I could already feel this starting to fishtail out from under me. I took a breath and tried again. "It's been a really hard few years. There are some things I need to know that only you can tell me."

"I can't," she said, lifting her chin. Her gaze was

set about five degrees off to my right, as if looking at me straight on would be dangerous. "I understand you don't respect our family or our God, so I wouldn't expect you to understand why I would choose to honor your father's wishes, but—"

"Yeah, I really don't."

"*But*. Your father is a good man."

"Is he?"

That seemed to strike home. Two bright spots of color appeared on her cheeks, red underneath the paleness of her makeup.

"You have no idea what sacrifices he has made for this family," she said. "You have no idea the troubles that the Lord has put on his shoulders."

I shrugged.

"Maybe someone could tell me," I said. "Know anybody who'd be up for that?"

"I will not speak to you," my mother said. Her scowl could have shamed stones. She set her shoulders and turned away, marching toward the grocery store.

"Please," my body said without me. It was always strange when it did that. Before I knew I had a rider, I figured it was just my subconscious taking action without bothering to alert my frontal lobes. I figured everyone worked like this. How could I have known otherwise?

My mother stopped like I'd yanked on her leash. I stood still, and the rider in me didn't do anything

else. My mother turned back slowly, as if unwilling
to but without the power to stop herself. She came
back slowly. There were tears in her eyes, which
was a first since I'd come back to town. And something else. Looking at her, it was like seeing a kid
on Christmas day coming downstairs to find a pony
standing by the tree. It wasn't happiness. It wasn't
delight. It was what came before that. Wonder,
maybe. Disbelief.

"What did you say?" she asked, and her voice
sounded like someone shouting from a long way off.
"What did you say to me?"

"Please," the Black Sun said with my mouth.
It reached out and took my mother's hand. She
stepped close, her eyes locked on mine now, staring
into me like she was looking for something. Like
she'd lost something important and thought she
might find it written on the back of my skull.

"You?" she whispered. "It is you? Are *you* there?"

When I answered, it was really me.

"I don't know. Help me find out."

Her hand dropped back to her side. A thickset
black man pushed a cart out from the doors behind her, nodded to us as he passed, and pressed
out into the parking lot with a metallic crash. He
might as well not have been there. My mother's attention was locked on nothing, her lips moving in a
conversation I had no part in. My nose had started
running, and the cold hurt my earlobes. I ignored

the discomfort. My heart was beating faster. I felt the gap between us growing thin. I could feel myself almost reaching her. Almost.

"I know you're not supposed to," I said. "Talk to me anyway."

"Your father is a good man," she said. "He's a good man."

"Except he's not my father," I said. Her gaze snapped to me. To me, not the rider, not the air beside my head. Not even the story she'd told herself about me ever since I left. For the first time in years, my mother was looking at me. Ever since a girl with the Sight had told me that my mother had had an affair, I'd had the suspicion take root, but I'd never said it. Not even to myself. "Dad. He's not my father. Is he?"

"Your father is . . . your father is . . ." she said, and it had the same intonation that she'd used before, except it broke. The sentence stuck there in her throat like a bone. For a moment her attention swam. "Your father was the devil."

It felt like a punch in the stomach. Or like victory. Or both.

"Okay," I said, nodding. "Tell me about that."

CHAPTER SIX

It wasn't a restaurant I'd been to before. I'd let Mom drive us there, trusting Chogyi Jake and Ex to figure out what was up and follow as best they could. I paid the girl at the front an extra hundred dollars for a booth away from everyone else and not to come over to us unless I called for her. Her eyebrows had tried to crawl up into her hair, but she took the money. Red plastic benches curved under us. The Formica table was an artist's interpretation of wood grain, recognizable but unconvincing. The radio in the kitchen was playing a country station. I didn't recognize the song, but the guitar work was good. The air was thick with the smell of grease and hot metal. I sat facing toward the front so that I'd see any assaults coming from the street and Mom wouldn't be distracted if someone we knew came in. I hadn't considered any of that consciously. Thinking that way was who I'd become.

She had a glass of iced tea clutched in her hand the way a desperate alcoholic might hold a glass of bourbon, and she poured packets of artificial sweetener in it one after the other until I was pretty sure she'd lost count. Her face was blank as a mask, and she was back to not looking at me directly. All animation was gone. Even her movements had a clockwork-like rigidity. I tried to connect all this with the woman I'd known as my mother, with her uncertainty and subservience, and at first I couldn't. And then I could. I didn't talk, didn't touch her. I let the moment have its own time, afraid that if I pushed, she'd jump up and leave. Even the air between us seemed fragile. I tried not to breathe too hard.

When she spoke, her voice was careful, slow, and emotionless. She sounded like someone being deposed by the police.

"God put Gary Heller into my life when I was eighteen years old. I knew the first time I saw him that we were meant for each other. Everyone at church knew him. They liked him. When he asked me to marry him, I felt truly blessed. I never had any doubt that I was supposed to be with him. Never for one minute, and I never have. Gary has been a true man to me. He's been better than I deserved."

She took a sip of the tea, opened another packet of sweetener and poured the white powder over the ice. Some sank to the sludge at the bottom of the glass and some hung suspended in the tea, gritty and cold.

"I didn't meet Eric until just before the wedding. He was the black sheep of the family. All I knew was he was a businessman, but he came to church like the rest of us, and he prayed as loud as anyone, and he spoke the name of the Lord with a smile on his face. I liked him. I did. He was funny and he was sweet. And he was a little better looking than Gary, though I was grateful to have the man I did. I love Gary, and I bless the day he found me. I bless it. I didn't understand what Eric was."

My belly was a little tighter.

"What was he?"

My mother opened her mouth, closed it, and brought a corner of her mouth up in a half smile that was as much cruelty as amusement.

"He said it was a surprise for Gary. He said not to tell him, and I believed. I went to his house. If it had been at night, I think I wouldn't have gone, but it was in the afternoon . . ."

She shrugged and drank a mouthful of tea through her teeth.

"There were candles everywhere, and smoke. The whole house was like someone breathing in my face, but someone with the sweetest breath. I made some sort of joke about it. I remember that I did that. I said something about making the whole place into a birthday cake. And he said no. That he was catching angels. I wanted to leave, but I didn't. I couldn't. He took me to his back room. The bed was tipped up against the wall, and there were . . . drawings on the floor. Symbols. He asked me to take my clothes off, and I did."

"Jesus," I said.

I'd thought I was ready to hear this. Really, even as we'd driven over from the Save-A-Lot, I was sure that I wanted to know everything she had to say to me. I'd been wrong, but there was no way to stop it now. No way to tell her to keep all this crap to herself. This was my mother and Uncle Eric, and I felt a little dizzy already.

"He anointed me with . . . oils?" she said, her intonation making it a question. "And he called forth an angel. He called an angel into me. It was like being in a dream. I was filled with her, and I was lifted up by her, and I saw the face of God. And when she left, I felt certain. I felt full of grace and love, like I had never felt before. He told me not to tell anyone. Not to tell Gary or Father Ryan.

He said that the angels were called to me for a reason."

Her eyes were bright now, alive with the memory.

"Every few weeks he would call me, and I would go to him. And they would come into me. And their names. Malphas. Wotan Irisi. Hadraniel. Onibaba. Each one would lift me up. They exalted me. I walked in the depths of the abyss and was not lost. I swam in a sea with no bottom and no surface with the angels of the infinite waters. My soul journeyed to places I had never imagined. I even found the beauty in death. I walked with the souls of the damned and found forgiveness in them. It was *beautiful*. And then I would come home to your father, and everything would be sharper and deeper and full of meaning for days. Maybe weeks. And then it would fade a little, and a little more, and before long I was a housewife again. Until Eric called me back and I felt the angels within me.

"I couldn't tell Gary about any of it. He wouldn't have understood. He only saw me as his wife, and I was the vessel of the angels."

There it was, then. For months at least, maybe years, Eric had used my mother as a testing ground to invoke riders, pull them into her body. Maybe he'd used magic to control her the way he had with Kim in Denver. And my mother had accepted it. Had loved it. Had put a frame around the experience that made it something good. At least at the time.

My throat felt thick, but I tried to keep my expression relaxed and calm. I wanted her to keep telling the story, even while I wanted it to stop.

"I grew apart from Gary," she said. "We sat with Father Ryan and prayed together every evening for a month. We had blessings on our marriage. He didn't understand why I was different. It was hard for me too, watching his hurt and confusion and not being able to reach out to him. But the work was so important. God had a plan for me just the way he did for Mary, and he was my Joseph. His faith restored me when the angels left me weak. But I was afraid he wouldn't be strong enough. I didn't tell him about my angels. Or about Eric. It was a secret, and I would have let myself be killed before I revealed it. Not until it was time."

"Time for what? Did he tell you what all this was for?"

"Time for revelation," she said, and her beatific expression faltered for a second. Her eyes shifted down to the table and she pushed her glass of tea away, the condensation leaving a wet track on the table. "I loved Eric. I thought I had married the wrong brother. That he would have been my perfect husband, but he insisted that this was all the way God intended. How could I disagree with him? He spoke the tongues of angels. Only . . ."

"Only?"

"Only he was the devil. Eric Heller was the devil

made flesh, and he seduced me with his magics and his vice. He ruined me."

"All right," I said. "How did that happen?"

My mother sighed.

"He found the angel he'd sought. She was magnificent. She took me to the desert, and I saw God as a pale sun in a vast sky, raining his blessings down over us all. He purified me. And she was there. She had wings as wide as the sky, with feathers like someone had plucked them out of the night sky. And sharp edged. Her face was beautiful. I wept when I saw her. Her beauty and her power. She filled me like none of the others ever had. I thought she must be the angel of the apocalypse, waiting for the trumpet to free her. And her name was Sonnenrad.

"When I returned to the world, Eric was so happy. He was so very happy. I lay with him then, with the angel inside me, even though I hadn't been with your father in months. Almost a year. And . . ."

"And me," I said.

She smiled. Her lips were thin. Bloodless. Her eyes seemed shallow and bright.

"And you," she said. "You were the fruit of my sin, and of his."

Eric Heller hadn't been my uncle. He'd been my dad. That alone would have left me dizzy. But there was also the Black Sun.

In the years we'd spent together, Aubrey had

taught me a lot about parasites and the logic of parasitism just by hanging around and talking. The rider had been in my mother's body. I wasn't sure, but I was willing to bet that was what brought the daughter organism into me. I'd been conceived by a possessed women, and the thing that lived in my body had been riding along from the time I'd been a zygote. It had always been with me.

"Gary found out, of course," my mother said, but I was only half listening. "He knew the baby couldn't have been his. I tried to explain to him that he was my Joseph. I tried to tell him that it was God's plan, and about the angels, and that I carried a child and an angel both within me. I believed then that I was without sin, and I told him that. I told him all of that."

"Can't imagine that went well," I said. It was more glib than I would have chosen if I'd been stable.

"His rage was justified. I'd broken my vows to him."

"What did he do to Eric?"

"Nothing. He didn't know."

"You didn't tell him?"

"Of course not," my mother said, waving the question away like it was silly. "I was the vessel of angels. I suffered and I endured. But I had her within me. And I had you. He couldn't kill me, and anything less than that, I could stand."

The door to the restaurant opened, and Chogyi Jake stepped inside. He looked over toward me, his smile as calm as always, then nodded and went to a table near the front where he could see me and my mother and the front windows too. He didn't seem to be in a hurry, so I figured the Invisible College wasn't about to attack. And if they weren't actively going to pull the trigger, I didn't have time for them. Not right now.

"Gary is a good man. We prayed together for a long time, and I came to see that I had wronged him. That Eric and I had both wronged him."

"And where was Eric while that was going on?"

"Gone," she said, her eyebrows lifting in a mask of wistfulness. "He vanished, and I never knew where to. Gary said that Eric had always been like that. Solid as stone one day, and gone the next. I'd heard that before, but I thought he would stay with me. I'd thought . . . Gary could have turned me out into the street. He could have asked for a divorce, and who would have told him no? After what I'd done."

A tear slipped down her cheek, tracking makeup along with it. I put my hand on hers, thinking a little comfort, a little contact, might make things better. She flinched back like I'd stung her.

"My husband is a good man. He forgave me my sins, and he took me back into his arms. And you. He took you as his daughter. He raised you as his own. He did everything to protect you. And you re-paid him with cruelty. I have never been so ashamed as I was the day you abandoned us."

Not even when you were screwing Eric, I almost said. I swallowed it. There was no point. For her, my leaving was an unforgivable sin. The choices she'd made didn't signify, because they were God's work. Beyond her control. And if Eric had been using the magic I was almost certain he had, then there was even some truth in it.

I'd left of my own free will. It had been a choice—my choice—and I'd made it. Mom had been at the whim of Eric and the riders and God only knew what else. I wondered, if I'd been in my father's position, if I'd have done the same. Raised a kid that wasn't mine and kept a spouse who wouldn't even tell me whose cuckoo I was support-ing. Honestly, I wasn't sure I'd have done it.

"He came back, though. Eric. He came back and he told Gary himself. Do you remember that? Your father came home and made each of us swear never to speak to Eric. Never to have anything to do with him again. He was so angry. With himself. With me. It was the only time he wouldn't pray with me. That was how I knew."

"I figured Eric was gay," I said.

"You were young," my mother said. Her voice was dry and brittle as slate. "You didn't know much."

"I'm sorry," I said, even though I wasn't. It was the right thing to say, and my mother nodded once in reply. "The angel? Sonnenrad? What happened to her?"

"She left me," Mom said. "No bonds could hold her forever. But she's in you. Isn't she?"

"Sort of," I said. "Something like her. I have a friend who'd call her a daughter organism. Did Eric ever tell anyone why he did it? What it was all about?"

"You must get rid of it. You have to cast it out of your body."

"I thought it was an angel."

"It is my sin. It's poisoned you because of me, but you can still be clean. You can put her back in me. I can be your sacrifice. I can carry it for you. I'll do that for you, because you are my child and I love you."

Now *she* was the one to reach for *my* hand, and I tried to pull back. Her fingers were stronger than I'd expected. Her eyes locked on mine. At the front of the restaurant, Chogyi Jake shifted in his chair, pushing back a few inches from his table in case he needed to come to my rescue. I didn't give him any signal, and he waited.

I tried to put the woman across the table from me together with the mother I knew. The mousy, quiet, subservient woman who accepted my father's anger. The meek one who told us all to make peace, to do as my father said. To obey and be good and be quiet. She looked the same. Older, but the same. And that was where the similarity stopped, because everything else about her was different.

"I think I need to go," I said, my voice shaking less than I expected it to.

"No," she said, loudly enough that the waitress turned to stare. There's a limit to how much privacy you can buy in a public space, and we'd reached it. "I am not Mary. I am not without sin. What you carry in you is corrupting you because of what *I* did. Give it back to me, and be pure. Let me help you. Let me make you pure."

I stood up.

"Thank you," I said, the words empty and automatic. I took a few light-headed steps toward the door, and Chogyi Jake rose in my peripheral vision. My mother's sobs rang through the place as I reached the door, pushed out into the cold air. The wind was like being slapped, and I welcomed it. Chogyi Jake put a hand on my shoulder, turning me gently, and I realized that the SUV I was staring at was mine. Ex was behind the wheel. I tottered over to the front passenger's-side door and lifted myself in.

"Back to the hotel?" he asked as I shut the door. Chogyi Jake trotted to a side lot where his rental was parked, nose out for a fast getaway. "Jayné?"

"Hmm? Oh. Right. Yes, back to the hotel."

Ex slid out into traffic, and I craned my neck. Mom was still in the restaurant. Still at our table. Her head was in her hands. The urge to go back to her was powerful and doomed.

"You all right?" Ex asked.

I'm fine fought with *Hell no*. The streets slid away under the tires, and I didn't say anything. He didn't ask again. All I could remember was my mother's face as she asked me to put the rider back into her; all I could see was the hunger there.

CHAPTER SEVEN

"I mean, I *knew* my family was screwed-up." I sat on the edge of my bed, one leg folded under me. The mattress made a soft huffing sound under my weight. Like an exhalation. "But oh my God. That was . . ."

"Kind of reframes your whole childhood?" Ex said.

"Does."

Chogyi Jake stood beside the little in-room coffeemaker, a black coffee cup in one hand and a tea bag in the other. The machine gurgled and spat heated water into a pot. Chogyi Jake's stubble was getting long again, his scalp fading into a dark halo. He'd shave it again soon. Ex's smile would have looked cruel and a little judgmental if I hadn't known that most of his judgments were on himself or the world. I knew these men well enough to read the way they held their bodies, the way they spoke, and dressed. We'd been in almost constant company since I'd arrived in Denver. Since I'd begun this chapter in my life. It was the kind of intimacy that you got with family. Small indications that grew into a larger whole, that drew along a whole cloud of implications behind it.

Except that apparently family could still surprise me. I could live with someone for years—live my whole life with them and know how to read their moods like a sailor reading the weather in a sunrise—and miss the huge, defining, central fact of their whole damn life. I thought of my father, even if he wasn't exactly my father, and his sullen anger. I thought about the times he'd yelled at my mother that I hadn't understood why. That made more sense now. But there were other things.

When I was eight, the whole family got the flu at the same time. The whole house was sick for a week and a half, and it was my father, suffering and weak, who brought me bowls of soup to eat in bed and medicine for the fever. Another time, when I was ten or eleven, I lost control of my bike and scraped a patch of skin the size of my palm off my left hip. Dad tended to the wound, and afterward he got his own bike out of the garage and showed me how to ride with my center of gravity lower.

If he wasn't really my father, if I was the cuckoo in the nest, and, more to the point, if he knew that, then all the little moments of caring—the Band-Aids and the kiss-it-and-make-it-betters and the birthday presents and the sticks of gum for a good grade on a test—changed too. They weren't the bare minimum.

If I had been the constant reminder of his wife's betrayal—if he'd swallowed the humiliation of raising another man's daughter not even knowing who the other guy was—then all of those moments of kindness, of love, became deeper and stranger and more profound than I had known. And my ignorance had been part of his gift to me. I was his daughter. His viciously controlled, better-damn-well-do-what-he-said, in-by-curfew, and sixteen's-too-young-to-date daughter, yeah. But his. And I'd never questioned that he was my father.

Even now, even knowing that Eric had provided the sperm donation that led to me, Dad was still my dad. I couldn't change that. And I couldn't change the resentment I felt toward him either. I could only know intellectually that it might not be as justified as I'd thought, and the dissonance was profound.

"Earth to Doris," Ex said.

"What?" I snapped.

"I asked if you wanted a cup of tea," Chogyi Jake said. "Several times."

"Oh. Sorry. Yes."

"Green?"

"Nasty-ass Lipton," I said, "if you've got it."

"Nasty-ass Lipton it is," Chogyi Jake said.

"So the question is what Eric was up to," Ex said, scratching Ozzie's ears and looking at her like she might know the answer. "It sounds like the Mark of Salim al-Assad. Binding different riders into the same host body until he got the one he was looking for. Only, instead of a goat, he was using a woman."

"That's possible. Having a host that had been ridden several times would make subsequent possessions easier," Chogyi Jake said. He handed me a coffee cup with the thin white string of the tea bag looped around the handle. "But that she was naked left me wondering about rites of Inanna."

"I just figured it was Eric getting his rocks off," Ex said with a shrug.

"Okay. Talking about my mother here," I said. "I'm feeling pretty freaked out already. It's not helping to imagine her as Eric's . . ." I waved my hand.

"Mind-controlled, sexually exploited lab hamster?" Ex offered.

"Yes, that. Not helping."

"But it's what she was," Ex said. "We knew that Eric was capable of atrocities. Looking away from it now doesn't win us anything. You aren't responsible for any of this. None of this is your fault. But you exist because Eric was willing to go to great lengths to make a child that would be possessed by the Black Sun from the moment of conception. He put a lot of effort into making that happen, and when he'd managed it, he moved on to whatever was next on his to-do list. There has to be a reason."

"That isn't what he's done, though," Chogyi Jake said. "Jayné isn't simply ridden by the Black Sun. Eric engineered the creation of a new rider. A daughter not only for the woman but for the mature Black Sun as well."

"Good point," Ex said.

I stood up and scooped the leather leash and my oversize sunglasses off the dresser. Ozzie's ears turned toward me, and she hopped on her front legs.

"I just took her out," Ex said.

"Yeah," I said. "This time she's taking me."

"Be careful. We didn't see the Invisible College following you today, but that doesn't mean they're not out there."

Ozzie and I walked down the corridor to the lobby. I had the leash in one hand and my coffee cup in the other. A television was set to FOX, where a woman in a pale blue dress was looking earnestly into the camera and talking about preparations being made for the New Year's Eve celebrations and wondering aloud whether three days would be enough time to get ready. Red and silver tinsel and fake holly clung to the front desk, and the man behind it nodded to me as I passed. I smiled back reflexively.

Outside, the world was getting colder. High, thin clouds scudded across the vast blue like they were in a hurry to get someplace. Or at least away from here. From the smell, I guessed there was snow coming. I led Ozzie out to the edge of the parking lot, and she trotted amiably along beside me. The traffic on the highway buzzed, the individual cars and trucks and semis all blending together in a single constant sound. I sat on the concrete curb, my elbows resting on my knees. Ozzie looked at me, chuffed once, and sat at my side. I counted windows, found where my room was, and then the one Chogyi Jake and Ex were sharing. I wondered what would have happened if I'd checked in with one of them. I'd heard more than one story of an unmarried man and woman being required to get separate rooms. Not corporate policy, just my little town.

There was something lonely about the hotel. It wasn't just that there was so little city built up around it, or the sparse scattering of cars in the lot. It seemed more basic. This was a building especially designed for people who weren't home, a place for being passed through. I'd lived a lot of places in the last few years—my dorm, a house I'd tried unsuccessfully to share with my college friends, and then easily a dozen condominiums and apartments and houses that I'd inherited from Eric. Probably as many hotels. Maybe more.

I hadn't had a real home since I'd left here. And now I found myself wondering if I'd had one then.

"You there?" I said to the rider. The Black Sun. My other self. "You have any idea what to make of all this?"

If it did, it didn't speak. Ozzie sighed, her breath a plume of white.

"You know," I said to her, "I was staying in much fancier places before I had a dog with me. There's a perspective why all this is your fault."

She wagged once and I put a hand on her back, scratching slowly.

I felt more than tired. I felt stretched thin, and I wanted it to be because of my father and my mother and the Invisible College. But the truth was I could hardly remember not feeling like this. I'd dropped into the middle of Eric's world after he died, spending months trying to inventory all of his belongings, find all of his places. I'd managed to build up a massive pile of information that I still hadn't really had time to digest. And then Grace Memorial, and the things I'd done there that I still didn't want to think about. And then the rider and New Mexico and now . . . now here. Being worn-out wasn't a response to the problems of the moment. It was a lifestyle choice that I'd made somewhere along the way, and that I didn't know how to change.

My telephone buzzed. I pulled it out of my pocket. It was the same number I'd had since I first learned what a phone number was. Home calling. I almost let it drop to voice mail; then, just before it did, I thumbed the green button and held the phone to my ear.

"Hello?" I said.

"Fucking Christ, sis," Curtis whispered. "What did you *do*?"

"Oh, a lot of shit, one time and another," I said. "Which one do you mean this time?"

"This place has been a zoo all day long. Dad's massively over the top. There was a bunch of money that showed up this morning? He burned it on the stove. Set off the fire alarm in the kitchen. And now he dug Grandma's Bible out and he's been yelling about how there's a curse on his family. And Mom looks like she's drunk or something. Jay came by with Carla to do some wedding stuff, and seriously, he came in, looked around, and just walked back out. Didn't even say anything."

I felt a stab of guilt. I'd almost forgotten about Jay's wedding and the effect my return was having on it.

"Yeah, kind of crap timing, I guess," I said.

"What's going on?" Curtis said, and I could hear the need in his voice. The confusion. Or maybe I was hearing myself in him. I didn't know what to say. There was no peace he was going to get from hearing about this, about me and Mom and Eric and the supernatural ecosystem of things that crept in from Next Door. But he was living in the middle of it. I couldn't shut him off, and I couldn't bring myself to lie.

"I tracked Mom down and asked her some questions about Uncle Eric," I said. "And it turns out there was a bunch of stuff that was connected to, and it all kind of got out of hand."

"And the guys with guns?"

"They're sort of connected to it too."

"Wow," he said. "I mean, just wow."

"I know, right? Look, all this time I've been sort of under the radar? Uncle Eric died a few years back, and he left me everything, and it got pretty complicated pretty fast."

"Holy shit. Uncle Eric's dead? What happened?"

I squeezed my eyes closed. This was going to be worse than I'd thought.

"Yeah, the guys with the tattoos and the shotguns? They killed him. And the more I look at it, the more it seems like he probably had it coming, only I didn't know that at the time, and I may have sort of gotten them pissed off at me too."

The silence on the line was profound. Maybe I shouldn't have gotten into this, but it was too late to pour the cream back out of that coffee.

"Was he selling drugs?" Curt whispered. I had to fight not to laugh. Drugs would have been so much easier. If it had all just been organized crime and corrupt DEA agents and a few million dollars' worth of heroin, my life would actually have been more comprehensible.

"I don't think so," I said. "I mean, I wouldn't put it past him. It turns out Eric was kind of a bastard, but the more I try to get the details of how it all was back then, the worse things seem to get."

"Are they going to come back? The gang guys?"

"I doubt it," I said. "I don't think they're after you."

"Are you going to be okay?"

"I'm sure enough going to try," I said.

"Look, if you need some money, I've got a couple thousand in my account. I've been working at—" An angry sound came from behind him. I couldn't make out the words, but I didn't need to. My childhood had grown up around sounds like it the way a vine climbs a trellis. "Nothing, Dad," Curt said. "I was just—"

The connection dropped. I hefted my phone for a couple seconds, then stuffed it back in my pocket. My mug of tea, abandoned on the pavement at my side, was already cold. I poured it out on the winter-killed weeds at the roadside and stood up. Ozzie creaked up too.

On one hand, I could hardly imagine how weird and awful things were for Curtis. On the other, I knew because I'd been there too. I wondered if I could swoop in and get him out of there. Maybe send him to school in Europe someplace on my dime. I had enough money to do it. The only thing standing in the way was that I was his sister, not his mom. And if Dad had burned the check I'd sent to cover new windows, I couldn't see him letting Curt have anything to do with me. From where my dad stood, I was as bad as Eric. And the truth was I'd committed some atrocities of my own along the way. So maybe he had a point.

I let myself back into my hotel room, the electronic lock cycling and the LED glowing green when I passed my card through. Chogyi Jake was by the window, looking out, and Ex was nowhere to be seen. Ozzie levered herself onto the bed, tucked her nose under her tail, and sighed.

"Where's Ex?" I asked, dropping into the desk chair.

"The other room. I think he was going to take a shower. He doesn't mean ill, you know."

"By taking a shower?"

Chogyi Jake sat on the edge of the bed. "He's been blunt with you. Sometimes cruel. But it's coming from a place of concern. And from his own anger with himself."

"Honest to God? I didn't notice. I mean, I guess when you say it out loud, the lab hamster line was maybe a little rough. But I don't think I have the spare cycles to care about it, you know? I know Ex cares about me. I trust him, even if that only means trusting him to be himself, right?"

"Right," Chogyi Jake said. "I wondered when you left if you were trying to make some space between the two of you."

"I wasn't. I was just trying to make some space. Coming home's weirder than I thought. I mean, check. You can't go home again. Message received. But the ways I can't go home again aren't the ones I was expecting."

"How so?"

"I thought there wouldn't be any room for me. That I'd have changed so much, and they'd have changed so much, that there just wasn't a Jayné-shaped hole anymore. We'd all have to hug and grow and learn. Instead, it's like all the things that happened when I was growing up didn't happen. Or they did, but *wow* did I not understand what they really were."

"I'm hearing you say that you thought the only thing at risk was the future. How you would relate to your family after they saw who you had become."

"And what?"

"And instead, you're finding that your past is just as threatened."

"Yeah," I said. "Like that. I wonder if Mom was always like this and I just didn't see, because how would I? And if Dad really was protecting us, or trying to, I can't really count it against him. Eric was a sonofabitch."

"He was," Chogyi Jake said. "And you weren't the only one he deceived. I think part of Ex's anger stems from blaming himself for not seeing Eric for what he was when we worked with him."

"What about you?"

"My anger stems from that too."

I laughed.

"I didn't know you had any anger," I said.

Chogyi Jake laughed. It was a warm sound, and it always relaxed me. Even when we were talking about things like this. Betrayal and loss and the emptiness that came from seeing the world you thought you knew crumble to dust. "I have a tremendous depth of rage. Massive. But I try not to take it too seriously. Eventually it will drain away."

"You think?"

"By the time I retire, I hope."

"Probably better than taking it seriously," I agreed. "I mean, what's the point of soul-crushing tragedy and betrayal if you can't get a laugh out of it."

"'The world is a comedy to those that think, a tragedy to those who feel,'" Chogyi Jake said, and I could tell from his tone it was a quotation.

"The Buddha?"

"Horace Walpole."

"Ah," I said. My fingers tapped against my

pocket, clicking against the hard rectangle of my phone like they were trying to draw attention to something. I didn't know if it was my subconscious or the rider in my body or even if there was a difference. I remembered Curtis offering me his money. There was a good example of something that was sweet and touching if I paid attention to how it felt to me, what it meant. But if you compared our bank statements, it was kind of hilarious. And the whole thing about whether Eric was selling drugs . . .

My fingers stopped tapping.

"What is it?" Chogyi Jake asked.

"Eric's money," I said. "How *do* you think he got it?"

CHAPTER EIGHT

"He inherited it, dear," my lawyer said. "Much the way you did."

"Inherited it?" I said, shifting my phone to the other ear. Chogyi Jake's eyebrows rose a degree and he leaned forward in his chair.

"Yes," she said. "The structures were a bit different, of course. Regulations on these things do change over the course of a few decades. But he came into possession in 1984, on the death of Michael Bishop Heller. He would have been your great-uncle. He was a charming man. I actually met

him once, but that was when I'd just started with
the firm. He still wore hats, and really men stopped
doing that after John Kennedy."

"Old-school."

"Very much."

"And—I'm sorry, but I have to ask. Where did,
um, hat guy . . . ?"

"Michael Bishop Heller came into possession on
the death of Amelia Norwich in 1966. She, I believe,
had it from Nellie Skinner-Bowes in 1944, who had
it from her father, Anderson Skinner-Bowes in 1927.
The original principal was put in trust in 1866, and
it was fairly large then, and primarily in gold. Of
course, the Civil War had just ended, so the assumption is that Elias Barker, who actually made the
investments, was relocating from someplace in the
Confederacy."

"And you just know all this stuff off the top of
your head?"

I could hear the smile in her voice when she answered. "You are our most important client, dear.
You must know that?"

"I hadn't really thought about it. So no one ever, I
don't know, got a gambling habit or lost a bunch of
money in a divorce or anything?"

"No," she said. "The investment strategy has
been very consistent. Long-term, medium-risk investments with occasional more speculative short-
term adventures at the client's direct instruction.

There isn't a five-year period when the overall capital has gone down. Your uncle, God rest him, was a bit more profligate than you are, but even his habits never threatened to cut into the capital."

"You mean he spent more than I do?"

"Considerably."

"Okay, in the last three years, I've bought a house, a car, a bunch of motorcycles, God knows how many plane tickets, and started an ongoing research grant. Like on whims. I just called and had you do it."

"The research grant was new," she said, her voice a little wistful. "That's mostly because it's an ongoing expense. But we put some language in the paperwork that gets us a share in any patents that come from it, so there may still be a return. But all in all, no, dear. You fly on commercial airlines, for heaven's sake."

"First-class, though," I said.

"Jayné, dear, I wouldn't *let* you fly coach. I believe in frugality, but there are limits."

I licked my lips. "How much of his expenditures do you have records of?"

"Well, I can't say what he paid for in cash unless he forwarded on a receipt. But for any large-scale purchases, of course I'll have full records."

"Going back how far?"

"I already said, dear. Eighteen sixty-six."

"You've still got the original records?"

"Yes."

"Can I . . . how can I review those? I mean, Eric's first, but if I can see all of them, that would be amazing."

"Come to Denver. I'll have the archives opened. Are you thinking of an audit?"

"Less of an audit," I said. "More of an overview. Orientation. Something like that."

"I would love to see you again, and I'd be delighted to go over any of our records with you. When would you like to come out?"

I looked at Chogyi Jake. His expression was the same calm smile as always. I wished sometimes he'd be a little easier to read. Or . . . no. That wasn't right. I wished sometimes he'd make a few of my decisions for me, just so I wouldn't have to. We could get in the car now and be there by morning. Going back to Santa Fe would have taken longer.

I had the visceral memory of the three tattooed wizards in my childhood home.

"There's something I need to clear up here," I said. "It may take a few days."

"The week after New Year's?"

"Let's aim for that," I said. "I'm not sure when exactly I'll get there, though."

"I'll pencil it in for now. Is there anything else I can do for you?"

"No," I said. Then: "Yes. Can I get a list of those

names? The people who had the money back from whenever?"

"Will e-mail do?"

"Sure," I said.

"It will be to you momentarily."

"Okay," I said. "Thanks."

We exchanged a couple rounds of pleasantries and farewells, and I dropped the connection and tossed my phone onto the bed.

"Well, that's interesting," Chogyi Jake said.

"Isn't it just? I've got to say, I feel kind of stupid for not thinking of this before."

"We aren't businessmen," Chogyi Jake said. "We fight vampires and demons."

"Ex kind of was living in a garage, wasn't he?"

"With a very nice car. He does like cars," Chogyi Jake said. "I take it we're staying for the wedding?"

"No. I mean, maybe. We're staying until I can find the Invisible College and make damned sure they leave my family alone."

He frowned. The light from the window caught the plane of his cheek, illuminating the spray of faint stubble there. A few whiskers down near his chin were coming in white.

"It may be difficult to find them," he said. "They are like you that way."

"Difficult for magic to track down," I said. "Well, we're clever."

"And pure of heart," he said. It was so deadpan,

no one who didn't know him would have recognized it as a joke. I laughed, though.

"So we should ace it, right?" I said. "Let's go tell Ex what's up. And maybe order a pizza. I know a really good pizza joint."

"Thank God for the native guide."

ELIAS BARKER. Toomey Conaville. Sarah Conaville. Elmer Bowes. Anderson Skinner-Bowes. Nellie Skinner-Bowes. Amelia Norwich. Michael Bishop Heller. Eric Heller. Jayné Heller. From 1866 to tonight. Turned out, I was part of a tradition. There was a line of people pressing back into history, and I had something to do with them. Some commonality. Literally, some *business*. I didn't have any idea what it was, but I would. All I had right now was the moments that the baton had been passed. I wondered if they'd all been as lost and confused as I was, or if there was some manual that was supposed to come with the fortune. Something that explained the riders and my relationship to them.

Nothing was going to excuse what Eric had done, but context might haul it up into explicable territory. That would be a start. It might even be enough.

I lay in bed that night, unable to sleep. Ozzie snuck onto the foot of my bed and I didn't have the heart to kick her off. She was snoring now, her legs twitching occasionally as she chased some dream-world squirrel. I wasn't sure I'd be able to sleep. In the hours since dawn, I'd found out I was actually Eric's daughter, that my mother had been possessed by the Black Sun and was still half-crazy from the experience. That Eric's money hadn't just been Eric's but had belonged to a long list of mysterious people leading back into the fog of history. I'd had whole years that were less eventful than today, and it left me feeling a little stunned.

Dad was not my father. I kept poking at the idea, waiting for it to explode on me. This was supposed to be where my whole sense of myself shifted, and it didn't seem trivial. But it also didn't change who I was. I'd been conceived in ritual sex magic orches-trated by my evil uncle while my mother was pos-sessed by a rider who was also quite possibly bound against her will. That was *way* creepier than the joy-less missionary-position indignity that I would have put my money on before, but it didn't seem to have anything to do with me. I'd had a movie-set child-hood where all the things I trusted in were lies and deceptions, but I kind of knew that already. What exactly was behind the curtain didn't change much.

When I'd climbed out my window and headed out for Arizona, I'd broken with the past. That it hadn't gone spectacularly seemed less important now than the bare fact that I'd done it. If everything back then seemed different now, well, so what?

Maybe it didn't really matter what past I'd broken from.

I shifted, pulling the pillows up over my head. In the corridor, someone tromped past, the squeaking of a suitcase's wheel as identifiable as a finch's song.

"Did you know?" I asked the darkness. "About Eric and putting all those different riders into Mom?"

For a long moment nothing happened. The footsteps outside my room stopped. The muffled sound of a door lock, a hotel door opening, then closing. Some random stranger whose life story intersected with mine just this much and no more.

"No," my mouth said without me. "I did not know what he did to our mothers."

Our mothers. Well, that was true. There were two of us and there were two of them. We'd been made together. Her mother and mine had both been bound, and we were both the products of that profoundly unclean ritual. I wondered if the rider was more upset than I was. I wondered if there was any way to comfort her. I turned the pillow over, putting the cool side against my cheek, closed my eyes, and willed myself to sleep.

I'd heard descriptions of people having strokes whose first symptoms weren't weakness or confusion, but an overwhelming sense of wrongness. Between one breath and the next, something like that washed over me. The pillow was the same, but the crisp, ghost-white cloth was suddenly nauseating.

The walls of darkened room seemed to be at subtly wrong angles. I turned on the light, thinking the brightness would push sanity back into the room, but the bulb seemed sickly too. Morgue light.

Ozzie lifted her head, growling deep in her throat. I sat up slowly, using both hands. I couldn't tell if I was dizzy or not, only that something felt wrong. That *I* felt wrong.

"It's okay, girl," I said, but Ozzie wasn't buying it. She jumped off the bed and started pacing the room, the growling getting louder. The hair on her back was raised, her lips pulled back to expose yellow, blunted teeth. She stopped at the window, her nose to the thick blackout curtains, and barked once.

"Shh," I said, rising uncertainly to my feet. "It's okay, girl. Keep it down or we'll wake the neighbors."

A sickening chill came over me, like the touch of a dead fish that had gone to rot. For a moment I thought I heard someone crying. Or maybe laughing. It was hard to breathe.

"Okay," I said. "This isn't just me, right?"

The rider didn't answer, but I imagined her perched behind my eyes, waiting and alert and ready.

Ozzie barked again, the angry sound of an animal defending its territory, and I walked to the window. The dog's barking was constant now, angry and wild and threatening. She didn't turn to look at me when I got to her side. Her full attention was on the window. I didn't want to pull back the curtains.

I pulled back the curtains.

Outside, the world looked the same and debased at the same time. The scattering of cars was just like it had been, but it meant something different. Decay, emptiness, the aftermath of disaster. The tires on the highway were a threat until they passed, and then they were hope retreating. I put my palms against the glass, and the cold bit my fingers. Dreams were like this. The way the meanings of things came unglued, and anything—an apple, a desert, the flicker of a match—could be a reason for bone-crushing fear. Madness was leaking into the world from the cracks, and I didn't know where the flood was coming from.

And then I did.

It stood at the edge of the parking lot, not far from where I'd been sitting when Curtis called me. It was small. Maybe three, three and a half feet tall. No bigger. It had the frame of a kid, a black rain poncho with the hood up, so that all I could see was the pale face. It was too far away to make out the details, but I had the sense of profound deformity. Of wrongness distilled into something so pure, the fumes from it burned.

It saw me, and a wide, toothless smile split its face. I was afraid it would wave at me or clap its hands, but it was still. A pair of headlights from a passing car played over the thing, making it bright for a moment. Ozzie's barking was a frenzy now, flecks of foam sticking to the glass. An unfamiliar voice was shouting at me to shut her up. It was like something from another world.

We stood there, the evil little thing and me, staring at each other through the glass, and then I was running across the room, out the door, sprinting for the stairs faster than a human body should have been able to. I vaulted the handrail, dropping to the flight below and out the door into the darkness of the night, charging the spot where it had been with a shout boiling up out of me, carrying the will of the rider along with my own. The pavement nipped at my bare feet, the cold slapped me, but I didn't care. In all my life I had never been so pure—or so ready for murder. It was instinct, and I didn't even want to restrain it.

The thing was gone.

"Come back here, you bastard sonofabitch!" I screamed in a voice that wasn't only my own but also something deeper, wilder. Not more dangerous, though. I was already feeling plenty dangerous. "Come back here and I will feed you your fucking *heart*!"

The last word came as a detonation. Behind me, three car alarms went off, their whoops and beeps like a pack of confused dogs barking because someone else was barking. It was too late. The unclean presence was already fading. The winter air was just air again. The wide sky above me lost all its malevolence and turned back into stars and clouds, impersonal and distant. The snarl on my lips wouldn't let go, though, and even with the cold I didn't move.

I heard Chogyi Jake and Ex coming from the hotel. Their footsteps were as identifiable as their faces. I didn't even turn to look at them, my gaze locked on the darkness, searching for the twisted little figure even though I knew it wasn't there.

"Jayné," Ex said. He had a gun in his hand. Chogyi Jake did too. They were both in pajamas. So was I for that matter. It wasn't the first time I'd been happy that I'd never gotten the habit of sleeping naked.

"Something was here," I said. "It was right here."

Chogyi Jake moved forward, his pistol held low but ready.

"You saw it?" Ex asked.

"From the window. It saw me too."

"You recognized it?"

I hesitated.

"No," I said. "No, I don't know what it was."

"But you came out after it on your own?" The disapproval was actually second to the confusion. Why attack it? And why go out on my own like I was taking on an army with my hands? It was a fair question.

"It scared the hell out of me."

Ex looked around. There were lighted windows in the hotel now. The silhouettes of people looking out into the parking lot at us. Ex put the gun's safety on and held it under his shirt. I crossed my arms and wondered if Ozzie was still in the room. I didn't have any idea if the door had closed after me. I counted windows until I saw mine. She was there, her paws against the window. From the slight shifting of her head, I guessed she was wagging.

"And this is how you react when something scares you?"

"Apparently so."

"Remind me not to pop any unexpected balloons around you."

"Don't pop any unexpected balloons around me," I said, because it was the right line to follow with. Something to let the tension slip. I couldn't let it stand there. "It wasn't like that, though. I wasn't startled. I was *afraid*."

"I have something," Chogyi Jake called. My feet were getting numb fast. The Black Sun had retreated back into my body and the adrenaline was seeping away, but my curiosity had cooked down to a solid need to know. I stepped into the scrub at the side of the road. There in the shadows lay a little knot of pale and black, like a crumpled sheet of ink-stained paper, only larger. I squatted down next to it, reaching out with my fingers. Something about it seemed strange and ominous and familiar all at the same time. I plucked at it, pulling it into the light.

"Well, I'll be damned," I said.

"You know what this is?"

"I do," I said.

My mother had always been the one to buy things for the house. Curtains, place mats, napkins. All of that had been hers. The dish towel lying on the soiled ground was the same blue-and-yellow kind that I'd used for years to wipe up spills and wash down counters. There were surely others like it all through the city, all through the world, but at that moment I'd have bet everything I owned that this one had come from my family's kitchen.

And half of it was stiff and dark with old blood.

CHAPTER NINE

"Are you *sure* it's your blood?" Kim asked from my laptop. Compressed into the Skype window, she and Aubrey seemed like news announcers, each ready for their turn at the camera. The morning sun was bright and low, and I'd pulled the curtains in the guys' room half closed, covering us all in an artificial twilight.

"Certain," Chogyi Jake said. "We've tried Bonewitz's consonance rites and the Dismas Ceremony. It's mine. I split my lip when they attacked, and that was the cloth I used to clean myself up."

"We figure they went back later and dug through the trash," Ex said.

Aubrey grunted his dissatisfaction. "I wish we could run the DNA all the same."

"You're just saying that because you have the equipment," Ex said.

"Well, we do," Aubrey replied.

Kim shook her head, but there was a smile with it. On camera, she looked fuller in the cheeks, not so pinched at the mouth. Aubrey was sporting the beginnings of a mustache that absolutely didn't suit him. Seeing them again—seeing them together—was more like coming home than coming home had been. I wished they were really there. But I understood why it was a bad idea. It hadn't been a full six months since Aubrey had been my lover and Kim had been his ex-wife. It only felt like years ago because so much had happened in between.

"If I had to guess," Ex said, "I'd say they were using the blood as a tracking focus. Jayné's damn hard to find using magic, but Chogyi Jake and I are just what we are."

"You have wards on your room?" Kim asked.

"Just the usual. Salt and ash. The Mark of Cyprian."

"That's it?" she asked.

"We're at a Best Western," Ex said.

"They allow dogs," I added. It seemed weak.

"Okay," Kim said. "So you're warded enough to

keep a human being from finding you. So the hypothesis is that a rider was using the blood, yes?"

"It felt like one to me," I said. "It felt . . . not big, exactly. It felt crazy."

"Crazy how?" Aubrey asked.

"Like, it-made-the-whole-world-mentally-ill-just-by-being-in-it crazy," I said.

"Let's take it as our hypothesis, then," Kim said. "We'll assume that a rider was using Chogyi Jake as a handle to find Jayné. To what end?"

I shook my head. The thing had come, seen me, and then vanished. It hadn't been an attack. It hadn't been a message. The only thing that seemed to make sense at all was that it was doing reconnaissance for something else. Something that hadn't happened yet.

"So let's table that," Kim said. "Was it the Invisible College?"

"I hate to invoke Occam's razor," Ex said, "but that seems like the safest bet. It was a rider. They're all riders. We know they're nearby. They made a weirdly half-assed attack on Jayné's family. Now we've got a weirdly half-assed approach on the hotel. I don't see what we get by assuming there's some mysterious third party involved."

"Could it be involved with whatever Eric was doing with me and the Black Sun?" I asked. "Whatever this all is, the Invisible College was after him from the start. I mean, they *got* him, right? They killed him. And they were hiding the *haugsvarmr* that he was trying to find. So whatever he was doing here, they were probably trying to throw a wrench in the works. If we understood what Eric was doing—"

Kim shook her head. "No."

"No?" Ex asked.

"No. We've got too many variables and not enough data. We can speculate all day. Make up as many stories as we want to. The fact of the matter is, we don't know enough yet to draw any conclusions."

"I don't know about that," Aubrey said.

"I do," I said. "She's right. Maybe if we nail down something, the rest of it will fall in line, but right now it's all just one damn thing after another. And the closer we look at it, the weirder it gets. There's two ends we can reach for. Either we go after the Invisible College and try to wring some answers out of them, or we go to Denver and hit the books about Eric's predecessors. I don't see anything else that makes sense."

The other four stayed quiet. I felt the weight of their reluctance, and I understood it. This was my call, and there were good reasons for it. We were in an untenable position, unwarded in a public building that even invitation-excluded riders like *nosferatu* and *cadaver sanguins* could waltz right into. The Invisible College had gotten the drop on us already, at least once and probably twice. We had no natural allies in the city. We had no clear way to find the enemy, and no good guess as to what was on their agenda.

In Denver we could sit in the middle of a bank vault if we wanted to, pile on wards so thick it would take weeks to find us and weeks more to force us out; and instead of looking for a bunch of gun-toting demon-possessed wizards, we'd have to read through historical documents. The only downside was that it left my family exposed to the Invisible College and the thing from the parking lot.

But it had been years since I'd been here, and the Invisible College hadn't bothered them in all that time. I had to think that if I went, they'd chase me.

"Okay," I said. "Pack it up, and let's get the hell out of Dodge." The chorus of agreement sounded like relief. "Kim. Aubrey. Thank you, guys, so much for putting your heads together with us. Is it cool if I call you when we get to Denver?"

"I think you should," Kim said. "I'd like to know what this whole damn thing was about."

"You and me both," I said. Despite everything, I really did like her.

We dropped the connection, and I sat back. Ex and Chogyi Jake looked tired. After our unwelcome visitor, we'd spent the night sleeping in shifts in their room, one person always awake with a gun in one hand and salt in the other. The only one who'd seemed happy about the whole thing was Ozzie. She preferred having the whole pack together, if only because she got more ear scratches.

"So. Occam's razor?" I asked. "Do I know that one?"

"It's not a spell," Ex said. "It's a philosophical law. Basic idea is that simpler solutions are more likely to be true. If the canary's gone and the cat's looking happy, there's not much reason to postulate a dog."

"You can explain it to me on the road," I said.

"I'd love to," he said with a smile. There was something about him that got more handsome after I'd seen or thought too much about Aubrey. So that was a great, huge, blinking warning sign.

"I'll go pack my stuff and settle the bill. If we get in the car now, we can eat dinner in Denver. Barring potty breaks."

"Don't look at me," Ex said. "Dog's the one with the weak bladder."

I laughed on my way out the door. Truth was, I wanted to leave. I was relieved to be going away again and putting my past in the past. Nothing about the return to Kansas was what I'd hoped, and a lot was worse than I'd feared. When I'd been off roaming the world, sneaking a call home to visit with Curt had been one of the ways I'd comforted myself. When things were bad, I'd been able to touch base with someplace simpler and safer. I'd told myself that in the whirl and madness of riders and magic,

supernatural beasts and tangled love, there was another world. Home had been a place of ignorance
and bliss. No one there knew how dangerous and
wild the world could be, and the idea that a place like
that existed had been enough to get me through.

Only, it wasn't true. Maybe it never was. All parents were kids once. All of them had their hearts
broken and betrayed. All of them carried secrets.
Probably I wasn't the only one who wanted to think
that her parents had been born before the inven-
tion of sex. But when I got to Denver, I'd probably
find how deeply that wasn't true. Name after name,
generation after generation, going back as far as
the records went, it could be stories of families like
mine. Seductions and rapes and madness and lies
going back through generations. Going back until
the papers ran out and the past streamed behind us,
unrecorded.

Because that was really what I'd taken comfort
in. Not my family but my past. The past seemed safe
because I'd survived its dangers. The truth was it
had never been safe.

And it still wasn't.

"Jayné!"

I turned, ready to fight. Jay was stumbling down
the corridor from the lobby. His eyes were red from
crying. He had on slacks and a white shirt that
looked like they'd been slept in. His face was the
waxy gray of exhaustion.

"Oh, thank God. Jayné, you have to help me. They took her. She's gone."

A sick chill ran down my spine.

"Who's gone?"

"Carla," Jay said, his voice breaking on the name. "Those people. The ones who broke into the house. They took her. And she . . . she *went* with them."

Jay put his arms around me, collapsing into me. Sobs wracked him. I had the visceral memory of being eight years old, when our first dog had gotten out of the yard and been killed by a truck. It was the last time I'd seen Jay cry like this.

"It's okay," I said. "My room's right here. Come on. Just tell me what happened."

I opened the door. Jay sat in the desk chair, running his hands through his hair and shaking his head.

"We were supposed to go to the bridesmaids' party. Her cousin was . . . her cousin was arranging it. I went first. With Dad. We waited, and she didn't come. She didn't get there. I tried calling her phone. Texting her. She didn't answer. When I went back to the house . . . Jesus help me. Lord Jesus, please help me."

His eyes screwed shut and new tears poured down his cheeks. He breathed hard through gritted teeth, his cheeks and forehead flushed red. I was half certain he was going to hyperventilate.

"Okay, talk to me now," I said. "You can talk to God anytime. I need you to be here with me now."

Jay swallowed his tears and nodded.

"When I got home, she was gone."

"Were there signs of a struggle?" I asked. "Did you call the police?"

"It won't help," Jay said. He paused, grabbed at his pants pocket, and took out a folded gray envelope. He held it toward me like a kid handing his mother a broken toy. I don't want to take that, I thought. I don't want this. I took it, opened the flap, and pulled out a single sheet of white printer paper. The handwriting was simple and clear, and the paper felt soft against my fingertips. I wanted it to smell of perfume, but it didn't.

> *Jay-bird:*
>
> *I love you. I love you so so much. You know I would do anything for you, but I have to go now. If it was only me, I wouldn't leave, I would stay with you even if you were going to face the devil. But I have the baby, and I have to take care of him. I'm his mommy, and I have to.*
>
> *There's a curse on your family. You saw what your sister did. The people who broke in were there to show me that she's a witch. Oh, Jay-bird, she eats babies. And you saw what she did. They're angels. They're guardian angels and they came to protect me and the baby and if I could take you too I would but*

I can't. They said I have to go where no one can find
me. I have to go away from you, and if it was only
me I wouldn't. But it's the baby, so I have to.

I am so sorry. I am so so sorry and I love you so
so much.

Don't look for me.

It wasn't signed. It didn't need to be. I said something obscene.

"I saw what you did," Jay said. "The way you
fought. It wasn't normal. Dad shot one, didn't he?
She said Dad shot him, and he caught the bullet."

"Yeah," I said. "That happened."

"And you fought them off."

"I did."

"A normal person couldn't have done that."

I sat on the bed, the letter soft in my fingers. Jay's
eyes were an accusation and a plea.

"No," I said. "A normal person couldn't have.
But . . . I'm not exactly a normal person."

"Are you a witch?" he breathed.

"No. I'm not a witch and I'm not a demon and I
don't eat babies. But she's right that there's something wrong with this family. I mean seriously
messed up. And I think maybe there always has
been."

We were silent for a moment. A few doors down,
Chogyi Jake and Ex were packing. Or maybe Ex
was taking Ozzie for one last walk before the road

trip. Out beyond that, Mom and Dad and Curt were
probably at the house, turning the place into chaos
over this new problem. Probably blaming me for it.
I handed him back the letter.

"Swear to me," he said. "Swear to me that it isn't
true."

"What isn't true? That I really don't eat babies?"

He grabbed my hand, squeezing it so tightly in
his own that it almost ached.

"Swear to me that you don't mean me or my baby
any harm. Swear to God, Jayné."

I shook my head. "I don't believe in God anymore, Jay."

"He believes in you. Swear it."

"Okay," I said. "If you need me to. I swear to God,
Jay, I never meant anything bad to happen to you or
to Carla or your baby. Or anyone. I never meant to
hurt anybody."

His eyes looked deeply into mine, like he was
searching for something. It was the same look I'd
seen on Dad when I went into the garage. That
sense of trying to read something deep inside of me.
I wondered if he could see the Black Sun in there.
If he could tell that she was looking out through my
eyes. He let my hand drop.

"Who are they?" he said. "You know, don't you?
Who took my wife and baby?"

"They are . . . they call themselves the Invisible
College. They're somewhere right in between a

society of warlocks and a hive of . . . I don't know. Demons. Or spirits. We call them riders."

"Riders?"

"Things from outside the world that come in and take over people's bodies. Like spiritual parasites. Vampires, werewolves, filth-lickers. They're all different kinds of riders."

His face went still. I couldn't tell if it was anger or courage or something related to both of them.

"Demons," he said.

"Sure," I said. "It's more complicated than that, but the term's as good as any."

"How do I find them?"

Outside, a semi pulled into the parking lot, its engine screaming like something clawing its way out of hell. The noise set my teeth on edge, and I was grateful when it stopped. I looked out the window at the place where the evil little thing had been. It wasn't there now, but it was somewhere. And it had my brother's unborn child.

"Jayné," he said, "tell me how to find them."

"You can't," I said. "And even if you could, there's nothing you can do to them. You saw what they could do. What *I* can do. I love you, Jay, but you're outclassed here. You're in the shit so far over your head, it looks like sky. That's just truth."

"I don't care."

And of course he didn't. I thought of Dad keeping me and Mom even after he knew I wasn't his.

Jay was cut from the same cloth. Dad had spent his life ignoring the humiliation of being a cuckold and treating me as his own. That he treated his own like they were subject-serfs who should obey him just because he was the patriarch of the house didn't seem to matter as much as it had once upon a time. He was a broken, weird, screwed-up man, and that demand for obedience and controlling anger had been a kind of love. Jay wouldn't do less for his own actual flesh and blood. For the woman he was going to marry.

This is my house, and my family. Any business you have, you can take up with me. And you haven't got any business with me.

If only it were true.

I'd told myself that they would chase me. That the danger that came to them sprang from me and that it would leave when I left. And even if I could convince myself that Carla was lost—and I really didn't want to think she was—Jay would get himself killed trying to either get her back or avenge her. And Curt, or if Curt ever got a girlfriend. A wife. If anything happened to Mom or Dad. Anything from this moment on that happened to my family because I'd stepped away was going to be my fault.

If Jay had just come an hour later . . .

"Okay, fine," I said, and pulled my telephone out of my pocket. Ex answered on the second ring.

"What's up?" he said.

"New plan," I said.

"Something happened?"

"Something happened."

"So we're staying and hunting down the Invisible College?"

I looked at Jay sitting at the edge of the bed. He looked old and desperate and tired. I wasn't feeling much better.

"We are."

CHAPTER TEN

Jay was a constant in my life. Like Mom, like Dad, he'd always been there. I went into kindergarten when he was a big, sophisticated third grader. I was a freshman in high school when he was in his senior year. We loved each other, and we took care of each other. We were never friends, and that was okay. We didn't need to be.

The years had made him physically more like Dad. Broader across the shoulders and belly, thicker at the neck. They had the same brown hair, the same curve at their jaw. I would never have mistaken the two of them for each other, but I'd never have doubted they were father and son. I couldn't help but wonder if people who didn't know us would identify us as brother and sister, or if the fact that we had different fathers showed in our bones and the way that we moved. He was my half brother, but more than that because our fathers had been brothers. There probably wasn't a name for exactly what he and I were to each other.

The last time I'd seen him, he'd been in college, a year from finishing his business degree and talking about whether he should go into the ministry. I had to assume he'd decided not to, because since then, he'd graduated, moved to Florida, fallen in bed with Carla, and come back. I'd been spending my time fighting ghosts and monsters and things from outside the world. It was hard to tell just at first glance which of us had been the most changed. I wondered what he thought of me, his prodigal sister. After all, what he knew about me was that I'd vanished under a cloud and reappeared with two men in tow, a lot of money, and heavily tattooed fiancée-abducting cultists coming after me. And he hadn't even seen the scars on my side or my arm.

I didn't know, as we followed his little gray Toyota through the residential streets, what it had taken him to come to me of all people for help. I wanted it to be because he trusted me. I wanted there to be some connection between brother and sister that had been forged without the need for speech and that had survived all our time apart, the differences in our lives and experiences. He knew he could count on me to stand by him and do whatever needed to be done.

I was afraid the logic was more like *When things get freaky, talk to a freak.*

I couldn't even argue against it. Mom and Dad. Carla's family. The pastors at church. None of them were better equipped to deal with the Invisible College. They'd come into it swinging wild, and they'd screw it up.

Which is to say, they'd be just like I'd been back in Denver when this all started. When the Invisible College had killed Eric Heller and I'd come in to avenge him.

Jay turned right, down a narrow, gray road, and pulled up at the curb of a small masonry-block house. I drew the SUV up behind him and killed the engine. Ex and Chogyi Jake slid down to the street before I did. My huge sunglasses weren't really hiding my black eyes. For a moment I wondered what I was going to do if I did find the Invisible College. After all, they'd bunged me up pretty good last time. That was a problem for later.

Jay fumbled with the side-door lock while Chogyi Jake and Ex walked a circuit around the outside of the house, heading in opposite directions.

"What are they looking for?"

"Whatever there is to be found," I said.

"Demon signs?"

I shrugged. "Sure. Or if someone dropped their wallet. We'll take what we can get."

The lock finally complied, the thin wooden door opening into a sparse kitchen. The round table in the center of the room looked lonely. I stepped in after Jay. Inside, the house was worn and scraped at the corners, but clean. The living room floor had pale carpet that remembered where the last owner had put their couch. The refrigerator was white, with an inexplicable drip of pale pink paint along the side. I pushed my hands deeper into the pockets of my overcoat and walked through the little rooms. This was my brother's house. And his life. These dim blinds, that secondhand television. I looked in at a nursery that was smaller than some closets I had. The mobile over the crib hung limply over the bare mattress. A sense of dread and depression seemed to outgas from the walls.

When I'd inherited Eric's fortune, it had come with a list of properties as long as my arm, and almost all of them were nicer than this. And even the ones that weren't could be forgiven as crash pads and hidey-holes to retreat to. I imagined the years stretching out before Carla and Jay. The late nights with the crying baby and nowhere to get away from the noise. The winters with the cold pressing in through the masonry walls. Everything about the place felt sad and oppressive. I opened the closet in the master bedroom and noticed almost automatically that it could be locked from the outside. I tried to imagine myself as Carla—newly pregnant, still unmarried, and transplanted from the people and places I'd always known.

It might not have taken strange magic to convince me to run away.

Ex came in the side door, and a few seconds later Chogyi Jake.

"What have we got?" I asked.

"Nothing," Ex said. "No wards. No sigils. No trace that I can see of any major pulls. If someone came in with a glamour on, I wouldn't have a clue, but I'd expect to see some sign if there'd been anything violent and recent done. And no one seems to be watching the place either."

"There is something, though," Chogyi Jake said. "Not specific, but . . ."

"Yeah, I feel it too," I said.

"Something like our unwelcome visitor?" Ex asked.

"I wouldn't be surprised if it had been here. Has the same ick factor."

Jay looked from one to the other of us, his brows crinkled into a mask of concern and confusion.

"Something came by the hotel last night," I said. "Something nasty. It feels like it's been around here too."

"'Feels like'?" Jay said. "What does that even mean?"

"Feels like means feels like," I said. "It's not one particular thing I can point to. It just . . . smells right."

"Did she take everything with her?" Ex asked. "Clothes? Things that had some sort of emotional importance?"

"It's all gone," Jay said, slumping down to the couch. "Everything's gone."

"If there was something with her blood," Ex said, "that would be best."

"You're thinking of tracking her down the same way they tracked Chogyi Jake?"

"What's good for the goose," Ex said. "They're warded by nature and practice. Whatever kinds of covers they put on her . . . well, just the three of us probably couldn't break them, but if you're other half will chip in . . ."

He said it casually, but I knew how much it was costing him. For Ex, the Black Sun was a demon, untrustworthy to the core, and a constant threat to my soul. To even bring up the possibility of asking her help was a betrayal of his principles. I met his eyes for a moment, and he was the first to look away.

"Did she leave a hairbrush?" Chogyi Jake asked.

"Did . . . No, I don't think so. There's a comb in the bathroom," Jay said. "What are you going to do?"

"Find her. That's what you wanted, right?" I could hear the defensiveness in my own voice. I knew what this looked like from his point of view. Magic, spirits, spiritual presences that weren't anything like what you'd expect in church. There was a revulsion in his eyes. And with it, fear of me and of what I'd become.

Chogyi Jake turned back toward the bathroom. Outside, someone honked twice. A door slammed open and closed. Ex stepped to the window to see what it was and then stepped back without raising the alarm. Just neighbors. Just people living normal lives while we did our work unremarked beside them. Chogyi Jake turned on the faucet in the bathroom, and the pipes in the kitchen sang.

"I . . ." Jay said.

"We're not going to hurt her," I said. "We don't eat babies, and we don't want souls."

"So you're working with angels?" Jay asked. He sounded confused and more than half disbelieving.

"We're working with whatever comes to hand," I said, and as if on cue Chogyi Jake came back in, his hand lifted high in triumph. A clump of something wet, dark, and slimy hung between his fingers.

"Shower hair?" I asked.

"They cleaned the top of the drain, but they didn't get everything from within the drain itself," Chogyi Jake said. "I unscrewed the cover and fished out a few hairs. These are the length I'd expect."

"No point in tracking Jay here," I agreed. "So you know how to do this?"

"I do," Ex said, pulling a folded map out of his pocket. He spread the paper on the little kitchen table, then drew a clear plastic box from his back pocket. A bit of red chalk rattled in it.

"What are you doing?" Jay asked.

Chogyi Jake put a hand on Jay's shoulder. "We're using the affinity of Carla's hair for the whole person it came from as a focus by which we can find her location. There's technically a second affinity between the map and the world that the map represents, but that rarely requires a great deal of concern."

"No," he said. "You can't do magic in my house. Magic is of the devil."

"Think of it as a really specific kind of praying," Ex said, drawing a circle around the table wide enough for the three of us to stand in. Chalk scraped tile.

"You don't have to be here for this," I said. "You can wait in the car."

Jay looked from the map to me and then back again. His face was pale, but there was a firmness to his jaw that gave me some hope that he wasn't about to call the cops on us. Or worse, Dad. "If this will help Carla, I'll do it."

"You don't have to do anything," I said. "Just don't stop me."

"Okay," Ex said. "We're ready."

Chogyi Jake had a length of braided twine with a
silver plumb bob at the end. Carla's hair was tied in
a loose knot just above the silver, wrapping around
the string. Chogyi Jake stepped into the circle, stood
across the table from Ex, and reached out his hand,
letting the string hang above the map. The streets
and rivers of Wichita stirred uneasily, the paper
catching some invisible draft.

When I crossed the chalk circle, it was like stepping into a vault. At first I thought sound had been
dampened, that I couldn't hear, but that wasn't true.
The traffic on the street, the whir and hum of the
furnace desperately trying to warm the air—even
Jay's ragged breathing—were all just as clear as they
had been before. Maybe more so. It was only the
weird oppression of the house that hadn't crossed
into the circle with me, and I was quietly grateful
for that.

I put my hand out to touch theirs and closed my
eyes.

"I represent the west," Ex said, and I felt a surge
come from his hand. Not heat, but something like
it. His living force was as familiar to me now as a
favorite book, and I welcomed the sensation.

"I represent the east," Chogyi Jake said, and an
answering surge came from him, cooler and gentler,
but strong and undeniable.

I gathered my own qi, drawing it up from the
base of my spine, through my heart and lungs and

throat, and out along my own arm as I spoke. "I represent the south," I said. My will mingled with theirs, the three different forces joining to become something larger. Stronger. I felt the twine begin to tug against us like a puppy ready to go for a walk, then lose its focus. One way and then another.

"I represent the north," the Black Sun said with my voice, "and I will not be denied."

If the surges of will before had been like the pressure of water coming out from a faucet, she was the fire hose. I gasped as the force of her broke against us. I felt Ex pulling back for a moment, stunned by the onslaught, but he rallied, steadied himself. I glanced at him, and his upper lip was beaded with sweat. He began to chant softly in Latin. Chogyi Jake picked up the rhythm after a couple rounds, and then the Black Sun and I, collaborating on the syllables, chanted with them. I could feel the twine even though it was between Chogyi Jake's fingers. I closed my eyes and it began to shift, tugging and spinning. Carla's face came to me like I was dreaming. I saw the distress in the corners of her eyes and the lines of her mouth. She'd been crying, but I didn't know why.

Yes, I thought. Her.

The pressure of our combined will pushed down, and something pushed back. We slid across it, string and hair and silver becoming only themselves again for a moment. Ex's voice, rough with effort, slipped into my ears, and I realized I hadn't been hearing him. Or anything. I bore down again, riding my rider as we brought the spell back into focus. Carla came to me again. A house. Green tile in the kitchen. A little porch out the front window with a swing on it. The smell of maple syrup and bacon. Breakfast for lunch. The string twitched, the wards pushing us away again.

No, I thought. Hold on.

The wards slid against us, drawing the silver away, and then, between one heartbeat and the next, they were gone. Carla was before me as clearly as if we were both in the same room. She had a scrape on her right hand, just below the knuckles. There were three pancakes on the plate in front of her. Someone was in the seat beside her, but I couldn't see who. They were nothing more firm than a presence, a ghost. I felt the weight of the river nearby, the moving water like a dead zone in my sight.

"Water," I said.

"Water Street," Chogyi Jake murmured from a long, long way away.

"South," Ex growled. "She's on South Water Street."

I was in the room with her, and I was also outside, looking in. There two more people there I couldn't see. Walking blind spots. The house was white with blue-painted houses to either side. A tree grew, not in the yard, but in the median between yard and street. There was a garage in back. I could find it.

"Carla," I said. She looked up, confused, and I was back in Jay's kitchen. The twine was whirring in a circle so fast it looked like a disk. Tiny drops of Chogyi Jake's blood spattered the map, and I saw that the largest of them had pooled on Water Street.

Chogyi Jake stopped the spinning weight. He looked pleased, I thought, but a little tired. I felt like I'd run a half marathon in a snowsuit.

"Are you all right?" Jay asked. His voice sounded small. I wiped the sweat from my forehead and grinned.

"Perfect," I said. "Never better."

"We found her," Ex said.

Jay looked from one to the other of us, torn between distrust and hope. Chogyi Jake stepped to the sink and ran water over his injured hand. I felt like the whole world was vibrating. I sat on one of the chairs and rested my head in my hands. Jay took a step toward me, hesitated, and then squatted down at my side. His hand on my shoulder felt almost cold. I expected him to say something, but he didn't. Maybe he didn't need to.

"It's the right place," Ex said. "You felt the holes where they were?"

"Yeah," I said. "Is that what I'm like too?"

"Similar," Ex said. "I didn't catch wind of their bloodhound, whatever it is."

"I didn't either," Chogyi Jake said, patting the raw spot on his finger with a paper towel. When he was done, he put the used towel in his pocket. "But I believe Carla sensed us at the end. They may move her if they know we've found them."

"Or they may be using her as bait," I said.

"Bait for what?" Jay asked, his voice gray and empty with dread.

"Me. Her. Us. Whatever," I said. "We're not going over there. Not yet."

Ex lifted his eyebrows.

"You sure about that?" he asked.

"Yeah. It's what everyone expects us to do, and you don't have to be Admiral Akbar to see it's a trap. Whatever they're up to, it's got to do with Eric and Mom and me. I'm betting Dad has a different perspective."

"Which he won't share with you," Ex pointed out, his arms crossed.

"I'm not the one asking," I said. "Jay is."

"I am?"

"If you want Carla back safe," I said.

My brother coughed and sat back.

"We have to go get her," he said.

"We have to find out what we're walking into," I said. "Running off half-cocked has been pretty much my basic mode, and it doesn't work as well as you might think. We'll go talk to Dad."

"You would really . . ." Jay shook his head,

started over. "You'd use this to hold Dad's feet to the fire. You'd exploit Carla to make him talk about whatever it is he doesn't want to tell you."

It wasn't how I'd thought of it. It wasn't how I'd framed it. I had a dozen arguments at my fingertips about why it wasn't like that, and none of them changed what we needed to do. I wondered whether Eric would have done the same: used the missing Carla as leverage, gotten what he wanted, and to hell with everybody else.

Silly question. Of course he would have.

And apparently so would I.

CHAPTER ELEVEN

We got back to the house a little after three in the afternoon, and the sun was already sinking down toward the horizon, pulling out the shadows of bare branches and promising that things would be darker and colder before dinner got served. A school bus trundled down the street, empty of everyone but an ancient-looking driver. I pulled my qi up to my eyes, and the old woman didn't change. She was just what she appeared to be, and I was a little paranoid. The air had been chilly before, but it was reaching toward cold now. I knew that, with the solstice behind us, the light was supposed to be coming back. It just didn't seem that way.

The damage to the house was almost invisible if you didn't know to look. The paint at the side of the front door was a good match to the original shade, but not perfect. Mom was never one to let the house look run-down, but the windows that had survived the assault were just a little bit dimmer than the flashy new glass. Darkened Christmas lights clung to the eaves, and a little patch of snow at the edge of the wall had been churned into mud and ice by the repairmen. I wondered how many favors Dad had pulled in to get it all done so quickly. Maybe there'd been people from church he'd appealed to. Maybe he'd just paid more for rush service. One way or the other, he'd made sure Mom and Curt didn't go into the new year with cardboard over the windows, and I had to respect him for that. I wished that there had been some way to convince Dad to let me pay for it.

Like extortion, maybe.

I pushed my hands deeper into my pockets, scowling all the way up the walk. Jay strutted beside me. I couldn't tell if we were a united front against Dad or if he felt like he was being marched to the gallows. Guilt and resentment at being made to feel guilty wrestled at the back of my head. Ex and Chogyi Jake came up behind us.

Jay rang the doorbell. For a long moment I

thought no one would come. Maybe they weren't home. Maybe they just didn't open the door to me and mine. Then the porch light came on, a pale echo of the falling sun, and the door opened.

"Hey," Curtis said. "Jayné. Jay. What's . . . ah . . . what's up?"

The forced casual tone, the way he didn't step aside to let us in. He was under orders. I understood that, and a flare of anger came up in me. It wasn't a position Mom and Dad should have put him in.

"Came to see Dad," Jay said. "Can you get him?"

"Sure," Curt said with obvious relief. "Hang on a sec."

He closed the door and his muffled voice came through it, calling for my father.

"Thank you," I said.

"For what?" Jay asked.

"For getting Curt off the hook. Not making him feel weirder about being the family bouncer."

Jay looked at me.

"What?" I asked.

"That's what you worry about? Whether Curt feels awkward?"

"It's one thing," I said. "Global warming kind of freaks me out too."

Jay shook his head. It was the same tight motion Dad used when he was angry and not safely at home where he could blow up. I shifted from one foot to the other, trying to decide what I'd do if they left us standing out in the cold. Go around to the back door, maybe. Or kick in the front and see if Dad shot at me. Not like I'd be the first. I felt like I was back at grade school, waiting to see the principal.

The door opened again and Dad was there. He crossed his arms and looked down at us.

"I thought I told you not to speak with her," Dad said.

"I need her help."

"You don't need anything she's got on offer," Dad said.

"Good to see you too," I said, and Chogyi Jake touched my shoulder. He was right. There was nothing I could say that wouldn't escalate things. I bit my lip and looked down. Dad was wearing cheap suede slippers with fake lamb's wool. Grampa shoes. I couldn't think why that should make me sad.

"I need to talk to you," Jay said. "And my sister does to."

"She's not your sister. Not anymore."

"She's my sister," Jay said, his voice growing stronger. "And I need to talk to you. Please let us come in."

Dad's face was set. He had more gray at his temples than I remembered.

"Carla's gone," Jay said.

I couldn't say what I'd expected, except that it wasn't this. Dad froze for a moment, like a video feed stuck on a single frame, and then for a moment his face seemed to cave in on itself. An enormous sorrow seemed to drown him, and I thought he might actually start to weep. It would have been slightly less strange if he'd grown wings and sang Ethel Merman tunes. The moment passed, and he was himself again. He stood back, nodding us inside.

"You and your friends can wait here," he said to me, nodding to the front room. "I want to speak to my son in private."

I ate the pain. There was nothing else to do with it.

The Christmas tree looked a little more disreputable than before. The needles were browning and falling away, and it left the tinsel looking cheap. Vulgar. A clown suit on a corpse. My mother appeared in the kitchen doorway, her eyes wide and hopeful. I sat on the good sofa and didn't look at her. I was afraid she'd offer to take my rider again, and I didn't want to see the desperation in her eyes once more. My father's voice cracked from the TV room like a whip, and she vanished. I leaned my head against the wall and closed my eyes. Chogyi Jake sat beside me. I knew him from the way he moved.

"You know where we could be right now?"

"Where?" he asked.

"Literally anyplace but here. Doesn't that sound great?"

Ex chuckled. He was by the picture window, looking out at the street. Jay and Dad were talking, low masculine voices like the murmur of a car engine on a long, unpleasant drive. I took off my sunglasses, and the room seemed unnaturally light.

"Is something bothering you?" Chogyi Jake asked.

I started to answer, paused, shook my head. There were too many answers to the question, and I couldn't even start to pick out just one to start with. It was Ex who spoke.

"You mean besides her brother's asshole guilt trip? She's worried that because she's getting as much information as we can before we hang our asses out in front of Jonathan Rhodes, she's just as bad as Eric." He turned and looked at me. His eyes were flat with outrage. "And her father's treating her like she's been dipped in shit."

"He's not really my father," I said, wondering how exactly Ex had gotten me in the position of defending Dad.

"He raised you," Ex said. "He's your father. And having met him, I think you turned out great."

"Thanks. I think," I said.

"He's had a difficult life," Chogyi Jake said. He was facing Ex, but I knew the words were meant for me. "Living with a lover who not only betrayed him but who was wounded by it. Raising the child of that betrayal as his own. I assume he took comfort in his faith, but many men in his place would struggle. Fear or sorrow or even love can come out as anger."

"Yeah, sucks to be a patriarch," Ex said.

"Guys," I said. "They're in the next room, right? Maybe cover this later."

"Sorry," Ex said. "Just a little pissed off right now."

My father's voice was raised now, and it had taken on a rhythm, like a preacher in his groove on Sunday morning. Jay's voice was a counterpoint, moving into the spaces and gaps. It was all like a grim, uncomfortable music, and it was as familiar to me as breathing. It would go up, spiraling louder and louder until it reached some kind of crisis, and then come crashing back down to that uneasy post-storm calm that passed for peace in my childhood. I tried not to listen, not to have my belly tighten in response.

"Okay, Invisible College," I said. "Any speculation about what they're up to?"

"Trap," Ex said.

"Trap," Chogyi Jake agreed. "Absolutely."

"Okay," I said, sighing. "Well, that took a few seconds. Anyone else got a way to distract me from this thoroughly awful day? Limericks? Crossword puzzles? Seriously, I'm open to anything."

"Have we considered whether they necessarily have ill intentions?" Chogyi Jake asked.

"Thought that was covered in 'trap,'" I said.

"Perhaps. But what do they believe they are trapping? You are the heir of Eric Heller. Once when we faced them before, we thought we knew what that meant. Since then, it's turned out to be something very different. Perhaps this doesn't have to be the situation we're expecting."

"Don't know about that," I said. "I mean, yes, Eric was a terrible, terrible person, but Randolph Coin did try to throw me off a skyscraper. Why he did it matters less than that he did, right?"

Chogyi Jake nodded at me to continue. Everything in his face and body said *Maybe*. I didn't want to, but the words came anyway.

"I mean, okay, that was after we killed his bodyguard and tried to shoot him, but . . . Ah, jeez. We're not the bad guys again, are we?"

"I don't buy it," Ex said. "The whole enemy-of-my-enemy-is-my-friend thing is naive. Sure, the riders fight against each other. Just because there's a war in hell doesn't keep the devil's enemy from being a demon."

"What do you remember about that battle? Anything that he might have said to you?"

"It was a long time ago," I said, "and I may not have been thinking my straightest. I mean, there was the are-you-sure-you-want-to-do-this? jazz where he offered to do some kind of binding pact where we didn't hurt each other. I figured that just meant he thought I might win."

"Did win," Ex said.

"Had some help," I said.

He smiled. "You're welcome."

"And anyway, I didn't go after them first. They killed Eric and, okay, maybe that was doing the world a favor. But the first time I saw any of them, they had guns in their hands. Four of them broke into that second apartment and started unloading at me."

Chogyi Jake nodded and pressed his fingers to his lips. I could almost hear him thinking, and it was hard not to follow my own path through the problem.

"There's a hole in that," Ex said. "How did they know you were there?"

"I screwed up the wards," I said. "Crossed the threshold without fixing the line behind me."

"Yeah," he said. "But how did they find *you*? You don't show up when people are using spells, remember? It doesn't matter what wards you broke when you came through. They wouldn't have seen you."

"The only other one there was . . . oh."

"Midian Clark," Chogyi Jake said. "Who is a vampire. And was plotting with Eric to assassinate their leader."

"Only then there I was too," I said. "And when they came to the house here, they were loaded with rock salt. Mundane, unaltered rock salt. So that if anyone did get shot, the chances were better that they wouldn't get killed. Unless, you know, high blood pressure. Shit."

I leaned forward on the couch. I didn't want it to be true. More than that, I didn't want it to be even plausible. Like a voice on an old tape, Randolph Coin came back to me. *You are determined to walk in his footsteps.*

And I even knew what I'd said back. *Yeah. Really am.*

"Hold on," Ex said. "I said it before. Yes, they were Eric's enemy. We always knew that, but that doesn't make them good. Whatever he was doing with the Black Sun and the *haugsvarmr* and you, standing against it doesn't make the Invisible College into angels and paladins. That thing they sent looking for us?"

I leaped for it. "That's true. I don't know what that thing was, but it wasn't good. Rotten to the core, more like."

"I wonder if there is a way that we could reach out to them," Chogyi Jake said. "Speak with them without the necessity of violence—"

"No," Jay said, stepping out from the kitchen. I realized belatedly that I hadn't heard Dad's voice for a couple minutes. I wondered how much of our conversation they'd listened to. I was pretty sure the whole demons, guns, and vampires bit wasn't going to help my standing in the family. "We're not doing anything to warn them that we know where they are. Or where Carla is. We do nothing that might put her in more danger."

Dad came in behind him. If I'd thought Jay was growing to look like Dad before, it was twice as clear with the pair of them standing side by side. Behind them, I saw Curt's legs pulling back up the stairs. So he'd been eavesdropping too. Well, it made sense. If I'd had the chance at his age, I'd have snooped too.

In the kitchen, Mom started putting away dishes, the familiar clatter of china and glass both commonplace and foreign. It was as if by acting like things were normal, she could force reality to be normal and regular and comprehensible. Maybe that was how she'd gotten through the last two or three decades. *Once I carried angels in my flesh, but now I need to get the boys to soccer.*

Someone had said to me once that the only people who called themselves crazy were sane. That anyone who'd really been down the road to madness only wanted to be normal again. I'd never thought to apply that to my own family. Or myself.

I stood up, pulling my overcoat straight.

"Jay tells me that Carla's gone off with the people that attacked you here," Dad said. "And that you won't help unless I do what you want."

"That's an extreme reading of the text," I said.

"Watch your mouth," Dad said. "You watch your *mouth* with me."

If he'd hit me, it wouldn't have hurt worse. I felt it in the space just below my rib cage. The anger was so raw, so vicious, and it was my dad. After everything and all the things I'd done, it was my daddy yelling at me. The shame ballooned out from it and I tried not to weep.

This is why I didn't want to come here, I thought. This is why I was scared to go home.

"I told you once you weren't welcome here," he almost-shouted, "and now you're back. You're already on thin ice with me, and I will *not* have you treat me with disrespect in my own house."

Jay put a hand on Dad's arm, and he sputtered into silence. His face was thick and flushed, his hands in fists. His eyes shifted over me like I was the enemy. Like he was looking for a place to strike. *Fear or sorrow or even love can come out as anger.* I felt the tears coming to my eyes, and I willed them away. I couldn't show weakness. I had to speak, but I couldn't. I had to bring him to a place where he could tell me what he knew, that he could save me. I couldn't do it.

The bloom started just below my sternum. It was a subtle thing—warm and close and secret. It pressed down into my belly, up into my throat. The hurt didn't fade. If anything, it came more clearly into focus. But my ability to stand it grew. I saw the sorrow in everything. In what my mother had suffered, and in what my father had suffered as a result. In the loving home they could have had, and didn't. In the childhood I could have had. And Jay. And Curtis. I saw the sorrow in the love behind the fear and rage my father's eyes. Love that had gone septic now. Unreachable as the moon.

"I'm sorry," I said. We said. "I do respect you, and I wouldn't have broken your rule if there weren't great need. I think Carla and her baby are in danger, and I need your help to save them."

Dad's eyes narrowed and his head turned a degree away from me, not trusting what he'd heard. I stood solid, a single line connecting me to the center of the earth. If he'd hit me with a truck, I wouldn't have moved.

Thank you, I thought. Her only response was a sense of wordless acknowledgment.

"What do you want from me?" Dad asked.

I took a deep breath, let it out through my nose just the way Chogyi Jake had taught me. It would have been so easy to say *I want to know about my real father*. The words were right there on the tip of my tongue, ready to fire. It wouldn't cost me anything.

"I want to know about Uncle Eric," I said. "Who he was. What he was into. How he went bad."

Dad's scowl deepened.

"He's gone, and you're in his place," Dad said. "What does any of the past matter?"

"Maybe it doesn't. I don't know. And I won't until you tell me what happened," I said. It was the truth, and something in Dad seemed to hear it. He ran his palm over his chin. For a long, breathless moment, no one spoke.

"Come with me, then," he said.

CHAPTER TWELVE

"You should go," Dad said as he stepped into the kitchen. Mom's eyes went wide, and she hesitated. Dad shot a look at her that would have peeled paint, and her face went pale. "Go upstairs and see that Curtis is doing his work. This isn't a conversation you need to hear."

Mom's mouth worked, her lips making a wet sound, and then she lowered her eyes. "Yes, dear," she said, almost too quietly to hear. She passed out of the room like a ghost. Dad gestured to the chairs. The table was new. The wood still smelled of sap

and varnish. Chogyi Jake and Ex and I sat while
Dad walked down the steps to the TV room and toward the garage.

"You leave too, Jay," Dad said. "This is between
me and her. You don't have to expose yourself to it."

"I don't care if we haven't said our vows yet. My
wife's in danger," Jay said. Dad stopped, looking
back over his shoulder. He might almost have been
proud of Jay's answer.

"As you choose," Dad said. He ducked into the
dimness of the garage and Jay took a seat at my
right hand. It was only a few seconds before Dad
came back. He had a massive book in his hand,
leather bound and ancient looking. I'd seen the
family Bible a few times. Usually, Dad read out of
a common, hard-bound Bible, but when something
especially momentous rolled through our lives, we
knew it because he pulled this out and read from
it. I felt an echo of excitement that belonged to a
little girl I hadn't been in a decade and a half: if
he's brought this out, things were serious. As if they
hadn't been before.

Dad placed the Bible on the table and looked
around. I realized we'd taken all four chairs, but
before I could do anything about it, Ex stood up and
offered his. Dad sat in it without looking at him. He
put his hands on the massive book, closed his eyes,
gathered himself.

"I had two siblings," he said, turning the book

over and opening the back cover. Blank pages flipped through his fingers. "Eric and Nadine. You wouldn't remember Aunt Nadine. She died when she was eight. Caught a fever. She was the oldest, and then Eric and then me."

He paused. There on the page a vast tree of names grew, written in different hands over the course of centuries. I hadn't known it was there before. And halfway down the page, I saw Nadine Heller, Eric Heller, Gary Heller. Of the three, only my father's name was linked to anything—Margaret Fournier—and then, from them, Jason Heller, Jayné Heller, Curtis Heller.

My hand reached out without me, fingers pressing the page. I didn't see it at first, and then I did. The names traced a line back up the page, not always connected, or not directly. Michael Bishop Heller. Amelia Norwich. Nellie Skinner-Bowes. Anderson Skinner-Bowes. Elmer Bowes. There was no entry for Sarah or Toomey Conaville. Nothing for Elias Barker, but for six generations, the men and women who had controlled Eric's money had been members of my family. Jay looked over at me, and I pulled my hand back. I felt like I'd cut open an apple and found a line of rot running through it.

"He was a good brother, when we were young," Dad said, leaning in toward the table. "He watched out for me. Saw to it that I went to church, even when your grandfather was too drunk to take us."

"But he changed," I said.

Dad shook his head. He wasn't disagreeing with me. He was denying the world.

"There was a lot that happened back then," he said. "My brother, Eric, was a good boy. The man he turned into wasn't the same person."

"How did it happen?"

Dad swallowed, his eyes fixed on nothing. His palm rubbed across the Bible like he was stroking a cat.

"I don't talk about this," Dad said. "But when Eric turned twelve, something happened. He said that he got an angel inside him. And he got where he could do . . . things."

"'Things'?" I asked.

"Miracles," Dad said, spitting the word out like it tasted bad. "He got up in trees there wasn't any way to get up. There was a fight at school. Big fella started swinging at this girl. He must have been fifteen, sixteen, because he had his own car. And she was just a little rabbit of a girl. Eric got between them. I was sure he was going to die, but he whipped that boy. Whipped him. And I swear it, he glowed when he did. Like the sun."

I looked over at Chogyi Jake. His smile was calm and encouraging. Gentle. His gaze met mine only for a second, but the message in them was clear. Eric had been ridden too.

"I don't know when Uncle Mike started taking

him to the special meetings," Dad said. "I remember the first time it happened, but I don't know how old I was. Or he was. Only, Mike would come by and talk to your grandfather, and they'd get a little drunk, and then I'd have to stay home and make sure the old man didn't get in trouble while Uncle Mike and Eric went off."

"What was Uncle Mike like?" I asked.

"He was everything my old man wasn't," Dad said. "He was smart and funny and he had all the money he needed. Everybody liked him, and he could drink all night and not even get tipsy. There were a couple times he spoke at church, and the way his voice got when he raised his hands to the Lord, you'd have thought he was a prophet.

"I do remember the last time Eric went, though. The last time the two of them were together. Eric was sixteen years old, because I'd just turned fourteen the week before. Eric and Uncle Mike went out the way they would, and didn't get back before morning. The old man was drunk asleep the same way he always was, but I was scared as hell. They never ran late, and I didn't know if something had happened. I was scared to call the police because I might get in trouble, and I was scared not to because what if something happened? I thought they wouldn't get help because I hadn't called. I told myself that if Eric wasn't back by the time to go to school, I'd call. Then I just prayed and hoped that it was the right thing."

Dad lapsed into silence. Jay sat forward, his hands in his lap. I couldn't read his expression, but it seemed almost as distant as Dad's, as if he were remembering something too. We had known this man our whole lives, and we hadn't known him. The flat tone of his voice now, the emptiness in his eyes, all spoke of years of pain so constant that it had stopped being a sensation and turned into an environment.

"He came back," Dad said. "Sort of, anyway. Uncle Mike drove up and let him out and then drove off again. Eric was bruised all over his body. I mean, all over it. And he looked sick. I stayed home from school and he did too. I tried to take care of him, but he wouldn't talk. Wouldn't tell what had happened. He just said that he'd been wrong about the angel. That was all.

"After that, there weren't any more miracles. It was like he was dead inside. He stopped taking care of me and the old man so much. Stopped going to church and school. I prayed for him. After a while, the old man prayed for him too. That's how bad it got. We didn't have much use for all that talk about depression and getting medicated, but we tried it. If it was going to bring Eric back, I think we'd have tried anything. Then the old man and Uncle Mike both died within about four months of each other. Heart attacks, both of them.

"Eric was out on his own by then, and I was working for the Ford dealership, helping build their computer network. Not that I knew much about computers, but I could run wire. And anyway . . .

"He came for the old man's funeral, and he was back. I thought the first time he was back to his old self. He'd thrown off that whole angel thing and come back up. He laughed and he stood up tall and his face wasn't gray anymore. I thought he was my brother. I was burying my own father, and it was the happiest I'd been in years because I had my brother back."

Dad snarled at the memory. Behind him, Ex shifted, leaning against the wall with his arms crossed. Upstairs a door opened and then closed. For all my father reacted, it could have been something on a different planet.

"He was different," Dad said. "I didn't see it at first, but he was different. He moved back here, started coming to church on a regular basis, just like Uncle Mike used to do. You kids won't remember it, but your mother and I were struggling for a while there right after Jay was born. Eric came in and paid some of my bills. Wouldn't let me pay him back either. Said it was the sort of thing brothers did for each other. Your mother was going through some hard times back then too, and he was . . ."

I understood. This was when it had begun

with my mother. The secret meetings. The riders. The long, unpleasant affair, if that was what we wanted to call it, that eventually led to me. I wanted to reach out to him, to take his hand. I wanted to comfort him, except I knew where that would lead. Shouting and accusations. Violence that stopped just short of hitting, if not the threat of it.

"There was some stuff happened. Your mother and I had a hard road for a while there. We were tested by God, and neither one of us came out as well as we should have," Dad said. "And after that, Eric was gone for a while. I didn't know where. Business, he said. I didn't have any reason to question it, and there were other things on my mind. Your mother was at church a lot then, and I had my hands full taking care of the two of you."

"*You* took care of us?" Jay asked.

"When she was at church," Dad said. "Someone had to make sure you didn't just rot in your own piss while she was gone. I mean, there were times that some of the ladies from the outreach committee'd come over and give a hand. But . . . but she was at church a lot. Man takes care of his children, so of course I did."

Jay shook his head. "I have a hard time picturing you changing diapers."

"I did what had to be done," Dad said, his voice sharp and hard with embarrassment. Shame. "Eric came through every couple years after that. Some-times he'd stay a while. Sometimes just a day or two. Work was steady by then, and I didn't need his money."

"What about the last time?" I asked.

Dad put both hands on the tabletop, steadying himself. His head still shook a little, shifting from side to side like the first tremor of palsy. He stared across at the refrigerator like it was an enemy. I wanted to stop, but I couldn't. It was what I'd come here for, and I needed to know.

"He came by," I said. "You went to dinner, just the two of you. And when you came back, you told us never to speak to him again. Forbade."

"Didn't stop you, though, did it?" he said. "Didn't keep you from getting all cozy with the bastard. You never respected *me*. You never followed the rules of my house. You ate my food, you slept in the shelter I provided, and you didn't listen to a single thing I said. Not a single goddamn *thing*!"

He slammed both his hands down on the table with a report like a gunshot. His face was flushed again, his eyes wide enough that I could see the whites all the way around. I'd pushed him too far. I'd made him too angry. He couldn't control himself anymore.

So I had to.

Help me, I thought, and the rider slid into my flesh. I took his wrist in my looped thumb and forefinger, pressing down against the back of his hand with my palm. The fist he'd been starting to form opened a degree, and he yelped.

"This isn't what we're going to do," I said. *I* did, with my own voice. I didn't know what the words were going to be until I was speaking them, but it wasn't her. This was all me.

"You don't order me around," he said. "I am your father, and you will respect—"

"What did he say? That last time you saw him. Tell me what he said to you."

Dad pulled his hand back, and I let it pull free of my grip. If I'd wanted to, I could have held him there for hours, and I saw in his expression that he knew it. The shape of his eyes changed to something like a wary respect, and that made me as sad as anything that had happened in the whole miserable trip. I'd shown my father I wasn't afraid of his violence, and *that* was what made him respect me. I wanted to leave this place and go home. The irony wasn't lost.

"He told me that you weren't my daughter," Dad said. "He told me that *he* was your real father, and that the time had come that he'd take the burden of you off my hands. You were his heir the way he'd been Michael's, and that I didn't have any right to you. He said he'd make it right with me. That he'd repay me for what he'd . . . done."

"How?" Chogyi Jake asked. His voice was like

a shock of cold water. I'd almost forgotten he was there.

"He had a bag with him," my father said. "It had . . . there was ten million dollars in it, and he just carried it into the place and put it on the bench next to him like it was nothing.

"I told him my kids were my kids, and I'd see him in hell before I gave up any of you. I told him that my soul wasn't for sale. He never crossed my threshold again. I thought . . . I thought I'd kept you safe. And I would have if you hadn't betrayed my trust. Only, now you're his, aren't you. You chose his path over God's. This is your fault. Everything that's happened has been your fault for breaking the commandments. You are to honor thy father and thy mother. Honor and *obey*."

"Yeah," I said, before I could stop myself. "I'm not supposed to kill either, so I'm falling down on a bunch of scores."

His mouth closed with a snap. The anger in his face retreated, and he looked me up and down like he was seeing me for the first time. I wondered if confessing to murder would have been an effective way to argue against his no-dating rules too. I was guessing not.

He wasn't telling me everything. I could feel it. There was something more, and I was willing to bet good money that it had to do with riders and magic and what he meant when he said I was in Eric's place. At the very least, he had to know about the money. But if he wasn't telling, I wasn't sure how to get it out of him.

"Did Eric mention the Invisible College or Randolph Coin?" Chogyi Jake asked, his voice as soft and warm as flannel.

"I didn't want to hear about his unholy ways," Dad said. "He wasn't my brother anymore. And she's not my daughter."

It hurt a little less this time, but I can't say it didn't sting.

"Did he use the word *haugsvarmr*?" I asked.

"He didn't talk about any of that devil worshipping. I wouldn't let him. He was taken by the devil. My brother was lost to the devil, and I couldn't stop it." There was a shrillness running through his voice like a wire. I'd pushed him past where he knew how to go. I'd made him look at the world he didn't want to see. If I stayed, I'd keep pushing until he broke. I wouldn't be able to stop myself.

"Okay," I said and pushed myself back from the table. "That's all. I'm done here."

Jay looked up at me. His lips were thin and bloodless. "Did you get anything that's going to help us?"

"I don't know," I said, because *Probably not* seemed too rude. I'd come wanting my father to explain it all, and the truth was he barely knew more than I did. But he'd told me enough. It wasn't about

Coin or Rhodes or what had happened to Carla. It didn't give me any insight into the political struggles of spiritual parasites trapped in the Pleroma. But it did give me something, and I could feel my mind shifting under the burden of the new information. From the time I'd walked into the apartment and the dead man on the bed had opened his eyes and started cooking, I'd been making assumptions.

No, since before that.

I felt things I thought I knew melting away, and as bleak as the truth was, it was better than the lies. I closed the family Bible, the leather covers enfolding the names of all the people who'd come before me. Burying them, and me with them. Putting it all in the past.

"Thank you, Dad," I said. "For this, and really for all of it. I didn't understand what you were doing, and if I had, I probably still would have taken off. But I know it was what you could do, and I appreciate it."

"You're like he was," Dad said. "You're lost to Satan."

I almost laughed.

"All right, guys," I said. "Let's go."

CHAPTER THIRTEEN

Darkness had taken the streets. I didn't have the luxury of my sunglasses to hide behind. All the wounds were going to be clear on my face, and I was just going to have to be okay with that. I sat forward in the driver's seat with Jay's headlights behind me. My mind felt like the thinnest part of a whirlpool, spinning too fast and drawn too far down.

"What's the plan, then?" Ex asked. It was a good question. I ignored it.

"You know what doesn't make sense?" I said. "Having a massive international empire and then leaving it to someone lock, stock, and barrel without bothering to tell them about it."

Ahead of us, a police car flew through an intersection, lights flaring on its roof, but without a siren to announce it. My knuckles ached on the wheel. I was hungry, and I needed to pee. Not the kinds of things that were supposed to bother an international demon hunter. I wished that I'd thought to hit the bathroom before we left the house, though.

"Eric's story is much like your own," Chogyi Jake said. "Taken under the wing of an older relative. And I have to think the miracles your father talked about were the work of a rider."

"So there's two points," I said. "Inherits fortune from uncle and has a rider on board either pretty young or since, you know, conception. Think that's enough to define a line for us?"

"Let's look at the differences too," Ex said. "He didn't keep his. Michael spirited him away and brought him back empty. No more miracles."

"But depression. A sense of loss," Chogyi Jake said. "Qliphothic."

"Okay," I said. "I've heard the term before. Remind me."

"Shells," Ex said. "Some riders, once they've been in a body, the person's not there anymore. Or they're there in some diminished way. There was one guy in San Diego, the rider was a *jé-rouge*, and when we got it out of him, he wasn't there. His soul was eaten or transferred to some animal we never found. Lost, anyway. That was an extreme case."

"It's always like that to some extent, though," Chogyi Jake said. I got to West Kellogg and turned right. The streetlights glowed around us, drowning out the stars. "Anyone who has had a rider becomes more vulnerable to other possession later."

"The filth-lickers hanging out around exorcists and going for the easy prey," I said.

"Exactly," Ex said. "So when Michael got the rider out of young Eric, it left him pretty bad off. And then he toddled off to wherever and left Eric hanging open."

For a moment I saw my mother's expression again and shuddered. An emptied shell, left on the beach for any crab in need of a place to pick up and use. I wondered what it would feel like, being alone in my own body. It had never been that way for me. I had nothing to compare it to. Only the people I'd known who'd been through it. In New Orleans, Karen Black had collapsed when her rider was cast out, but Joseph Mfume had carried the same beast, and he'd been able to make himself whole. Mostly. Except that he loved the killer after it left him. Longed for it and the sense of peace that it brought him.

No one touched by riders was whole afterward. Even the people who found a way to live with them—a balance that brought rider and horse into a kind of partnership—paid a price for it. *You will outgrow me, so we should be ready*. The phrase had come up in conversation recently, but I couldn't remember where. It seemed important at the time—

"You're speeding," Chogyi Jake said.

"Thanks," I said, and let up on the gas. We were almost at the Walmart. The lights in the parking lot rose up higher than the street lamps. Fake holly hung and bright red bells hung from them. I was surprised to see so many people there so long after dark, and then I checked the time. Five thirty. Most folks weren't even home for dinner yet.

"So Eric had some kind of use for someone who'd been emptied."

"No," Ex said. "Just the opposite. Michael had some reason for casting the rider out of Eric, but we don't know what that was. And Eric didn't do that to you."

I hit the signal and slowed, preparing to turn into the parking lot. Behind me, Jay's blinker started going too. I turned.

"He could have been aiming for it, though," I said. "The *haugsvarmr* under Grace Memorial? It could have kicked the Black Sun out of me. It would have, if it had had little more of a chance. Only it couldn't see me, because . . ."

Because whatever weird thing made me hard to see with magic had left the massive rider blind to me.

"And what would the point be of making qli-photh?" Ex asked. "Why'd Michael do it? Why would Eric do it? What is there to gain from it?"

It didn't hang together. Not yet. But I was closer than I had been. I was sure of that. There were still pieces missing. Like why the people who'd killed Eric were spiriting away my brother's pregnant fiancée.

One thing at a time, I told myself. We'll get there if we just take one thing at a time.

It took me a couple passes to find two parking spaces next to each other, but I managed it. Jay pulled in beside us and killed his engine. He was out of his car before my feet hit the pavement.

"What is this?" he demanded, waving a hand toward the store. "I thought we were going to find Carla!"

"We are," I said. "We just need some things first."

Ex and Chogyi Jake both closed their doors. The sound was deep and metallic. Like a jail cell closing.

"Things? Like what things?" Jay said.

"Shotguns," I said. "And a bathroom."

SOUTH WATER Street was exactly the worst kind of place to do reconnaissance on an enemy. It was in the middle of a wide residential area, no fences to lurk behind, and not many hedges. Two-lane streets of gray pavement, the cracks filled with black tar. Winter-bare trees lined the street on both sides, bare branches reaching across toward each other like fantastic fingers. There weren't many cars on the street, so if I parked the SUV close enough for us to see the house from the vision, we'd also catch the local attention like a fire at a preschool. If we parked far enough away that we couldn't be seen, we also couldn't see anything. Jay's car was more nondescript than my massive black apartment on wheels, but it was also the car that Carla would recognize on sight. Given what she'd said in her note, I wasn't assuming she was going to be on our side. At least not at the start. I might be wrong. The Invisible College might have forced her to write it, and she could be desperately waiting for us to break down the door and pull her away.

I was open for a pleasant surprise, but I wasn't counting on it.

We wound up parking one street over, near the corner where we were most obscured by the houses. Chogyi Jake and Ex got out to walk around the block, not using any glamours, but trusting to the darkness of the night to obscure their faces. The guns we kept in the backseat. I thought about leaving the engine running so we'd be able to use the heater, but I couldn't find a way to do that without keeping the running lights on. So we sat in the darkness, Jay and I, while Chogyi Jake and Ex headed out. The cold seemed to press in from the windows, and I folded my hands in under my jacket and watched the traffic pass. Jay shifted nervously in his seat, his hand tapping at his knees, at the door. He sighed often and without seeming to know he was doing it. Eventually I had to talk to him. It was that or let him annoy me to death.

"She'll be all right."

"I don't believe that," he said.

"They don't have any reason to hurt her. If they're after me, she's no good to them dead."

"How about hurt?" Jay snapped. "Or taken over by demons?"

"Yeah, okay," I said. "Those would suck."

"I can't believe you did this to us. I just can't believe you'd be so selfish."

I turned to look at him. The heat of our combined breath was fogging the insides of the windows, and he looked like a silhouette of himself in front of privacy glass. A streetlight another street away caught the window behind him, giving him a false halo.

"Guess I don't see it that way," I said, then turned back to watching the street. Lights were on in the houses. Men and women going about the rituals of their lives. Getting ready for parties or watching TV or putting the kids to bed. All of it going on while I froze my ass off waiting for the chance to lead a strike on a nest of demon-ridden wizards who probably wanted me dead. Damned selfish of me, all right.

As if he could hear me thinking, Jay tapped his palms on his knees, shook his head, and spoke.

"I'm sorry," he said. "That was out of line. I'm kind of freaking out here. I just don't understand all what's going on. I mean . . ." His voice broke. "I'm supposed to be getting married next week. I'm supposed to be worrying about getting a job that makes enough money and what kind of fucking diaper container to use so we don't stink up the house and making sure Carla's not miserable because we're back here instead of Florida with her family."

"Well, given our family, Wichita is kind of a hard sell," I said. "No offense."

He laughed. It was a small sound, and bitter, but it was more than I'd expected, and I was glad to hear it.

"I sooo didn't want this," he said. "Seriously, this wasn't in the plan."

"How'd it happen?"

Jay rolled his eyes.

"Well, sometimes when a man and a woman love each other very, very much, they give each other a special kind of hug," he said. I punched his shoulder.

"Not what I meant. How about . . . I don't know. How'd you meet her? What's she like when my bullshit drama's not jumping through the windows?" I said. And then a moment later, and more plaintively than I'd meant it to sound, "Are you happy?"

A car drove past, blue or brown or black. Between the fogged windows and the night, I couldn't tell. Something dark. Jay was quiet so long, I thought he wasn't going to answer. When he did speak, his voice was soft. Almost gentle.

"She's great. Smart and talented. And beautiful. She got here, and she made friends with everyone at church right away, even though she's . . . you know."

"Hispanic and knocked up?"

Jay lowered his head to his hands.

"Yes," he said. "That."

"I'm not throwing stones," I said. "She's cool with me."

"Thank you," he said, laughter in his voice. "I'm glad my crazy sister with her porn star SUV and coat and scary-old-man entourage isn't freaked out."

"What're you talking about, 'porn star SUV'?"

"It's a porn star SUV," he said. "The only things its missing are a wet bar in the dashboard and a bunch of little cameras in the backseat."

"Shut up," I said, and punched him again. "How do you know what porn star cars look like anyway? I thought you were all Jesus all the time."

"You thought that, did you," he said. "You noticed I'm in a shotgun wedding, right?"

"Fair point," I said.

"I don't love her."

He said it so easily, his voice so calm, so conversational. The words hung in the air between us, implications trailing out behind them. He was going to have a wife, a baby, a home, a life. Decades stretching out before him sharing his days and nights with a woman he seemed to like. I wanted to say something comforting and wise. Something that would make his situation better, or if not better, at least better than that. I put my hand on his.

"What about you?" he said. "The blond guy. He's in love with you, isn't he?"

"He thinks he is," I said. "I don't know. Maybe it's even true. That issue's got a lot of complexity in it."

"Because of the angel inside you?"

I opened my mouth, closed it again. This wasn't a conversation I'd been planning to have. Ever. With anyone.

"Sort of," I said, feeling my way around the syllables like they might have sharp edges. "She's not an angel, though. Or a demon either."

"So what is she, then?"

"She's what I've got to work with," I said. "And it makes Ex a little scared for me."

"And the other guy? The Asian?"

"He's harder to unease," I said.

"Do you love them?"

I ran a hand through my hair.

"I have an unhealthy thing for Ex," I said. "By

which I mean, I think it's probably a bad idea and I'm probably reacting to a bunch of things besides him. But it's there. Chogyi Jake's . . ."

"Like a brother?" he asked, a smile in his voice.

"More like a mom, actually," I said. "He's just so *nurturing* all the time. I mean, it sounds kind of creepy when I say it out loud, but it's actually really nice."

"So they're your family now." There wasn't any rancor in the question. No outrage at the idea that I might have made a family different from the one I'd been born into. I sat with it for a few seconds. Ex. Chogyi Jake. Aubrey. Kim.

"I guess so," I said. "I guess they are."

"And are you going to church at all?"

"I'm not," I said.

I looked out the side window. The house nearest us had its Christmas lights on still, a half dozen bright colors blinking on and off. Inside, the blue flicker of a television danced like a fire.

"I wish you would."

"It's not really who I am these days," I said. "Maybe later. When things have calmed down a little."

"I'd appreciate it," he said. "It was hard when you left. There were a lot of things that got thrown into the air. Plans had to change."

"Mostly plans about what college I'd get my 'MRS' degree from," I said.

"Well, that too," he said.

"Yeah? So which plans were you thinking of?"

Jay shrugged.

"I always pictured you being around, is all. Mom and Dad are going to get old. They'll get sick and need us to take care of them, and I figured it would be the three of us together. You and me and Curt. And, you know, I figured your kids and mine would be going to Sunday school together. Or, you know, at least Christmas services. When you stepped out of the picture, it blew everything up."

"I didn't mean it to," I said. "I just . . . I needed to go, you know?"

"I do," Jay said. "I know exactly. I remember when Mom called me and told me that you'd gone to Arizona even though Dad said you couldn't. Honestly, the first thing I thought was *She can't do that—can I?* But by then I was almost done with my degree, and after I had that . . . well, I could go anywhere."

"So you went to Florida because I went to Arizona?"

"I don't know if I'd say that," he said. "But part of what made me think I could go out in the world was that you already did it. Only, it didn't work out all that well, did it? I mean, here we both are."

Something shifted on the sidewalk about half a block down. I tried to wipe the steam from the inside of the windshield, but it was already half frozen, so instead I scraped it with my fingernails, tiny white threads of frost falling to the dashboard. Chogyi Jake and Ex. I rolled down the window, and Ex stepped up.

"Got them," Ex said. "The place is about a block and a half down on the east side of the street. There's a truck in the front, and I'm pretty sure they've got the motorcycles in the back. I'm only seeing Rhodes and the woman. Idéa Smith. If Martinez is there, he's not near a window."

Chogyi Jake opened the rear door. By the dome light, he started gathering the four new shotguns.

"And Carla?" Jay said. "Is she there? Did you see her?"

"Didn't," Ex admitted. "But we weren't getting too close. They have wards on the place. When we come in, they're going to know it."

"Okay," I said. "Here's the plan. Chogyi Jake and I will head for the front and see if we can pull them out to the street. You and Jay get his car parked on the next street over and come in at the back. If they try to get her out, you can grab her. If they don't, you can go in after her. Invoke Calling Malkuth so the magic's not as effective, and then use the guns if you need them."

"'Calling Malkuth'?" Jay asked, his brows furrowed.

"Special kind of prayer," Ex said. "And once we have her, where do we go?"

"Airport and out of town," I said. "Wherever the first flight's going."

"Wait," Jay said. "What about—"

"It's on my dime," I said. "If you're not here, I've got one less thing to worry about."

"And you?" Ex asked.

"There're some things only your enemies know about you," I said. "I'm going to try to distract them and get them to talk to me. Maybe get something useful out of them before it all goes down."

"You know they have guns too," Ex said, scowling.

"Didn't say it was going to be easy," I said.

CHAPTER FOURTEEN

There are a lot reasons that dealing with riders felt like crime. The first one—the most important one—is that I never wanted the police involved. I've got nothing but respect for cops. They've got a rough job, and an important one. But when they're around, they're the authority. Explaining that they shouldn't arrest me because the guy I just shot is really a demon from another plane of existence would actually be worse than just insisting on speaking with my lawyer. I had faith in my ability to buy my way out of almost any amount of legal trouble short of murder, but it was always easier to stay out of the legal system than to get out once I was in it.

Another reason was that most of what I did and had done for years now involved doing something other people—often violent and powerful people—didn't want me to do. Abducting a girl before a New Orleans voodoo cult could put a rider in her, for instance, although that one hadn't really gone as expected.

But the thing that made my job and criminal work most similar was this: I didn't care what other people wanted. For a thief or a murderer, that was because very few people are up for being robbed or killed. Really taking into account what the person on the other end of the knife wanted, including them in the dialog, pretty much meant you weren't a thief and murderer anymore. For me, it was more complex. I could want the best for the people I dealt with, but I couldn't assume they wanted the best for themselves anymore.

Riders are like any kind of parasite. They change the organism they're living in. A caterpillar parasitized by some kinds of wasp larvae will defend the larvae even while they are eating it alive. *Toxoplasma gondii* bacteria make its host mouse like the smell of cat in order to get the mouse eaten and the bacterium into the cat's gut, where it is happiest. An ant with fungal parasites will climb to the top of a blade of grass and wait for a cow to come eat it. People with riders don't have free wills the way normal folks do. They are puppets on strings, and if they are even still in their bodies, they may not even know they are being controlled. For all I knew, Rhodes and his buddies hated the things they were doing now.

For that matter, if I hadn't had a rider, I might never have fallen from grace with the church. I might not have left home. All the choices I had made in my whole life were suspect. I knew it, and it didn't change anything. I had to pretend that I had made all my own choices at the same time that I was willing to put theirs down to being controlled by spirits and ghosts. The irony wasn't lost on me.

I stood at the corner, looking down the dark street. My right hand was in a cheap vinyl duffel bag, my fingers wrapping the stock and trigger of a Remington 870 Express. The nice thing about shotguns, at least for me, is I didn't have to have great aim. Chogyi Jake stood beside me, blowing warmth into his cupped hands.

The house looked different in the night, but not so much that I didn't recognize it. The single tree close to the road. The porch and porch swing. Darkness had turned the white walls to gray, and the blue of its neighbors almost black. It was the same house I'd seen in the vision, though. No doubt about it.

"Are you all right?"

"About to walk into a trap," I said. "Feeling a little nervous."

"We still have options," he said. "We can call the police. Report her as having been kidnapped."

"Wouldn't do any good," I said. "And it would put a bunch of innocent people in danger."

"Better if the people in danger aren't innocent?" he asked, and I smiled.

"If they're shooting at anyone, better that it's us. At least we know to expect it."

He shifted, swinging his own cheap duffel bag off his shoulder, putting his own hand in to match my own.

"This isn't your fault, you know," he said.

"It's my responsibility, though. That's close enough. I'm trying to take a lot of comfort in the fact they were packing rock salt before."

"Is that working?"

"Not really," I said. "You ready?"

Chogyi Jake nodded and we started down the street. The cold and the dark meant there was no one else out. I stopped at the sidewalk across the street from the Invisible College's safe house. The shotgun felt heavy and unpleasant in my hands. The lights burned white in the windows, and I could feel the force of the wards pushing my awareness away. I remembered being in science class in middle school and having the teacher—a short, mean woman with red hair and bad teeth—show us that we all had a blind spot. She went on about how everyone had a little glitch in their field of vision where the optic nerve was attached to the retina, but I was just sitting at my desk, playing at making the tip of my finger disappear. Move it an inch, it appeared. Shift back and it was gone. The house was like that too. There and gone. It made my head ache a little to look at it.

"They get to shoot first," I said.

"Is that why you asked Ex to stay with your brother?"

"You don't think Ex would let them take a free shot at me?"

"I think he wouldn't."

"I think you're right," I said. I didn't want to cross the street and step directly into their wards and devices. I didn't want to stay here and slowly freeze until they noticed me. Or if they had already, until they did something about me. "I feel like Lloyd Dobler."

"Who?"

"Guy in a movie. Never mind."

I was sure by now they'd noticed me, but nothing kept happening. It was my move, and their home court advantage. I drew my will up, letting the force of it pool in my throat. The Black Sun didn't add anything to it. Whatever I started with, it would be only a human effort. I imagined her waiting in the space behind my eyes, as tense as I was and watching for our next move.

"Hey," I called, pushing the word out. It was invisible, but I felt it break against the wards and shatter. That was fine. I hadn't meant to get through, just knock. Maybe ten seconds later the door swung open. My gut went tight. Even in the dead of winter, my palms were sweating against the shotgun. I smelled overheated iron, like an empty skillet left too long on an open flame, and a vast pressure of qi curled over me. Whatever the riders were in those people's skins, they were strong. And worse, they were smart.

He came onto the porch. Jonathan Rhodes in blue jeans and a thick knit sweater. If it hadn't been for the intricate tattoos, he could have been anyone. Instead, he looked like a refugee from some deeply disturbing carnival. When I had killed Randolph Coin, it had been with an enchanted bullet. I hadn't shot him with it, even. Just pressed the ensorcelled metal to a wound and kicked the rider in him loose. He hadn't stopped breathing all at once. For the first time I wondered if that meant the man—the shell—had been alive at the end, empty of its rider and wounded past all hope of survival. I wondered whether Jonathan Rhodes had any bullets like that one, and if there might be a rifle trained on me right now.

"You're Rhodes," I said, lifting my voice. I didn't

put any magic in it. It was just me talking loud enough to carry across a narrow street.

"Jayné Heller," he said. I thought he sounded nervous, but I was probably flattering myself.

"You wanted me here," I said. "So I'm here now."

He nodded. He had his hands in his pockets, and I had the sense he was holding something as tightly and with the same faux-casual attitude that I held the Remington. A pistol. A charm. Whatever it was, he hadn't used it against me yet. We were two dogs circling each other, not sure yet how the fight was going to start. Who was going to take the first bite.

"We know what you've been doing, Ms. Heller. It stops tonight."

"We can talk about that," I said. "But I think you may not be up on everything. Or maybe I'm not. But you have to let the girl go."

"She's under our protection," Rhodes said. "Her and the child she's carrying. You can't have them."

"Not a negotiating point," I said. "But maybe if you—"

The shots came from the back of the house. Two shotgun blasts with maybe half a second between them. Someone screamed, but I couldn't tell if it was a man's voice or a woman's. I brought up my shotgun, still in its bag, and started running across the street.

This wasn't how it was supposed to go. Ex was supposed to use the spell called Calling Malkuth;

he was supposed to damp down their magic before anything else happened. The fact that he hadn't meant the firefight was starting with the bad guys at full strength. It was happening too early.

On the porch, Jonathan Rhodes pulled his hand out of his pocket and gestured at me. A fine arc of gray dust puffed out, thin as ashes. It felt like a sledgehammer to my chest. I staggered back, gagging, and then I wasn't driving anymore. The Black Sun dropped to one knee on the dead brown lawn and lifted a hand palm out toward Rhodes. His snarl was made of anger and fear. His teeth were deformed, carved into strange, inhuman shapes.

He came off the porch, launching himself straight at me and blocking the path to the doorway. Chogyi Jake appeared from my right. He'd taken his gun out of the duffel bag, and its barrel was trained on Rhodes's head. He might just as well not have been there at all from the attention the tattooed man paid him. I raised my own weapon.

Time seemed to slow down. I saw his eyes grow wide, not with fear or surprise but a kind of joy. Like this was the battle he'd been waiting for, and now, at last, he had it. The marks on his face shifted, remaking themselves under his skin. I pulled the trigger. The shotgun kicked like a car wreck, and the end of the duffel bag blew open. Rhodes was five, maybe six feet from the end of the barrel. It was as good as a mile. Hundreds of tiny sparks flashed around him, the bright metal of the buckshot vanishing. He grinned, stepped forward, and kicked at me. My body dropped back, letting the gun fall to earth, and caught his ankle against my crossed forearms. Chogyi Jake fired, and the flash came again. If Ex had managed his cantrip—if the powers of the riders had been pushed back—it would have shredded Rhodes's skin. Or at least drawn blood.

He pushed down with a shout, landing on the foot he'd kicked with and twisting forward, driving his elbow toward my temple. Even with the unnatural reflexes of my rider, the blow glanced off my skull. I staggered back. Chogyi Jake racked a fresh shell and fired again. He was at point-blank range now. I saw the hot gasses from the muzzle flash make ripples in Rhodes's shirt, but he still ignored it. I jumped back from a kick that sank his heel inches into the dead brown sod. Another scream came from the back of the house. Unmistakably a man this time.

Ex.

I broke away, racing for the back of the house, legs pumping with so much force I felt the grass under me sliding. I ripped out divots.

A single exterior bulb cast a harsh pool of light in the space between the house itself and the shed in the back. It was like a lit theater stage in the dim night. Ex knelt in the middle of the circle, steadying himself with one hand. His shotgun lay on the ground in front of him. His head hung forward, the cascade of loose hair hiding his face. His left leg from the knee down was soaked with blood. I was at his side in seconds, and it was still too long.

He looked up, his face pale and stony with pain. I tried to speak, but my body wasn't my own. Instead, I put my arm around him, staring into his eyes in mute fear. For a moment he seemed not to find me, his attention swimming. He found me, his eyes focusing. His smile was tight.

"Well, that could have gone better."

I tried to ask about Jay, about Carla, about what had happened, but the Black Sun wouldn't give me control. Instead, she looked back. Jonathan Rhodes was walking down the side of the house toward us. I was aware distantly of lights in the neighboring houses, of voices raised in fear. Somewhere nearby, a car engine roared and tires shrieked against pavement. I hoped it was Jay, and I hoped he had Carla with him. It would suck to die like this for nothing. Ex shifted, tried to stand, and yelped in pain. Rhodes came to the edge of the light. His eyes seemed to glow.

Something moved on my left. The other man, Eduardo Martinez, stepped out of the darkness. I turned around. The woman, Idéa Smith. I'd made the classic mistake. I'd come too far forward and ignored my flanks, and now they were all around me. I felt a growl low in my throat. Ex shot out a hand, reaching for the shotgun, and the woman gestured. Her will was like a whip, and the shotgun ripped itself out of Ex's hands and stuck hard to the icy earth. My body went still, waiting for an opportunity I wasn't sure would come. These were the people who had killed Eric. They knew what they were doing.

They opened their arms, and I felt the web of energy sparking between them, pressing against me like a cage. The Black Sun turned, shuddering, but the circle was complete. There was no way out. The three began chanting, and the invisible net grew stronger with each syllable that locked into the ones behind and before. Rhodes lifted his arms. The black ink shifted in his skin, words in arcane languages forming, growing sharp, and then breaking apart. The vast flow of meaning burned off him, pushing me back to the center of the circle. Ex took my hand. His fingers were cold.

"By your name I bind you," Rhodes said, and his voice was dry and vast and older than the flesh it rode in. "Puer Mórtuus, I bind you."

The cage grew closer, pressing in against me. His tongue was black now, his eyes bright and nacreous, like mother-of-pearl. He took a step in, and the other two stepped in with him. The air thickened, and I struggled to breathe. The stink of overheated metal overwhelmed me.

"By your name I bind you," he said. The words

tapped against me like hailstones, and I felt the division between reality and the Pleroma thinning, the mindless, blind spirits thrashing in distress. "Abraxiel Unas, I bind you."

Ex was shouting at me, his lips pulled back with the violence of the call. I couldn't hear him. Everything was silent except the deep, constant pressure of the riders pushing against me. I rose to my knees, then sank again, my head bowed. Ex tried to shake me. The blood on his hands was wet and cold.

They were close now, their fingertips almost touching. Arcs of power danced between them, so powerful they were almost visible. My hands clenched in fists, fingernails digging into my palms, and I was also trapped in the tight space behind my eyes.

Rhodes's voice rang with triumph and joy.

"By your name I bind you. Graveyard Child, I bind you."

The trap was complete. I felt it close for the last time, and then wash away around me. Together, the Black Sun and I looked up into his eyes. They were the common brown of a human being now. The marks on his skin were only ink again. His smile spoke of exhaustion and pleasure and victory.

"Those aren't my names," I said.

There was a moment of shock and fear in his expression, and my body unfolded, legs and gut and back twisting, every muscle firing, bones creaking with the strain of sinking my right fist, knuckles down, into the soft place just below his rib cage. Ex rolled forward with a cry, scooped up his shotgun, and fired wild. The woman ducked back, her hand up to cover her face. Rhodes doubled over, his breath whooshing out of him. I got my feet under me and brought an elbow down hard between his shoulder blades, and he fell. Martinez tried to rush me, but the Black Sun danced out of his path and kicked at the back of his knee as he passed.

I scooped up Ex, holding him to me like he was a child. He didn't seem to weigh anything at all. He lost his grip on the shotgun, and it clattered to the ground behind us as I sprinted out into the dark. The SUV wasn't far. Chogyi Jake's shoulders and head were a shadow in the driver's seat. The running lights came on and a great puff of white rose up from the tailpipes.

Ex clung to me, his hands around my shoulder, his head pressed against me.

I ran.

CHAPTER FIFTEEN

The emergency room at Wesley Medical Center wasn't the worst I'd been to. Which meant, in part, that I wasn't actively worried about people trying to kill me. The halls were clean and bright, the intake nurse was calm and professional, and they got Ex into a room within ten minutes of our pulling up to the front door. The triage nurse and a couple of techs in blue scrubs cut away Ex's pant leg and washed it down while I held his hand. I claimed to be his fiancée and that was enough to get me into the room with him, while Chogyi Jake was stuck in the waiting area.

Ex's color was coming back, though he was still pale. Swaths of dried blood were flaking off his hands and cheek. Between his black eye and mine, we looked pretty rough, which I didn't figure was likely to make the doctors more responsive. If I'd seen us, I'd have dialed straight to drug-addicted spousal abuse too. The nurse on duty came by after an hour and sprayed something on his wounded foot that seemed to take the edge off the pain. They weren't dosing him up with any pills more powerful than Tylenol, probably on the assumption that we'd shot him in the foot ourselves in a bid to score pain medication.

Somewhere nearby, a woman was groaning and calling for someone named Steven. Over the previous few months and years, I'd been in more hospitals than I liked, and other than making me feel profoundly self-conscious and unwelcome, this one wasn't bad. A nurse came and drew some blood for routine testing. She had a discreet bandage on the side of her nose to cover up the piercing there.

I held Ex's hand while she did it, more for myself than him, and I didn't let go when she left. After a few minutes his breath got heavy, slow, and regular. I assumed he was sleeping until he spoke.

"What is it with your family and firearms?"

"My family and . . . You mean *Jay* did this?"

"What we get for bringing civilians in," he said. "We were waiting just past the shed. The warding was light there, and we had a decent line of sight on the back of the house. They brought her to the back when you showed up on the street. I figured the longer we could put off using the cantrip, the longer it was until they noticed us. Jay went up the back steps and waved at her through the window. She came out, and he put his gun under his armpit and blew my foot off."

"It's not off," I said. "It doesn't even look all that bad."

"It looks like a sausage with a dozen little raisins where the blood's clotting."

"I was comparing it to blown off," I said. "It looks better than that."

Ex smiled without opening his eyes, and I smiled with him.

"They got away?"

"I think so," I said. "He's not answering his cell."

"And the homestead?"

"I don't think Mom and Dad are likely to accept my calls anytime soon," I said. "What about the other shot? I heard two."

"After he shot me, the other two noticed we were there. I tried to slow them down."

"It worked," I said.

"Sort of," Ex agreed. "The trap. They were working a binding, weren't they?"

"Trying to," I said. "They didn't do a great job of it."

"Well, thank God we're all the Keystone Kops," he said.

We waited. The woman who was calling for Steven had stopped. I texted Curtis to see if he'd heard any news, and Chogyi Jake to let him know that I hadn't. I listened to the nurses talking at their station, I paced quietly beside the bed. The monitors said that Ex's heartbeat was regular, his blood pressure a little high. I wanted to go find Jay and Carla, wherever they were. I kept suffering visions of them in some dark place, caught by Rhodes and his cabal. Of course, if I left, I'd start imagining the Invisible College coming to the hospital to finish the job. We were too scattered, and we didn't know enough. One worry followed the next, anxiety building on anxiety, and behind it all was the sense that I'd forgotten something. Something important.

The doctor arrived about three hours later, and I had to tell myself that the long delay only meant that Ex's condition wasn't bad enough to get worried about. He was a young man, probably not more than a year or two ahead of me, but he affected a world-weary attitude. Maybe he'd even earned it.

"So you did this to yourself, or did you have help?" he asked.

"Little help," Ex said.

"That was my guess," the doctor said.

"Is he going to be all right?" I asked.

"Sure," the doctor said. "We'll numb him up, dig

the shot out of him, and send him home. We see this kind of thing every night. Only thing that's strange about this one is that he came in sober. There's going to be a form to fill out, though. Police like us to let them know when someone comes in shot. In case it matches up with something that happened."

"Ah," I said.

"That wouldn't be the case here," he asked, "now, would it?" I didn't know what to say, and a few heartbeats later the doctor shook his head. "Well, I'll need to fill out the form, so you two start thinking about what you want to say on it."

"We're not as bad as we look," I said.

He smiled at me. His eyes were gentle.

"If I was one to pass judgment on people, I'd be in the wrong job," he said. Honestly, I could have kissed him.

The whole thing start to finish took another four hours. I left during the extraction of the shot, since they wouldn't let me stay in the room. Chogyi Jake had gone across the street and gotten McDonald's. I didn't realize how late it had gotten until I saw he'd ordered off the breakfast menu. I still hadn't heard from Jay or Curt or my parents, and I still had the growing unease that came from something only half-forgotten. Something I was supposed to take care of and hadn't.

We got back to the hotel with the late winter sun just beginning to lighten the sky. Ex's foot was wrapped with pads and gauze until it looked almost like a cast. He'd been given the option of a crutch but turned it down. The doctor hadn't offered pain medication, and Ex hadn't pushed for it. When we went in through the lobby, I had my arm around him on one side, Chogyi Jake had his arm around him on the other. The woman at the counter looked a little alarmed but didn't say anything.

When we got to their room, Chogyi Jake used the key card. The electronic lock wheezed open. The first thing that struck me was the smell of shit and rank urine. Both beds had been stripped, the coverlets pulled to the floor. A pillow had been ripped apart, the stuffing strewn on the carpet.

I knew what I'd forgotten.

"Ozzie! Oh my God," I said. "What did you *do*?"

Her claws tapped against the bathroom tile, and she came trotting out, tail wagging so hard it swung in a circle, tugging her hips along after it. She looked from me to Ex and back, her canine expression caught between worry and delight.

"In her defense," Chogyi Jake said, "we were gone much longer than we expected."

"I know, but she trashed the place!"

"She was worried," Ex said, scratching her behind the ears. "Weren't you? Weren't you a worried dog?"

I flapped my hands in wordless distress. The truth was I felt guilty. How was I going to save innocent people from the overwhelming power of riders when I couldn't get it together enough to look after a Labrador?

"Any chance we could bunk in your room?" Ex asked.

"Yes," I said. "Of course. Take her too. We didn't feed her either."

"Where are you going?" Ex asked.

"To give housekeeping a *lot* of money."

By the time I got back to my room, Ex was already stretched out on the second bed and snoring softly. Chogyi Jake lay beside him, eyes closed in what could have been meditation or sleep. Ozzie was curled up on the foot of my bed, chewing contentedly on her right front paw in a way that meant all was forgiven—on her end, anyway. I put the Do Not Disturb thing on the door, changed into some sweats, and crawled into bed.

I hoped that sleep would come quickly, but I was disappointed. My mind kept looping back on itself: Where was Jay, was Carla all right, what if the Invisible College went after Mom and Dad and Curt, didn't people get blood clots in their feet and die from it and what if that happened to Ex, why didn't the binding spell Rhodes put on me work, was I a bad pet owner . . . The waterfall of fears and anxieties promised to run on forever. I stared up at the ceiling, watching tiny web works of light that snuck in at the edges of the curtain shift and brighten and fade as the sun rose. I tried to meditate the way Chogyi Jake had taught me, but I'd fallen out of practice and I couldn't seem to maintain my focus for more than a few seconds at a time.

What had they called me? Puer Mórtuus? Abraxis something or other? Graveyard Child was the only one I remembered for sure. I felt like I'd heard the term before. Like it had something to do with the constant fighting that went on between riders in their own environment. I couldn't place it.

When my phone rang, I was the only one awake, and I answered almost immediately.

"Jayné?" Jay said as I crawled out of bed and slipped into the bathroom, closing the door behind me so I wouldn't wake anybody up by talking.

"Where are you?" I said.

"I'm okay. We're okay. I did what you said. I got Carla on a plane. It took a while, but she's going to Memphis. I gave her enough money to get a hotel for a few days. They won't be able to find her there, will they?"

"They might," I said, "but I don't think they'll have reason to. Their plan failed, and bait's not much use without a trap."

"What . . . what happened?"

"You mean after you shot Ex?" I asked, more sharply than I'd mean to.

The line was quiet for a moment.

"After that. I'm . . . I'm really sorry about that. I

should have been more careful. And . . . I shouldn't have left him behind like that."

"Well, yeah, they're going to take away your gun safety merit badge," I said. "But getting out was the right thing to do. The whole point of being there was to get Carla out safely. Ex knew it wasn't safe. We all knew."

"Thank you," he said.

"Don't mention it," I said. "Turns out this is what I do these days. I'll need to talk to Carla, though."

"Why?" Jay asked.

"See what she heard. What she saw. She was with the bad guys for hours, and they might have been in touch with her before she went."

"They were," Jay said. "They told her that you were possessed by a demon and that it was going to leave your body and take over the baby. That whole thing at the house? They did it to force you into doing magic in front of her, so that she'd believe them. She said she texted them when you showed up at the house. She's sorry about it now, though. Really."

"It's a big world," I said. "Everyone screws up. It's all right. Still, when she's somewhere she can use the phone, I'd like to ask her a few questions."

"She's not going to want to do that. She's scared of you, sis. And no offense? You're kind of scary."

I looked at myself in the bathroom mirror. I hadn't turned on the overhead fixture, since it would have meant cranking up the exhaust fan with it. The only light coming off my phone. Between my bruised face, hair that spoke of a night at the ER, and the pale glow spilling across my cheek, I did look like a poster for the sort of movie that parents don't let their kids see.

"We'll work something out," I said. "Where are you?"

"I'm at a friend's house. He's out of town for the holiday, and I had a spare key so I could water his plants. I figure they wouldn't know to look for me here. Also . . . I hope this is okay. I called Dad. I told him that the guys who broke into the house were still around, and that he should be careful. I hope that's all right?"

"It is. I'd have done it myself, if he was taking my calls," I said. And then, a second later, "You didn't go with her."

"I didn't, did I?" Jay said ruefully. "I thought about it. They're still here, though. Those people. I told her I was staying until I had everything with them resolved."

"Yeah, that's going to be tricky."

"I'm not sure it was true when I said it. I don't know if we're going to get married after all."

"What about the baby?"

"I don't know." The words were so simple, and the way he said them was so rich, so complicated.

"You know what you're hoping for?"

"No," he said. "I don't even have that."

I wished he were with me instead of talking across the phone. I wanted to see his face, take his hand. Offer some kind of comfort. He was trapped. If he stayed with Carla and the baby, he would be living a life he didn't want in a loveless marriage. If he didn't, he was going to spend the rest of his life hauling along the knowledge that he was the kind of guy who'd get a girl pregnant and leave her.

"Sorry," I said. It sounded powerfully inadequate, even to me.

"What about you guys?"

"Holed up. Licking wounds, figuratively speaking. I've got some things I need to follow up on."

"The bad guys? Did you . . . are they still around?"

"I didn't kill them," I said. "Got away, though. And I have some things I want to look into. They were doing something, and they did it wrong. If I can figure what they were trying for, I'm hoping it'll aim me in the right direction."

"I want to be in on it," Jay said. "Whatever you wind up doing, I want you to let me know."

"You're feeling guilty about shooting Ex, aren't you?" I said, teasing him.

"I am," he said. "And I also just got my sister back. I'd rather not have her just vanish again."

My tears weren't a surprise, really. I should have expected them.

"I love you too," I said. "You know that when I said these guys were my family now, I didn't mean that you weren't, right?"

"Of course I knew that," he said. "Dummy."

I laughed a little. "We'll get through this."

"We will. We'll track those bastards down wherever they go."

"Yeah. First, get some rest. Can I reach you here when we're up?"

"Absolutely. I'm going to try to get a little sleep myself."

"Take care of yourself," I said.

When I crawled back into bed, my brain felt less like an accident in a fireworks factory. Talking to Jay, knowing he was safe, even for very narrow definitions of safe, calmed me down. I pulled the blankets up to my chin and snuggled down into the pillows. Ozzie stood up, walked around in a circle, and lay down again with a contented sigh. I knew what she meant.

In the darkness, I listened to Ex's soft snoring and Chogyi Jake's slow, deep breath. I felt every time Ozzie shifted, chasing dream rabbits. My mind started to drift. I was glad, I decided, that Ozzie had wrecked the other room. If it had just been me and her in the place, it wouldn't have felt right. Part of that came from spending the last day fighting and afraid, but part was just that these were my people. This was my pack, and having us all together in the

same room was right. This was the way it was supposed to be.

I reached my mind down, deep into my body.
Thank you, I thought. The Black Sun didn't re-
spond. Maybe she was asleep too. I didn't know if
riders did things like that, but I couldn't see why
they wouldn't. She was part of my pack as well. Part
of my self.

Back in college, a deeply unethical teaching as-
sistant had told me that there were two kinds of
family: the one that you're born into, and then the
one that you make for yourself. He'd been trying
to seduce me at the time, but that didn't make the
sentiment wrong. I had made myself a family, and
it was one that I liked a lot. I would always be my
parents' daughter. That was just history, and there
was nothing that could change that. But what
that meant was up to me and the people—and the
dog—I kept with me.

I closed my eyes and listened to the cars on the
highway, the voices in the hall, the breath of my
family. I slept.

And when I slept, I dreamed.

CHAPTER SIXTEEN

I stood in the desert at night. Wind whipped the bare earth, but I wasn't cold. The sky was black and starless. A dark scorch mark ran alongside me as I walked or ran or floated through the emptiness. I knew both that it wasn't real and that it was the result of my abortive efforts to exorcise the thing living inside me. I looked at the damage with a real curiosity. If they could put me in one of Oonishi's fMRI machines back in Chicago, would they be able to find what part of me had died in order to make this scar? Or maybe this wasn't a sign of death. Only change.

And then she was there with me. Or we were there together. Or I was doubled. There wasn't a good word for it. I cast two shadows in the light from an invisible moon.

Her face was cracked. The Jayné mask that had been so perfect for so long had black marks running through its cheeks. I lifted my hand to her, and I also pulled my head back so that she couldn't touch my damaged self.

It's okay, one of us thought. *I won't hurt you.*

Fingertips brushed against the broken mask, and more of the pale ceramic fell away. There was flesh under it, dark as the midnight sky. I kept peeling away the mask, uncovering her and being uncovered. The air touched my dark cheeks for the first time. The Black Sun looked at me with eyes like my own set in an inhuman face. Inhuman, but beautiful.

I will outgrow you, she said. *Not yet, but not long from now. The change has begun, and we can't escape it. We can't even slow it down.*

The elation I felt was human. I took her hand, and her false skin shattered, letting our fingers entwine for the first time ever.

It's all right, I said. *We're ready. We will be ready.*

I'm frightened, the rider said in a voice that was soft as a whisper and vast as mountains.

"I'm not," I said with my real voice, and, by saying it, woke myself up.

"You're not what?" Ex asked.

The hotel room was still dim, but someone had shifted the curtains so that a little bit of sunlight came through. It wasn't the full-on cave darkness that it had been. More a kind of winter twilight. The water was running in the bathroom, the shower splashing. I put my hand to my hair, suddenly aware of how much I smelled like sweat and unwashed me, and wondered if hotels ever ran out of hot water. At my feet, Ozzie raised her head. Her tail thumped against the mattress twice. I leaned forward and put my hand on her side, scratching her ribs. She put her head back down with a contented canine smile.

"I'm not awake," I said.

"You can keep sleeping," Ex said. "We've only been down for a few hours."

"No, I'm fine," I said, and yawned so wide my jaw cracked. "I heard from Jay while you guys were asleep. He's fine. Carla's safely out of town."

"And your family?" Ex said.

They're mostly in the room with me, I thought. "Dad's warned. I don't know what more we'd do, even if we could."

"I don't like it," Ex said.

"I'm not thrilled either," I said, yawning again, but less prodigiously. "But it's what I've got. How's your foot?"

"Swollen. Has a bunch of holes in it. So what's

our next step here? Is it time to head for Denver and hit the archives?"

I pulled the blankets back and sat up. My body felt sore and achy and the ghost of a headache was floating somewhere at the back of my neck. Given how bad last night could have gone, I felt pretty good about it.

"Not yet," I said. "Do you remember much of the binding spell Rhodes and his buddies tried on me?"

"Some of it, yes," Ex said.

"The names they tried to bind me with, Puer Mórtuus. Graveyard Child. And the other one."

"Doc," Ex said. "The last one you can never remember is always Doc."

"Doc sounded more like Abraxis something."

"Abraxiel Unas. I remember that much."

The shower water stopped and I heard the metallic hiss of the curtain opening. I pushed my hair back. I really wanted that shower next.

"Ring any bells?" I asked.

"No," Ex said. "But I've been looking around on the online resources. I'm seeing some footnotes in the London resources. Nothing solid, though."

I laced my fingers together. What had been a half-formed suspicion slid into my consciousness like the back of my head was serving it up on a platter. If Ex couldn't find information on a rider, either it was the most obscure entity in the catalog or something else was going on.

"Go outside our resources," I said.

Ex frowned. "To where?" he asked. "Eric put together the most comprehensive collection of occult literature and theory maybe in the world. Seriously, any one of the places we've visited had caches as good as the best museums and universities."

"I know," I said. "That's why I want to go outside of them."

"Still not following," Ex said.

"Indulge me. I have a hypothesis."

The bathroom door opened, and Chogyi Jake stepped out. I was past him in a second.

"What's the plan?" he asked.

"Two-fisted tales of research," I said.

"Does it include eating?"

"As long as it isn't room service, go wild," I said, and closed the door.

The hot water didn't run out, and I gave it every opportunity to. I stood under the steaming blast long past when I needed to. The heat of the water relaxed the muscles along my back and shoulders, and the steam fog felt like luxury. Slowly, I felt my mind becoming clearer, more focused. The long night of fear had scrambled me, left me ignoring anything that wasn't happening just then. Now it was over, and I could start putting the pieces together. There had been so many mysteries in my life for so long, I'd gotten used to ignoring things that didn't fit. Now, maybe for the first time, I was starting to see a pattern that put everything in place. It was ugly, but that was all right with me. I'd faced ugly and I could do it again. What I needed was true.

The Invisible College had tried to bind me. It had failed. And that was the piece of the puzzle that made everything else make sense. Eric's childhood. My childhood. The ritual hollowing out of my mother. The more I looked at it, the more sense it made. Certainty settled around me like a cloak.

I got it now. I *knew*.

The only thing that was left was confirmation.

When at last I got out and toweled off, I felt better than I had in weeks. Maybe months. Grounded. I put on my robe and waited for the steam to clear off the mirror. I heard Ex and Chogyi Jake talking in low voices. Ex puzzled and annoyed. Chogyi Jake calm but perplexed. Something equal parts dread and excitement tightened my chest.

The scent of chicken in garlic sauce and curried shrimp filled the room as I stepped out. The white folded cardboard boxes lined the black dresser. Chogyi Jake was in the little overstuffed chair by the window with a white paper cup of what I assumed was green tea in his hand and a plate of food on his knee. I picked one of the containers up, grabbed a pair of cheap break-them-apart-yourself chopsticks, and folded myself back into bed. Outside, the sunlight seemed wrong. It took me a few seconds to realize that, after waking up and taking a shower, I was expecting it to be morning instead of afternoon.

"What have we got?" I asked, and popped a piece of broccoli into my mouth.

"I don't know how you figured out that it wouldn't be in our books," Ex said. He was still on the bed, his injured foot propped up under four pillows to help it drain. "You were right, though. I sent an email to Carsey and Tamblen."

I nodded. "And what did the Vatican's best have to say?"

"Not a lot, but they'd at least heard of it," Ex said. "It's a *gamchicoth* form."

"And for the people playing along at home, that means . . . ?"

"It's unpleasant," Chogyi Jake said, "even as these things go."

"It's called a devourer," Ex said, "but that's kind of a misnomer. From what Tamblen said, it's more like slaver ants. It's a rider that uses other riders to do its work."

I felt myself growing still as they went on.

"It's got a reputation for being viciously intelligent, as long-lived as a *varkolak* or a *ravana*. Strong, mean, more than a little sadistic, but also risk averse."

"Is it a species or an individual?" I asked.

"We don't know that yet," Chogyi Jake said. "Tamblen recommended checking an archival source in Vienna. He's trying to get up permission, but with the new year coming up we may not hear anything until next week. So, with the old financial records in Denver, that's two great huge stacks of records to go through."

"One's a massive collection of arcane secrets and obscure references, and the other one's in Europe," I said with a grin. "How do you kill it?"

Ex and Chogyi Jake exchanged a glance. "We don't know yet," Ex said. "You had a hypothesis. How does this all fit into it?"

"Unfortunately, pretty well," I said.

"Walk us through it," Ex said, scowling.

"All right," I said, holding up the chopsticks like a pointer. "Here's what we know. Eric got a bunch of money that's been getting passed down through my family since forever, and when he died, he passed it on to me."

"So are you thinking that the wealth itself is carrying the rider?" Chogyi Jake asked.

"No. Hold on. I'll get there. The next thing we know is that Eric used my mother to build someone who'd been possessed since literally before birth," I said, raising my hand. "And he was looking to cut a deal with a massive rider that could, in theory, have been strong enough to bind the Black Sun on a permanent basis. The *haugsvarmr* bound her in the 1940s, remember?"

"That seems like a lot of work to wind up where you started from," Ex said. "Invoke the Black Sun, create a daughter organism, then track down something to get rid of the daughter. How does that get you anything?"

"It gets you a shell," Chogyi Jake said, nodding.

"Right," I said. "And if we think about what happened to Eric, it sounds like the same song in a different key. He got ridden young. Not as young as me, but still when he was a kid. And the rider got shucked out of him. And the one thing we know about folks who've had riders is that they're more open and vulnerable when the next one comes."

"You're saying that Eric was preparing you to be possessed by some other spirit?" Chogyi Jake asked.

"I'm saying there's been a rider crawling down my family tree since God knows when. And each generation, it grooms some poor new kid, puts a rider in them, lets it get comfortable, then shucks it out and leaves the kid open, vulnerable, and gasping."

"Only, that didn't happen to you," Ex said.

"Didn't, did it? Because Eric got killed before

I was ready. I still had a tenant, and I didn't even know. But everything else was in place. The money came to me. The property. All the things that the Graveyard Child's been hoarding over the past who knows how many generations dropped into my name, just like they'd dropped into Eric's when his uncle died. And I'll bet you dollars to donuts we can trace versions of the same story all the way back to forever.

"Eric left me everything he had but didn't warn me about anything. Also, Eric wasn't stupid. That looks like a contradiction."

"Unless . . ." Chogyi Jake said.

"Unless I wasn't supposed to be the one in control of the body when the money all came," I said. "Someone else was supposed to be driving. Someone who already knew all about the money and the resources and the big, big picture. I was being groomed to be the next one eaten literally since before I was born."

We all let it stand in the air for a second. It changed everything.

I'd started off thinking of Eric as a demon hunter, and of myself as his heir. Even when I'd figured out he was an evil sonofabitch, I didn't cast him as a victim. Not until now. And with the money and the weird magical powers, I'd cast myself in the hero's role. I was the kick-ass enemy of darkness, just like my idealized uncle. I could fight and win every time. I could get any outfit I wanted, go anywhere I chose. Other people whose lives were touched by riders were the ones who were really in trouble. People like Aaron the cop being ridden by a *haugtrold* or Dolores in New Mexico with the *akaname* or, it turned out, my mother. They needed help because they were powerless. Because they weren't like me.

Only, even with being able to beat everyone else in the room when it came to a fight, even with the kind of money that made Bruce Wayne feel like he needed a nicer suit, I'd still been set up. The power that had been going back for generations and leaving women and men destroyed and broken in its wake didn't care if I could win a fistfight. I was just another kind of tool to it. I'd gotten incredibly lucky, and what the luck earned me was the time to figure that out on my own.

Now that I knew, I was going to have to get smart.

"The reason that there's no resources on the Graveyard Child," Chogyi Jake said.

"Same as the reason Jayné didn't get scheduled for orientation," Ex said. "You don't need to tell someone what they already know. The one rider that the Graveyard Child would never need to research is the Graveyard Child."

"And the Invisible College is still looking to take me out," I said, "because whatever grudge they had against the Graveyard Child, they don't think it's finished. They think it got out of Eric and into me."

"Which may be why they'd try to keep Carla away," Chogyi Jake said.

"If they thought her baby was getting lined up to be the new sacrifice, sure," I said. "I don't know if the Graveyard Child did something in particular to piss them off, or if the riders in the Invisible College are naturally predisposed to hate it, or if it's some kind of weird altruism thing. But they've been trying to break the cycle. First by killing Eric, and now by threatening its hold on Carla, using her as bait, and trying to bind it."

"But because the Black Sun was never cast out of you, the Graveyard Child never got in," Ex said. "The binding failed."

"Exactly," I said. "Now they may figure that out on their own. Or they may not."

"They've kept trying for years at least," Chogyi Jake said. "It would seem odd if they gave up the effort now. I mean, assuming you're right about all this."

"And so the next attempt could be some clever bastard with an enchanted sniper rifle," I said. "I will be under threat from a huge magical conspiracy for the rest of my life unless I can get them to call off the hunt."

They were silent for a moment. I could see both

men thinking it through, looking for cracks in the theory. As the seconds passed, I felt more and more sure they wouldn't find any. It was still only a theory, a story that fit the facts, but maybe not the only one that did.

"We can go back to the Water Street house," Chogyi Jake said. "Or get someone to deliver a message to it. If we can arrange some kind of parley, maybe—"

"Or they can use that to set a new trap with a different outcome," Ex said. "And that's assuming that they haven't taken off. If I were in their position, I don't know that I'd be hanging around, waiting to see if Jayné had a truckful of fertilizer and diesel she wanted to park outside my place. If Eric was possessed by the Graveyard Child, it made him kind of a prick about that kind of thing."

"Agreed," I said. "We have to assume they're on the lam. The longer it takes for us to confirm this, the more likely it is that something bad's going to happen. And by that I mean worse than me assassinating their head guy."

"Having done that does make a simple conversation seem less plausible," Chogyi Jake said mildly.

"Twelve hours ago, they were here. In Wichita," I said. "They're scared, and keeping a very low profile is what they do best. We aren't going to get a better chance than this. Not anytime soon. We have to hunt them down now."

"Agreed," Chogyi Jake said. "But do you have any thoughts as to how it might be done?"

I picked up my cell phone. My lawyer answered on the third ring.

"Jayné, dear. Is everything all right?"

"It's a little messy, actually," I said. "But body and soul are still more or less together."

"What can I do to help?"

I took a deep breath. After all this time, I still felt like I was asking permission.

"I need a miracle," I said. "The three top-ranking members of the Invisible College were in the city last night, and I think the chances are pretty good that they've made a break for it. I need to find at least one of them, and I need to do it very, very quickly."

"That's going to be difficult," my lawyer said. "The week between Christmas and New Year's is always difficult, and those particular ladies and gentlemen are surprisingly challenging to keep track of."

"You remember how you said I didn't spend as much money as Eric used to?"

"Yes, dear?"

"I don't care if we break the bank doing this. If it means spending everything down to the floorboards, I'm okay with that. I just need these people found."

The line was quiet for so long, I thought I'd lost the connection. Or that she'd hung up on me. When at last she did speak, I could hear the smile in her voice.

"Well, dear. That's a horse of a somewhat different color, now, isn't it?"

CHAPTER SEVENTEEN

It was snowing as I drove out of town. The traffic on the highway was sparse, and made mostly of long-haul truckers throwing gray slush up behind them as they sped to make time. Low gray clouds held in the light from the city even as it faded away behind me. The oncoming headlights caught the swirl of huge, feathery flakes. The red brake lights before us seemed softer and farther away. The radio was infomercials, canned sermons, pop songs, and one lonely sex advice show relayed in from the West Coast. I cycled between them incessantly until

Chogyi Jake stopped me by putting in some Pink Martini.

It was almost midnight. It was the twenty-ninth of December. If the year had a dead spot, this was it. The long, cold hours when everything that had been going to happen in the long, slow trip around the sun had already happened and nothing new could quite begin. I felt like we'd stepped outside time, outside the ebb and flow of the normal human world and into a kind of bleak, surreal mindscape. The night had been directed by David Lynch.

I hunched over the steering wheel, my knuckles aching. The heater's white-noise thrumming rose and fell as I accelerated or braked. I was pretty sure it wasn't supposed to do that. The sense of anticipation and fear crawled up my spine. I wanted to go faster, to be there already, and I wanted to slow down for fear of what was coming.

We passed through Newton and Herington. Junction City was still twenty minutes ahead of us. We were coming close.

"Are you certain you want to do this?" Chogyi Jake asked.

"Nope," I said.

"And are you determined to do it regardless?"

"Yep."

"Can I ask why?"

I glanced over at him. His face was calm, but he looked older than he had back when we'd all started together in Denver. As if the years had been longer for him than for the rest of us. I wondered what he would have done if it hadn't been for me and Eric and the fortune that I'd used to hire him and Ex and Aubrey. Whatever it would have been, I hoped he didn't regret missing it.

"You mean besides the obvious not wanting to be hunted by a cabal of riders?"

"Yes, besides that."

I grinned. No one else would have moved past me so gracefully or been able to put me at ease while he did it. It was what I loved him for.

"I want to know if I'm right," I said.

"Is it important that you be?"

"It changes who Eric was. If he was being ridden, it changes why he did everything he did. To my mother. To Kim. To me."

Chogyi Jake made a small sound in the back of his throat. "So we're trying to save Eric. Not the man himself, of course, but what he meant."

Half a mile later I answered. "Would that be a problem?"

"Not at all," he said.

Leaving Ex had been difficult, not just because he'd insisted that he was well enough to come but also because part of me badly wanted him there. We'd gone through so much together that leaving him behind seemed like going to the fight unprepared. It wasn't true, but it seemed that way.

In point of fact, the list of reasons to leave him behind was as long as my arm. The first one was he'd been shot in the foot a day before, and the rest of them didn't matter. If things went pear-shaped at the motel where—according to my lawyer—a credit card associated with Jonathan Rhodes had been used to guarantee a room, I couldn't have him bursting in on his bloody foot and trying to save me. It was a scenario that commanded the ugly place in the Venn diagram where ugly overlapped with plausible.

In the end, he'd agreed to stay with Ozzie if we promised to call him before we headed in and again when we came out. With his hair pulled back, he'd looked like some kind of very severe bird, and I'd seen in the way he held his shoulders and the lines at the sides of his mouth how much it cost him to let me go on alone. I knew how much it meant to him that he protect me, even when he couldn't. Maybe especially when he couldn't. Giving the concession of telling him when the parley, if there was a parley, started and ended was a small price. It gave him a sense of being in control when he wasn't. Not that he'd be able to do anything if it went bad. For one thing, I'd taken the car, and he wouldn't have been able to rent one before morning. And by morning it was all going to be over.

One way or the other.

The GPS informed me that my turnoff was

coming up on the right, and my gut went tighter. It was too soon and it couldn't happen soon enough. I put on the blinker, watched, and then drifted to the right, turning onto a thin road that was already slick with ice and snow. I slowed the SUV down to thirty and it still felt optimistic.

American Eagle Lodge and Motor Hotel sat half a mile off U.S. 77. Twelve units squatting in an L around a gravel driveway. Except for the lights in the office building and two of the rooms, it would have looked abandoned. It didn't even have the neon Vacancy/No Vacancy sign that I'd assumed was a guild requirement for creepy old motels.

We were a little over two hours from Wichita, in the middle of nowhere. The land was flat and any-one coming off the highway would be visible from the office, at least, if not the rooms. It didn't mat-ter. I hadn't come here to be subtle. I pulled to the side of the road and killed the engine. The sudden silence was profound. I rubbed my palms together, but the anxiety lighting up my spine was the kind that came after you've already jumped off the high dive. Turning back wasn't an option for me now. I was just wondering how big the splash was about to be.

I took my cell phone out of my pocket. There were still two bars. Pretty good, considering. I'd already programmed in the number for the hotel. Now I called. It rang four times. Five. Six. I started to wonder if the American Eagle looked on a post-midnight presence as a luxury when I saw a flicker of movement. In the distant office, someone was coming to the desk. From this distance I couldn't tell if it was a man or a woman, but I saw them scoop up the phone, heard the click on the line.

"Hello?" the voice said. A man's, and slurred with sleep or alcohol or both.

"You have a guest," I said. "A young man traveling alone. I need to speak with him. It's an emergency."

"Miss, we get a lot of young men traveling alone one time and another. I don't make a practice of waking them up."

"This is the credit card number he gave you," I said, and read off the account number, expiration date, and three-digit confirmation code. I went slowly enough that he had time to pull up his records, fast enough that he didn't have space to interrupt me. "I don't know which room he's in, but I need to speak with him, and I need to do it now."

"Are you with the police?" the man asked.

"Not yet," I said. "But you should put my call through."

"I can take a message, miss, but it's pretty late at night."

I was tempted to make threats. Have him look out his window and turn on my headlights so he could see that I was right there. That even if he called the cops, I'd be there before help could arrive. I wanted to use the Black Sun's power to scare him into doing what I wanted. Instead, I took a deep breath.

"Please," I said.

The tiny sigh on the other side of the connection meant I'd won.

"If I get in trouble for this . . ."

"You won't," I said. "Thank you so much."

I watched him make some small movement on his desk. My phone clicked, went quiet, clicked again, and the ringing started. I watched the rooms to see if a light went on, but nothing changed. The ringing stopped. He didn't speak.

"Jonathan," I said. "It's Jayné. We need to talk."

The sharp intake of his breath was weirdly gratifying. Some part of me liked being the scary one in the scenario, if only because it meant he thought I might be dangerous.

"How did you find me?"

"Bribes," I said. "There are probably half a dozen people who are going to be a little more corrupt and a lot richer in the new year. Look, don't freak out on me here."

"What do you want from me?"

"To talk," I said. "That's all."

"Okay. I'm here. So talk."

"I think this is more of a face-to-face thing," I said. He was silent. "If I wanted to kill you, you'd be dead now. You know that, right?"

"You won't break me," he said, and I had the sick image of Rhodes downing a bottle of cyanide to avoid being captured by the enemy. That would be just great.

"I want to talk truce," I said. "We got off on the wrong foot. Mistakes were made. I'm not looking for a higher body count, and I think you aren't either."

He was quiet again.

"You know it's not in me," I said. "I'm not the Graveyard Child."

"All right," he said, the syllables trembling a little. "Okay. I'll meet with you. But I decide the time and the place."

"Yeah, that's not actually going to work for me. I was thinking more like right now."

A moment later the curtains on the room at the far south end of the motel shifted. It wasn't much. Just enough for someone to look out. I thumbed on the engine, lighting up the headlights, and then killed it again.

"Hi," I said.

He laughed, and it wasn't in victory. I'd heard the I'm-so-fucked laugh coming out of my own throat often enough to recognize it.

"I'm not seeing a lot of options," he said.

"Make a break for your car and try for an extensive chase sequence," I said. "Works in the movies."

The lights went on in his room.

"Come in," he said.

"Thanks," I said, and dropped the connection. I drove to the parking lot. I didn't understand why the crunching of gravel against the tires sounded so loud until I realized I hadn't turned the music back on. Chogyi Jake reached into the backseat and brought up his shotgun. Of all the ones we'd bought at the Walmart, his was the only one left. I put the SUV into park.

"If I don't call or come out in five minutes," I said, "or, you know, in the event of bloodcurdling screams . . ."

"I understand."

I undid my seat belt. It hissed against me as it retracted. Even the smallest thing was grabbing my attention now. It was strange to watch myself being afraid without actually feeling it. I wondered if it was her influence or just where my head was. Or if there was a difference between the two.

"If I don't make it out, take care of Ex and Ozzie for me."

I'd meant it as a joke, but even then as a ha-ha-only-serious one. Chogyi Jake put his hand on my wrist for a moment, then let go. "Are there any other messages you'd want me to pass along?"

I paused for a moment, wishing he'd taken the line a little less seriously. Was there anyone I'd want to pass a message to? I thought of Jay and Carla. My parents. Little Curt about to graduate high school.

I thought of Aubrey, who had made the transition from lover to ex-lover to nice guy I used to sleep with so gracefully that it sort of called everything that had come before into question.

"No," I said. "I'm good."

"Be careful."

I opened the door and slid down to the ground. As I closed it behind me, Rhodes opened his door. He was wearing a pair of blue jeans and a shirt that looked like it had been slept in. He hadn't bothered with a glamour. He was thinner than I'd remembered him. The thin stubble of hair on his scalp showed that he was balding a little. If he'd been human, he'd have passed for a junior system administrator. He stepped back as I came close, gesturing me in. I nodded. As I passed through the door, I felt the echo of his wards like a change in the air pressure.

The room was if anything more squalid than the exterior promised. The greenish wallpaper showed its seams, and the bed seemed to apologize for itself. The lock was mechanical, and the chain looked like it had rusted where the links touched. I sat at a tiny writing desk, and the chair groaned under me. Rhodes closed the door but he didn't lock it. We both knew that if it came down to unpleasantness, a couple cheap locks and a hollow-core door weren't going to make a difference.

"Well," I said. "This is awkward. I think we

got off on the wrong foot. You and the others. You've got something against the Graveyard Child, right?"

Rhodes didn't speak, just stood there, arms folded across his chest. His lips were pressed thin, and I couldn't tell if it was from fear or anger. The markings on his face acted like a mask, obscuring all the fine details of his expression.

"Okay," I said. "So here's the thing. I'm not the Graveyard Child. I have a rider in me, but it's not that one. And I think maybe we're on the same side."

He shook his head in a gesture of disbelief.

"You've got brass ones, I'll give you that," he said. "So now we're on the same side again, are we? You broke the temple. You killed Coin. And now you think you can waltz in here and smile and pretend it never happened?"

"Yeah. I know. That was a mistake, and if I could take it back, I would."

"No," Rhodes said. "You don't get to switch sides every time the wind blows. You made your choice and you acted on it, and now the consequences are your problem."

It was fear. It showed when he spoke and in the way he moved, but it was also standing firm in spite of the fear. He was scared of me, but he wouldn't let it rule him.

"Let me explain," I said. "I didn't even know

about riders until Eric died. All I knew was that he'd been killed and that Coin had been part of it. I thought I was protecting myself. And yeah, okay, there was a kind of vengeance kick too, but I didn't know what was—"

The sound was something between a laugh and a cough. He stepped close to me, his eyes flashing. His hands were balled into fists.

"God*damn*. You really thought you could lie your way out of this? I was there. I was with you. Did you think I wouldn't remember you, or did you just forget about me?"

I had planned out a hundred different ways this conversation could go. Everything from apocalyptic battles that ended with me watching everyone I cared about die, to hugs and beer and pizza. This hadn't been on my list.

"You were *with* me?"

"I saw you take the oath. You knew *everything*."

I could feel the power radiating from him like heat.

"Okay, the only thing I don't understand is every word you just said."

He blinked. Under his mask of skin, his expression shifted, changed. He tilted his head and narrowed his eyes.

"The induction," he said.

I held up my hands, palms open, and shook my head. Rhodes sat on the edge of the bed. Springs squeaked under him. I couldn't imagine how any-body could sleep on something that loud.

"Holy shit," he said. "You really did forget me, didn't you?"

"I'm guessing we ran into each other before somewhere?" I said.

He pressed his hand to his mouth. His eyes flick-ered in the middle distance, like he was looking for something in the empty air. I had the uncomfortable feeling that I'd been left behind, but I waited for him. He did the laugh-cough thing again.

"You really . . . you don't know?"

"Really don't," I said.

"I met you . . . God, was it ten years ago? Not the last induction, but the one before."

"The one before?"

He nodded.

"We came to you when you were leaving church on the Thursday before the rites. You came with us. I gave you that flower. You don't remember any of it?"

I felt a little dizzy. If this was a trick, a way to get me disoriented and off my guard, it was working pretty well. The Invisible College held their induc-tions every seven years—prime number. Like cica-das. Midian Clark had told me that. The ceremony I'd broken up had been in August. Right over my twenty-third birthday, in fact. So seven years before that would have been . . .

Sixteen. Oh, holy shit, it would have been my sixteenth birthday. The one where I'd lost two days.

I felt the world drop a little, like an airplane hitting a rough patch of air. I was suddenly deeply aware of the half-finished tattoo at the base of my own spine. The one that I didn't remember getting. The one Uncle Eric had helped me hide from Dad.

"What happened?" I said.

CHAPTER EIGHTEEN

"All right," Rhodes said, running his hands over his scalp with a sound like paper against paper. "This is going to be . . . So the Invisible College? It started off as a group of natural philosophers in the 1630s. They were looking at what makes living beings different from just normal matter, and in the course of their experiments they found riders. We all made a deal. The society acted as hosts for the riders—a way to reach the physical world—and in return, the same riders would bring their knowledge and experience to new generations of the society.

The idea was that we could continue research over more than one lifetime. Normally all the knowledge and experience and insight that someone gets in the course of their life either gets put in books and essays that maybe keep five or ten percent of what they actually know, or else they're just lost. We got around that."

"So wait a minute," I said. "Who are you, really?"

"I'm Jonathan Rhodes, really," he said. "But I have access to Marian Cunningham, who was host before me, and Emile Canna, who studied the kabbalah in the 1920s, and Sean Korrigan, who was a biologist and undertaker and artist in Baltimore in the 1890s. I have the things they knew and the way they saw the world. We're all part of one longer life than any single body could carry. Or at least than it could carry without ossifying. You need to get a young person in every now and again to see things in a different way. Sean Korrigan was a decent guy for his time, but his stance on women and blacks wouldn't fit too well in the modern world. We're different people, but we're part of the same continuity."

"Okay," I said. "I think I can follow that."

"Abraxiel Unas was one of us. Not a person. A rider. A continuity of people through time."

I felt my heart start to beat a little faster. I felt like I was on the edge of something, like unwrapping a present on Christmas morning, except without the joy or sense of safety.

"Something went wrong?"

"It did," Rhodes said. "You don't remember us telling you any of this?"

"Nothing," I said.

"Because I was there when Master Coin told this to you. I was sitting as close to you then as I am now."

"I remember I was going to a sleepover at Monica Smith's house and I came to in a hotel room with a tattoo and Uncle Eric. He said I'd called him from a bar, and that I'd been crying about someone named Sidney. I didn't even know I had a tattoo until he told me about it."

Rhodes's face was pale under the ink.

"Yeah. That wasn't true."

"Picking up on that," I said. "But the Graveyard Child?"

"Right. Sorry. It was a rider like the one I've got, but it went mad. One of the people it was riding was a man named Willis Ford. No one's sure whether he drove the rider mad or if it broke him. He split from the College and started his own research. Gathering power to himself. Without the sigil work to keep him in control or the induction to help him move from generation to generation, he had to prepare bodies that would be easier to move into."

"Qliphoth," I said.

"He made shells. At first he'd do it by torturing someone. Traumatizing them until they were spiritually vulnerable and then keeping them in captivity until his last body grew old or infirm. Then he would move into the new skin."

"The rider, you mean."

"The rider and the man. Ford was a part of the new person's consciousness just the way all my old hosts are part of mine. But each time it happened, it moved into a new mind that was broken. Every new life it stepped into was miserable and shell-shocked and angry. The illness of generations built up in it, along with the cruelty and the distance from whatever humanity Ford had possessed in the first place. Eventually it learned how to force other riders into bodies and then pull them back out. It began with small ones. *Geisten* and *kobold*. And then, over time, it moved to more and more powerful riders. Sometimes it would force several riders into the same body. Or induce possession and then exorcise the spirit, and then induce possession again so that whoever the host was to be might have gone through a dozen rounds of being ridden and having the rider ripped away."

"Sounds like the kind of kid who tortured animals for fun."

"No. Not fun. For knowledge. It was a vivisectionist of souls, and it learned things on its own that would have taken those of us who weren't as bloody-minded ten times as long to discover. If we ever would have. Its plan was to eventually return to the College when it was strong and knowledgeable enough to put itself in the central position. That may not make sense, but the College centered on a single individual. Master Coin, until—"

"Yeah, really, *really* sorry about that."

A shadow seemed to pass over Rhodes's face, but he didn't stop.

"Master Coin kept track of where it was and what it was doing. Three times he reached out to it. Tried to bring it back where we could help it. By then it had taken on the Graveyard Child's name and started investing that with power. And then, eventually, the threat grew too great. We all agreed that it had to be stopped. And so we came to you."

"Because I could stop it?"

"Because we saw that you were being made its heir. We thought we could help you escape. He'd already placed a rider in you. Something young but, we thought, powerful. We . . . well, we abducted you. Sorry about that."

"In the big picture, I kind of see why. It's weird how much all of this looks like crime, isn't it?"

Rhodes leaned back on the bed, the spring groaning and complaining. "I hadn't really thought about it that way, but now that you say it, yeah. It does."

"Anyway, you drove by in the creepy windowless van and forced me in or whatever," I said.

He looked uncomfortable at the phrasing. "We took you to the gathering, and we explained what we were. What *he* was. The danger you were in."

"Must have been a hard sell," I said. "I idolized Eric. He was the good guy through my whole childhood. The only sane-looking one in the family. I mean, put it in a different frame and it's a very different picture. But—"

"No. You believed us at once. You told us that he'd always struck you as . . . off. That there was something wrong with him."

I couldn't say why that piece of information— that, among all the horror and violations that my history had become once I started looking—should be the one that made my flesh crawl. It was crawling, though. My lost weekend at sixteen was a story. Before it had been about acting out and getting too drunk to think straight. Now it was about a power struggle between generation-spanning spiritual parasites. Okay, big change. My mother had always seemed meek and broken in a way that I put down to my father and the excesses of faith. Turned out it was about shame and ritual abuse. It changed the story about who she was and what her relationship was to me. Dad, it turned out, wasn't my bio-dad but my real uncle, and my uncle was my actual dad. Even that hadn't changed my sense of who I was. Of the life I'd lived.

There had been some version of me that had known or guessed that something was wrong with my uncle. I didn't remember that. Whoever that Jayné had been, she'd been wiped out of existence, and even knowing that she'd been there couldn't bring her back. All the way back, I had loved and admired Uncle Eric. I'd trusted him, looked to him as an example of how things could be better than they were at home. Only, maybe that wasn't true. Maybe, along with the memories of the Invisible College, Eric had done something more to my mind and memory. It left me feeling uneasy and unclean.

The door burst in with a bang like a gun firing. Rhodes leaped to his feet, the sudden squall of his will filling the room. His hands took on a wild, unearthly glow. Chogyi Jake stepped into the doorway, the shotgun in his hands and a snarl on his face that belonged on a wolf.

"Wait!" I shouted, leaping up from my chair. "Stop! Don't shoot anyone!"

Chogyi's eyes didn't shift from Rhodes. The shotgun was aimed squarely at the young man's head. Chogyi Jake's chest worked like a bellows, and the stink of overheated iron filled the air.

"More than five minutes," Chogyi Jake said.

"Yeah. Sorry about that. I got distracted."

Chogyi Jake's gaze flickered over to me for a second. It was enough to carry annoyance and amusement and chagrin. He looked back at Rhodes.

"Well. This is awkward, then," Chogyi Jake said between clenched teeth.

"We've all been kind of tense recently," Rhodes replied gruffly, the glow in his hands pulsing like a heartbeat.

"We should probably both put our weapons down."

"I think we should."

The two men didn't move for a long moment, their eyes locked and ready for violence.

"Oh, for Christ's sake," I said, and stepped between them. Chogyi Jake didn't resist when I took the shotgun from him. I turned back to Rhodes and lifted my eyebrows reprovingly. The glow faded to nothing. "All right. My mistake. Sorry, but let's all just take a couple breaths and calm down, okay?"

A few seconds later Chogyi Jake shifted back, looking at the door. "I think I broke the frame."

"We'll buy a new one," I said. "Not the worst thing that could have happened tonight. Jonathan. We were back at my shitty sweet sixteen."

Chogyi Jake looked astonished. I nodded toward the dresser. He propped the broken door closed as best he could, then went and leaned against it, his expression back to the almost unreadable calm it usually was. I took my seat again, the gun across my lap. Rhodes shifted between the two of us, then sighed.

"We had a safe house ready for you. People who were ready to see to your well-being. We talked about taking the rider from you, but we were afraid that it might leave you open to the Graveyard Child. So instead we erased you."

"My tattoo," I said. "It's why I'm hard to see magically. That was you guys."

Rhodes spread his arms, displaying them. His smile was rueful. "Skin sigils are pretty much what we do," he said. "We couldn't use any of the standard Marks. The Graveyard Child knew them all. We fashioned one specific to you and tied it to your own qi for its power. So long as you lived, magic would not see you. Only, then you vanished."

"Eric swooping down and doing whatever he was doing to mess with my head," I said.

"Apparently," Rhodes said. A gust of freezing wind blew the door open. He pushed it closed and moved a standing lamp to block it. "We didn't know that at the time, though. We thought you might have been in league with Eric the whole time, playing along with us in a way that gave him information about us and gave you the Mark that would make it even harder to track when the rider had moved to you.

"We kept track of you, but the Graveyard Child

defended you like his own. When you left for Arizona, we thought that you were trying to escape him, and we tried to reach you, but he laid a trap for us. We almost succeeded in taking away his heir. I believe that was what moved Abraxiel to take action. He planned for the next induction, when he knew where we would be."

"And so he got Midian Clark to be the focus for him. The idea was to kill Coin and take his place."

"Only, Master Coin reached him first."

For a moment I was with Midian Clark. The rueful smile on his ruined lips. The yeah, you-got-me shrug when Aubrey and I had realized he wasn't a cursed human but a rider trapped in a corpse. I wasn't about to tell Rhodes that I still thought of the old vampire as a friend. But even if I liked him, Midian's agenda had always been his own. I wondered how much he'd known about Eric, and about the Graveyard Child, that he'd never bothered to mention because it suited him to leave me in the dark.

"And I took out Coin, thinking he was a demon-possessed monster who'd killed my loving uncle," I said. "And everyone assumed that the Graveyard Child had shucked out whatever was living in me and taken up residence. So the whole thing started over. Jay got Carla pregnant, and it looked like the cycle might be beginning again. So you grabbed her, lured me into a trap; except, instead of the Graveyard Child, you got the Black Sun."

"The Black *Sun*?" Rhodes said, his jaw actually dropping a centimeter.

"Well, the Black Sun's daughter," I said. "But yeah."

"And here we are," Chogyi Jake said, "and we don't know what happens next."

"That is the question, isn't it?" I said. "Is this something where we can shake hands and chalk it up to experience, or do we still have a problem?"

Rhodes sat on the bed again, his hands on his knees. He seemed so thin, almost too fragile for the power that was in his flesh. I wondered whether I should have felt the same about myself. I wasn't as twiggy as he was, but the Black Sun was orders of magnitude more powerful than I was. Maybe I should have felt too small for what was in me, but I didn't. I felt at home with her.

"You and I are fine," he said slowly, "but I am not the Invisible College. Eduardo and Idéa have as much status in the body as I do. I can take everything you've said to them, and they might believe it too. But you are the one who killed Master Coin. Not Eric Heller. Not even the Graveyard Child. You. And that may not be something all of us can overlook."

"What about a pact?" I asked. "When . . . God, I feel like a terrible human being. Okay, when I was fighting Coin, he offered to make a pact. A binding. If I didn't act against him, he'd let me go. At the time that sounded like a kind of spiritual slavery, and I was still pretty bent about Eric, so I turned him down. Any chance the offer is still open?"

"Maa—aaybe," Rhodes said, pulling the word out to three syllables. "If you're serious, it might be something we can do. But if you have the Black Sun in you as well—"

"I will consent to this," my mouth said without me. "The *sabiendos* are no enemy to me."

Rhodes's eyes went round and wide enough that I could see the whites all around the irises. It was hard not to smirk a little.

"Was that . . . ?"

"Yeah," I said. "That was her. So what do you think. We have a deal?"

Rhodes seemed lost in thought, but his voice was as sharp as ever. "It would need to be binding on your allies as well. No offense."

"None taken," Chogyi Jake said. "I am willing, but our friend Ex may be more difficult to convince."

"I'll talk him into it," I said. "We can make this work. But it needs to cover all of you guys. And that freaky bloodhound thing too. I don't know what that was, but seriously, if we do this, I want it kept on a leash."

Rhodes shifted his focus to me. The wind blew the door against the standing lamp with a clunk, and then another one.

"Bloodhound?" he said. "What bloodhound?"

A chill crawled up my spine and I felt a fear that was deeper and colder than anything I'd felt on the drive out here.

"The thing that tracked us to the hotel," I said. "About a head and a half smaller than you? Black poncho. Creepy as hell. The one that was using Chogyi Jake's blood from the big battle of the kitchen table?"

Rhodes shook his head. "We didn't track you. We'd convinced Carla you were dangerous. There was nothing else we needed to do."

"All right," I said. "Then what the fuck *was* that thing?"

The silence lay over the room for a long moment, each of us thinking the same thing, but none of us willing to say it. To make it real.

"It's not dead," I said, and the words were stark. "The Graveyard Child. You killed Eric, but *it* didn't die. It's here. It's here, and it knows I'm here too."

Rhodes went pale under his ink. "That's not good news. It has to have found a host. Someone else who'd been prepared besides you."

I rose from the chair, clutching the shotgun. Chogyi Jake wasn't leaning against the dresser anymore. I saw my own alarm mirrored in his face.

"It knows where we're staying," I said. "Ex is alone."

"I think we should leave," Chogyi Jake said. "I think we should leave now."

"Be in touch, okay?" I said to Rhodes over my shoulder as I walked out. "Your people call mine. Like that."

"Yes. Of course. But be careful. If it is Abraxiel and he manages to empty you after all, you won't be able to keep him out of you."

"Yeah," I said. "Spiffy."

CHAPTER NINETEEN

I bent over the wheel, trying to will the SUV faster. The engine groaned and roared. The snow made a tunnel that was almost but not quite aligned with the road. I could feel the surface of the highway in the small movement of the steering wheel, the slickness and the growing ice. Two hours out to Rhodes's hideout; forty-five minutes, more or less, talking to him; and now two more hours back. I plucked my phone out of my pocket, keeping one eye on the red glow of the brake lights on the trailer in front of me. It was hardly doing fifty, and there was just slightly too much oncoming traffic to pass.

"Let me dial," Chogyi Jake said. "It won't help anyone if we wreck on the way back."

"Okay," I said. A pickup truck blew by, heading the other direction, and I pulled out to pass the trailer just as a new set of headlights appeared, coming toward me. I said something obscene and pulled back. Chogyi Jake put the phone on speaker, each ring tightening thc knot in my stomach. The call dropped to voice mail.

"Call him again," I said.

At the second ring of the second call, I lost patience and pulled onto the shoulder, gunning the engine and passing the trailer on the right to the music of his outraged honking. I pulled back onto the road proper on the fifth ring, and I only fishtailed a little bit.

"Here," Ex said. "I'm here."

"Are you okay?" I snapped.

Ex's reply came slowly. Hc soundcd drugged. "I'm fine. Are you all right?"

"Put up any wards you can. The Graveyard Child's alive," I said. "It knows where we're staying."

"All right," Ex said. "Was there a reason we thought it was dead? And what's it want with us?"

I brought him up to speed in short, telegraphic sentences. Before I was half done, I could hear the small sounds of his preparations. The hiss of a match head as he lit candles or incense, the clattering of the curtains on their rails as he closed them, the squeak of the spout on a container of salt. It took me less than two minutes to tell him the bare bones of what he needed to know.

"Okay," he said. "I'm going to let you go and focus on getting the wards up."

"We'll be there as soon as we can," I said.

"All right, but don't push too hard. It looks nasty out there, and I don't want to have the state patrol pulling your corpses out of a ditch because you hit a patch of ice."

I glanced over at Chogyi Jake who was looking back at me placidly. I let the speedometer drop back down to the speed limit.

"I'll be careful," I said. "Just really try to be alive and whole when we get back, okay?"

"Depend on it."

He dropped the connection and Chogyi Jake put the phone away. I went back to focusing on the road and trying not to let the speed creep too high up on me.

"We should have brought him with us," I said. "Ozzie too."

"And who else?" Chogyi Jake asked. "Your brother and his fiancée? Your parents? Would you have brought Curtis with us too?"

"The whole damn pack," I said. And then: "I could rent a bus."

The minutes clicked by, each seeming longer than the one before. The snowfall thickened and slacked off and thickened again. Through good luck and viciously focused control, I didn't manage to slide off the road before Wichita, and it was still the deep darkness when I pulled into the motel parking lot and let the engine die. All around us, the world was silent, the snow consuming what little noise there might have been. About an inch had accumulated on the pavement, and my tire tracks were the only things to mar the whiteness. I got out of the car and swept my gaze across the edge of the lot. I more than half expected the evil little figure to be there, grinning at me like it had just crawled out of its formaldehyde jar. My shudder had nothing to do with the cold. I turned to go inside.

"Jayné," Chogyi Jake said.

"Hmm?"

"You're carrying a shotgun."

I looked down at my hands. I didn't remember scooping it out of the backseat, but clearly I had. I tried to imagine what the lady at the counter would think when the girl with the black eyes who'd come in that morning fresh from the ER with her friend who'd been shot waltzed through with a firearm in her hands. Still, I hesitated.

"If it comes to that," Chogyi Jake said, "it won't be enough to help."

Reluctantly, I put it back in the car, locked the doors, and shrugged deeper into my coat. The clock behind the main desk said it was almost four a.m.

My driving time hadn't been as good as I'd hoped. At the door of my room, I knocked. There was no answer. My mind flooded with images of Ex and Ozzie gutted and bits of their bodies thrown around the room or else missing. When I opened the door, the room was empty, the beds made, and fresh towels in the bathroom. I felt myself starting to panic, but Chogyi Jake only nodded toward the corridor.

"He may have moved to our room," he said.

When we got there, Ex let us in, and I had to restrain myself from yelling at him for switching rooms. It wasn't that he'd actually done anything wrong, but I was stressed and tired and anything was ready to set me off.

"Anything?" Chogyi Jake asked.

"All quiet," Ex said. "Nothing got past the wards, and as far as I can tell, nothing tried."

Ozzie was stretched out on the bed that was still made. I noticed that the room didn't stink and the ruined pillows had all been replaced. I gave a small prayer of thanks to whatever gods or saints watched over hotel cleaning staffs and sat at the table, my phone in front of me, uncertain what I should do next. Having come this far, I wanted nothing more than to get in the car, drive back to the house outside Santa Fe, and board it up like we were waiting for the apocalypse. Just knowing that the evil, grinning little thing was out there, that it had destroyed my family generation after generation—that it was in some repulsive sense my father—made me want to get out of the world and collapse the tunnel back. And after that, maybe shower for a year or two.

I wasn't sure what it meant that, even with that, it felt weird calling people at four thirty in the morning. The only thing I could guess was that I was compartmentalizing the hell out of things. Yes, an arcane evil from beyond the grave that had stalked my family, broken my mother's mind, and made the rest of our lives into a living hell—the thing that seemed to squeeze all the sanity and rightness out of the air just by breathing it—was alive and in the city. But four thirty a.m. was an inappropriate time for phone calls.

I started with Jay. His phone rolled straight to voice mail without so much as a ring.

"Hey, big brother, we've still got problems. I found out what the Illustrated Man Fan Club was actually doing, and turns out they aren't the biggest threat. Call me when you get this."

When I called home, Dad picked up, sounding groggy and pissed.

"Who is this?"

"It's Jayné. Look, there's a problem. The demon that was in Eric when he did all those things? It's here. You need to get the family and—"

"Don't call again," he said, and hung up.

"Great," I said to the dead connection.

"Problem?" Ex asked.

"Nothing I should be at all surprised by."

I sent Curtis a text: Bad shit coming. Call me but don't let Dad know. B careful.

It was woefully insufficient, and I knew it. But it was all I had to work with. I wished now that I'd told Curtis more about riders and magic and the surreal messes I'd found myself in when they were happening. He'd been my safety valve. My touch-stone with some other, safer world. But that had been an illusion, and there was only one world after all. I'd thought I could shield him from the ugly truths of possession and magic, and all I'd actually managed was to make sure he wasn't ready when trouble came. I put away my phone and took out my laptop, checked a few news sites and a couple of Web comics. Fidgeted. Put the laptop away. Chogyi Jake was on the bed next to Ozzie, and it wasn't perfectly clear which of them the snores were coming from. Five in the morning. The snow was still falling.

Ex leaned over from his bed and put his hand on my shoulder.

"You should sleep," he said. "It'll be all right. I'll keep watch."

"That's what you do, isn't it?"

"Sometimes," he said. "When it needs doing."

He didn't take his hand away, and I didn't want him to. The simple warmth and weight of a human hand felt like the best security blanket in the world just then. It wasn't the prelude to anything else, nothing about it was flirtation or foreplay. That was what made it all right.

"It had a plan," I said. "It was going to hollow me out and take over my life, and when that didn't work out, it had something else it could fall back to."

"You sound jealous," he said.

"I am. I can't remember the last time I had a clear idea of what I'd be doing next week. This thing plays with decades. With lifetimes. Can you imagine what it would be like to have that kind of time to plan through?"

"I'm supposed to be planning for my immoral soul," Ex said. "But honestly, no. I can't imagine living on that kind of time scale."

"It's got to be pissed off that I got its stuff, though," I said. "Maybe we should go out and spend everything quick before it . . ."

Ex turned me around slowly, the hand on my shoulder drawing me back until I faced him. Then he took his hand away. In the light from the desk lamp and the backsplash of city lights from the snow, he looked younger. His black eye was already fading toward a weird green. I wondered what mine looked like. Whether my nose was going to be the same shape it had been before Rhodes broke it. I wondered if anything was ever really the same after it broke. Even things that healed were different. I felt a rush of exhausted tears come to my eyes.

"I wish I had a plan," I said. "I wish I knew what I was doing next."

"We'll decide in the morning."

"I don't mean just that. I mean . . . I mean where do you see yourself five years from now? Or ten? Or twenty? I'm pretty sure I'm not going to spend the rest of my life bouncing from crisis to crisis and emergency room to emergency room. But I don't know what that looks like. And it does."

Ex stretched his neck, the vertebrae popping like a wet stick.

"It's also apparently mind-warpingly crazy and evil besides," he said.

"But with a solid investment portfolio," I said. "Did you ever see it? I mean, you worked with him. I'm sure you didn't think, Hey, this guy's clearly possessed. Would you look at that? But from here, looking back, were there signs?"

Someone in a nearby room turned on the shower. The pipes sang.

"No. I didn't suspect anything at the time, and I can't think of anything that in retrospect should have looked suspicious. He seemed like exactly what he claimed to be. Whatever this thing is, it can pass for human. It may take years to track this thing down. It may take our whole lives. But we can do it."

"Do we have to?"

"Yes," he said, and he was right. I had come

into this thinking that Eric had been some kind of spiritual fixer, the guy who came in when there was trouble and faced down the demons. He'd been just the opposite, but that didn't change things for me. If anything, it confirmed it. The Graveyard Child. The *haugsvarmr*. The body-hopping serial killer that had ruined Karen Black. They were madness, and I was in a position to do something about them. And so yes, I had to.

"And the Black Sun?" I asked. "Are you going to have to fight her too?"

"She's a demon," Ex said. "Sooner or later, yes. That's going to be a problem. But she's not at the top of my to-do list."

I chuckled.

"Suppose that'll have to do."

I rose and walked to the window, put my fingertips to the glass. The cold pressed through, but not as badly as I'd expected. The world was the soft orange-gray of city lights captured by the snow. I let the future fade away for a second. The need for a plan, for certainty. I just took in the moment and let it be beautiful. My hometown, in snow.

"Can I ask you something?" Ex said.

"You can ask me anything."

"You don't seem freaked out. Why not?"

"I don't seem freaked out?" I said, laughing a little through the words. "Seriously?"

"Well, maybe a little. But compared to what I

expected . . . I mean, in the last few days you found out that your father wasn't your real father, that your mom was ritually abused by your uncle, and you're the product of that abuse. That your mother is probably insane because of what happened to her. That you had your mind altered by this Graveyard Child thing; that you almost escaped the whole thing once, only you don't remember; and that the thing that's responsible for it all is not only still alive but it seems like it may be tracking you. By just about any scale, that's a pretty bad week."

"True," I said. And then a moment later: "I've had worse."

Ex sighed and Ozzie sighed with him. "You have, haven't you? You know, I think back to the girl I met in Denver."

"You mean when you were helping hide the corpses of the Invisible College people I'd helped Midian kill?"

"That was the night."

"And what do you think about when you think about that girl?"

Ex's expression went sober. "That she was fragile. And she was lost. When you found out reality wasn't what you thought it was, it shook your world. All of it. Now it's happened three or four times in as many days, and you're wondering what your long-term plan should be. You're not the same person you used to be."

"I am, though."

"All right," Ex said. "Then maybe I'm just seeing how much better you are at being her. Now, lay down and close your eyes. You don't have to sleep, but you do have to rest."

The pillow felt better than it had any right to. I kept looking outside for the first light of dawn, but it would be hours yet. There was traffic, though. Men and women going to their work, the city pulling itself awake after another long night's rest. I felt my mind beginning to wander. I wondered what Jonathan Rhodes had done about his broken door and whether Jay would ever find a way to be happy married to Carla. If Curtis would have the courage to go to a secular university, and whether it would be easier for him because he was a guy and the youngest.

My closed eyes felt perfectly comfortable and my body still and calm. Somewhere inside me, the young Black Sun might be resting or thinking or waiting for some event or opportunity. The more I'd learned about her, the more I trusted her. Not a perfectly rational response, I thought, but at least it's mine.

Ex was right. I *had* changed. I thought of the things that had uneased and unsettled me, not just when I got to Denver. When, in Arizona, my boyfriend's circle decided to eject me from their clique, it had been devastating. I'd dropped out of college because I'd been distracted by something that didn't matter to me now at all. When I'd found out, after falling into bed with Aubrey, that he was technically still married, I'd thrown a fit. When I'd met Karen Black, just standing next to her had left me feeling inadequate.

I could remember all those events, all those feelings. But I couldn't imagine having them now. Even coming home, seeing my parents again, seeing Jay. It hadn't been easy, but four years ago it wouldn't have been possible. The thought was comforting. I liked the younger Jayné who'd made her decision and stuck by it. I liked the one who'd decided to let herself be seduced by a man she basically didn't care about as a rite of passage into the new life she'd chosen. I'd made some stupid decisions, but they were mine, and there was as much to love about where they had brought me. Except for the hiding behind wards in a hotel room. That part wasn't an emblem of success.

I heard Ozzie jump off the other bed and pad stolidly across to the bathroom. She drank out of the toilet. Voices came in the corridor and went. I drifted by degrees down toward sleep.

And then I sat up, my heart pounding and my blood electric. Ex turned to me, alarmed.

"What's the matter, Jayné?" Chogyi Jake asked from the other bed.

"I never told Jay where we were staying," I said, "and he found us here anyway."

CHAPTER TWENTY

We drove to Jay's house in the rising light of dawn. The streets were filled with the traffic of the city. The snowstorm was only getting worse, wind whipping the traffic signals until they swayed. Ozzie, in the backseat with Ex, whined softly under her breath, and I didn't know if she was worried by the weather or if she was just picking up on my fear. I hadn't told anyone where we were staying. And then the evil little bastard had used Chogyi Jake's blood to find us. And then Jay had appeared. I'd been so focused on the Invisible College and Carla that I hadn't questioned it.

"We aren't certain yet," Chogyi Jake said. "There may be another explanation."

"He's my older brother," I said. "He was born before Eric broke off his whole angels-in-America thing with Mom. It had plenty of chances to put a rider in Jay and pull it out again. And it didn't crawl through my family through the whole twentieth century with a few extra decades on either side by not having a backup plan. I should have seen this."

"The opportunity was there," Chogyi Jake agreed. "I'm only saying we should be certain before we do anything drastic."

Drastic. He meant we shouldn't kill Jay out of hand. Well, fair enough. We shouldn't. I needed to get Rhodes and his pals together to bind the thing. The only comfort I had was that someone knew a way to beat this thing, even if that some-one wasn't me.

A particularly vicious blast of wind caught the SUV broadside and rocked us a little as I swung around in a wide left turn. Another two miles and we'd be there. I wished now that I hadn't called Jay, that I hadn't told him about meeting with Rhodes or that I knew about the Graveyard Child or any of it. But if I was right, it still wouldn't know I'd figured out who it was. I had to hope that tiny advantage was something I could use.

"I'm a little surprised, though," Ex said. "I made the mother for it."

"She is certainly qliphotic," Chogyi Jake agreed. "On the other hand, if it had been in her, she wouldn't have seemed so desperate to take in Jayné's rider."

"Fair point," Ex said.

"Guys," I said.

The little house loomed up from the blowing snow like a ghost. A single light was on. His car wasn't there. Ozzie's whimpering grew louder, and she pawed Ex nervously. I got out of the car, my senses straining for anything. A smell, a movement, any sense that something was there. The malaise I'd felt the last time I was here seemed less like a reflection on Jay and his impending loveless marriage. It seemed more sinister, like the nature of the building itself had been changed by being too near something evil. I walked up the unshoveled walk. The ghosts of footprints still showed, slight indentations in the gray snow. Chogyi Jake trudged up behind me.

I rang the doorbell and waited. The cold felt like a slap. Chogyi leaned to look in past the closed blinds. The freezing wind whistled and shook, driving snowflakes sharp as powdered glass against us. I dug my phone out of my pocket and called Jay's number again, listening for the ring coming from the house. I hung up without leaving a message.

"Not here," Chogyi Jake said.

"Nope. So where?"

We stood, looking at the closed door for a few more seconds, then he turned and headed back to the car. I started to do the same, but then my body stopped. Without my willing it, my feet took two steps in toward the door. The Black Sun pressed my ear against the wood. I heard Chogyi Jake's footsteps creaking in the snow behind me. I heard the shifting, restless wind. And then I heard what the Black Sun had wanted me to hear.

I heard a woman sobbing.

"Carla!" I shouted over the storm. "Are you in there? Please, Carla, open the door! I know what's wrong. I can help!"

The sobbing grew more violent—louder but not closer. I looked at the dead bolt, the frame of the doorway. I put my hand against the freezing metal. There. It was small but unmistakable. The house was warded.

"Carla," I shouted. "I can't break the door in. You need to come open it."

Nothing.

"Carla, it's Jayné. I can help you, but you have to come talk to me. There's going to be something in there. A line of ash or salt in front of the windows and doors. You have to help me get across that. I can help you."

I pressed my ear to the door again. It was quiet. I imagined her on the other side, maybe inches from me.

"I can help Jay," I said. Nothing. "I can save the baby, Carla. Open the door, and I swear in the name of Jesus Christ, Lord of Lords, that I will help you save your baby. I swear it in His name."

The trick is to know your audience. The lock clicked. The knob turned and Carla pulled the door open. She looked like hell. She wore a dirty nightgown that showed how big her belly had grown. The dark, exhausted circles under her eyes were as dark as the blood pooled under mine, and the whites of her eyes were pink. Her skin looked gray and her wrists were red and angry. Ligature marks. Sometime recently she'd been tied against her will, and I was pretty sure it hadn't been when she was with Rhodes.

"What did you do?" she asked. "What did you do to him?"

"Made him nervous, I think," I said. And then, simply, "There's a demon in him. It's not Jay. It's the thing inside him."

Tears tracked down her cheeks. The cold was making gooseflesh on her arms and legs, but she didn't seem to notice.

"I want to go home now," she said.

"All right," I said. "I can help you do that."

She shook her head slowly and opened her arms. I walked across the threshold and embraced her. Her body felt hot as a fire, and she folded against me. "He's the devil," she murmured. "He's the devil, he's the devil, he's the devil."

I turned to look back. Chogyi Jake stood in the snow. He wasn't smiling.

"I think we've got confirmation," I said.

"I believe we do," he said.

We didn't pack her anything, just put a coat over her nightgown and took the car. When I looked for her purse, she told me it was gone. Her ID, her money, her cell phone. Everything was gone. After Jay got her from the Invisible College's safe house, he'd taken everything away.

The Best Western, despite having the most forgiving cleaning staff in Christendom, wasn't safe anymore. I didn't know where to take her, so instead I drove, as if movement by itself was a kind of defense. As if the Graveyard Child couldn't find us.

"He told me that he'd kill me if I left again," she said. "He said that I was his. I didn't mean to hurt him. I thought I had to go. The tattooed man said that . . . my baby . . . and that you were . . ."

"The tattooed man and I kind got our wires crossed," I said. "We're cool now, though. Nothing bad is going to happen to you now. We're going to make sure you're all right."

She licked her lips and looked up at me.

"How?" she asked. I didn't have an answer. I needed shelter. Safety. I needed a base of operations I could count on being secure.

I needed a home.

"Gentlemen?" I said. "I am open to suggestions."

"Are we thinking short term or long?" Ex asked.

"Either. Both."

"A sacred place," Chogyi Jake said. "In the short term. After that, it will depend on the situation with Jay."

"We can go to church," I said, but Chogyi Jake grunted softly and shook his head.

"Someplace we thought the rider unlikely to have been already," he said. "Better if it was someplace he wasn't familiar with. A Buddhist temple would be best for what I have in mind."

"We're in *Kansas*," Ex said. "Where are we going to find a Buddhist temple *here*?"

"Fairmount," I said. "That's where the Zen center is anyway. I think there's one out on South Hydraulic by the exit from 35 too, but I'm not sure about that."

The silence in the car was broken only by the wind, the engine, and Ozzie's steady breath.

"That was my prejudices showing, wasn't it?" Ex said.

"We love you anyway," I said, making a careful U-turn.

At the temple, Chogyi Jake spoke quietly with a kind-faced woman who listened to him intensely. Ex and Carla and I sat in a waiting room, drinking tea from Dixie cups while the wind howled at the windows. Now that Carla was out of that oppressive, grim house, she seemed to be rallying a little.

There was more color in her cheeks, and the fever-heat that had radiated from her before was lessening. Despite all that, she looked empty and lost and alone. I wondered if I'd looked like that once myself. Seemed likely.

"He woke up this morning and listened to his voice mail," she said. "That was the last time I saw him. He just left. He didn't tell me where he was going. He said that I had to stay in the house. He took my shoes. He took all my shoes away so I wouldn't leave."

"I'll get you new shoes," I said. "Did he say where he was going?"

"I asked. He said he didn't answer to me," she said.

"Has he been like this before?"

"Sometimes," she said. "But then he's so sorry. He's so sweet. He's my little Jay-bird."

Ex stood up. I could see the anger in his expression, even if Carla couldn't.

"I'm going to take the dog for a walk around the block," he said.

"She's not going to thank you for that," I said.

"I know," Ex said, limping manfully back toward the door.

I watched him go.

"Did I piss him off?" Carla asked. Her voice sounded tired.

"You didn't," I said. "He blames himself because

he didn't keep this from happening to you. He does it with everyone."

"That's dumb."

"He's dumb sometimes."

Chogyi Jake came in and nodded to me. As I walked out into the hall, the kind-faced woman went in behind me.

"The good news is that they have had some experience with riders here, and have connections with a women's shelter. I believe they will be able to keep her safe until we can arrange a way to get her safely back to Florida and her family."

"The Graveyard Child can buy plane tickets too," I said. "I'm not sure there will be any place safer than here. Hell, for that matter, I'm not sure where *we* can go. This thing is a bad one."

Chogyi Jake paused, leaning against the yellow-brown wall. The inked calligraphy behind him reminded me of Jonathan Rhodes. The air had the faintest ghost of incense.

"It is," he said. "I believe the time will come when we have to confront it. But now isn't that time. It has the advantage of its own environment. It has places of physical and spiritual power to draw from. And by the nature of its host, it has certain protections we don't."

"You mean that, since it's in Jay, I won't kill it," I said.

"And it won't hesitate to kill us. Yes. I think the

time is right for a strategic retreat. We go to Denver and research its habits, learn about its goals and its strengths and weaknesses. Consult with the Invisible College and Sabine Glapion. Aubrey and Kim. Tamblen and Carsey and the rest of Father Chapin's exorcists. We have a network of support that we can bring to bear on this problem. If you and Ex and I can't solve it, the others will find a way."

I felt myself frowning. Everything he said made sense, and I hated it. I wanted to make Carla and her baby safe in some long-term, permanent way. The truth was that no one gets that, ever. The bad guys might come after her, or she might get cancer, or escape from Jay and the Graveyard Child and fall in love with some other, more mundane abusive asshole. The best I could do was the best I could do.

"I don't have to like it, though, right?"

"No. You don't," he said.

"So wait for the storm to break, then gas up and get out of here?"

"And we will need to make a call to your lawyer," Chogyi Jake said. "Roshi Annabel is an uncompromising negotiator, and I'm afraid we've promised her a great deal of money for taking care of Carla."

"Well, there's that, anyway. If we can't beat the bastard, at least we can spend its money in ways it wouldn't approve of."

I pulled my phone out of my pocket, ready to

make the call. A tiny numeral 1 was next to my texting icon. Somewhere in the drive, I'd missed the alert chime. It was a response from Curtis:

Help me. Its here.

THE SUN was gone, the day as dark as the night had been. Every third thing on the radio was a severe weather warning or someone advising anyone that didn't need to be on the roads to get off them. I drove home for the last time. The curbs were starting to vanish under the depth of snow, and only the bigger streets were clear enough to drive on. I'd gotten the SUV to drive through the snow and ice of northern New Mexico. If we'd been in one of the little sports cars Ex liked, we'd have been walking.

I felt calm but not peaceful. I wasn't ready, and I knew I wasn't ready, and I was going in anyway. To their credit, Ex and Chogyi Jake hadn't asked me to reconsider or wait. We were rushing in where angels feared to tread because there was no option. When it came to possession and riders and evil things from outside the world, we were the pros from Dover. I knew where the panic was in me, and I could chose not to feel it. Later, if there was a later, I could break down. Not now, though. That wasn't the person I'd become.

At the house, the windows were all bright. The Christmas lights blinked and glowed blue and red and yellow and green under the thickening snow. Icicles as long as butcher's blades hung from the eaves. The family home at holiday time. It should have been beautiful, but it seemed obscene.

In the backseat, Ozzie growled. When I stopped the car, she looked from me to the house and back, her eyebrows raised. It was the perfect pantomime of you're-not-going-in-there-are-you? I reached back and scratched behind her ears.

"Okay," I said. "Here's the plan. I'm heading in. I'll distract it. You guys go around the outside and come in the back. When you hear the signal, we'll try to beat the sonofabitch down enough that Ex can run an exorcism."

"And what will the signal be?" Chogyi Jake asked, hefting our one remaining shotgun.

"I was thinking something like 'Get him,'" I said. "Simple, direct."

"Works for me," Ex said. "Let's go."

"Wait," I said. "If there's a question . . . if it looks like we can't stop this thing without hurting Jay . . ."

I couldn't say the words. They were there at the top of my throat, too thick and hard to speak. For more than a century, this thing had been eating my family. The math on the sacrifice was obvious. Lose one person to stop the death and degradation of dozens more. But it was my big brother.

"It's not going to come to that," Ex said. Chogyi Jake didn't say anything, but I knew what was in his mind. Whatever happens, happens. We may die. We may kill. Terrible things or wonderful or both together, inextricable as milk poured into tea.

"I just needed to say it," I said. "You know."

"All right," Chogyi Jake said.

I got out of the car, and before I could stop her, Ozzie clambered out with me. She pressed her body close against my knee and looked up expectantly.

"Okay," I said. "But you're not going to like it in there."

We went up the walk, me and my dog. I didn't bother knocking or ringing the bell. The door wasn't locked.

As soon as we stepped in, Ozzie started growling low in the back of her throat. I felt it too. Everything was as it had been, but it was wrong. A parody of my childhood home. A grotesque version of it. The smell of gingerbread filled the air so thickly, it nauseated. The dead Christmas tree was decaying in its stand. I gathered my will and pressed out, making a warm place at my heart and expanding it like a bubble all around me. The sense of transcendent madness and evil lessened a degree, even if it didn't evaporate.

From the kitchen, something laughed. It was a sick sound, wet and phlegmy. I walked in. They were at the table. Mom, Dad, Curtis, and the small, twisted tumor of a thing that had once been my brother Jay. Thick nylon rope bound all of them except it. Bright red Christmas stockings were stuffed in their mouths as gags.

The Graveyard Child's grin split its face, and it cackled obscenely.

"Hey there, sister," it said, and smacked its massive frog-like lips. "I was *hopin'* you could come."

CHAPTER TWENTY-ONE

"Abraxiel Unam," I said.

"Sure, whatever," it said, waving a hand like it was shooing a fly. Its skin was pale as maggots, its hands larger than a grown man's, and thick. Its knuckles seemed to sink into its flesh. "Call me that. I'll call you Little Janie Pees-Her-Pants. Or whatever. Your Royal Majesty if you want. Might as well fuck a horse as a supermodel where I come from."

It shuddered. Its black eyes quivered. Ozzie barked once, and the Graveyard Child barked back, spraying spittle across the room. Ozzie got behind

my knees but didn't retreat past that. I could feel
her growling. The thing at the table was madness.
Not stupid, not out of control. It was vast intelli-
gence gone necrotic. It hopped down from its chair
and reached for a plate of cookies beside the stove.
Everything it did seemed rich with meaning and
menace. Even putting a cookie in its toothless
mouth.

"You want some, sister? They made them for
everybody but you. You're the fucking Whore of
Babylon," it said, then winked massively. "I should
know, right?"

"What do you want?"

"I want what's *mine back*!" it shouted, its mouth
a square of rage. "You took my things. You took my
stuff. Do you have any idea how long it took me to
build all that up? All those places, all those houses?
All that lovely, lovely money? Because you know
what money is? It's power."

It sighed.

"So here's the deal. You get out of my sister's
body, and I won't kill all these people. Sound good?"

"You're not talking to her," I said. *I* did, not the
rider. "You're talking to me."

"Sonnenrad! Darling! Why the cold shoulder? I
know you're in there. I fucked you into her," it said,
then pressed fingers to its lips. "Oh. Hey. Was that
rude? I never know where the line is."

It took the plate of cookies and trundled back

to its chair, chewing with its mouth open, unself-conscious as a baby.

"Let them go," I said. "You don't have an issue with them. You have it with me."

It reached down with one foot, hooked an ankle under the rungs of the chair Dad was tied to, and tipped it back. Dad's eyes went wide as he fell backward. I shouted and moved forward, but I still heard the thump when his skull hit the floor. It popped another cookie into its mouth and looked up innocently.

"No? All right," it said, its deformed face a picture of wide-eyed guilelessness that melted into a leer. "How much do you think it would take?"

"I am not here to bargain," my voice said without me.

"Didja come to mud wrestle? Because I'm all for that shit. Of course you're here to bargain. That meat suit you've got on is mine. I tailored it. You only got to borrow it for a while, and then you were supposed to give it back. I mean, honey. I'm your daddy, right? You wouldn't steal from your own daddy?"

"I have no father," the rider said, and I could feel the power of the words in my throat. "I am the Black Sun and the Black Sun's daughter. You are no part of me."

"Okay, not daddy, then. Favorite midwife. It doesn't matter. The thing is, all my toys are tied to that meat sack. And I want 'em back. You can crawl up out of there and give her to me, then you can swim on back to the Other Side and all these poor bastards can fall into lives of denial and alcoholism, or I burn them all and you besides. Jayné Heller turns into that icky Ball Park frank that's been in the cooker since last August, and her fortune goes to her only living relative, her poor brother Jay-bird."

"I don't fear you," the rider said.

I didn't see it move. It was that fast. The Graveyard Child was at the table, popping another cookie between its toothless gums, and then it was on me, its massive hand around my throat, banging my head against the kitchen wall with a violence that cracked the plaster. My hands dug at it, trying to find space between its finger and my flesh. Even with the strength of the rider, I couldn't do it. I tried to join my will to hers, tried to help. I felt the plaster crack against the back of my head, the hot/cold trickle of blood coming down my scalp. I swung my leg out, hammering at the arch of its foot. It ignored me. I twisted, bringing my elbow hard across its throat. Nothing. It seemed to go on forever, slamming me like a rag doll. Its breath smelled like old meat. Somewhere, Ozzie was barking in a frenzy. Somewhere, Curtis was weeping from wide, horrified eyes. Somewhere else. The world went gray. It would keep doing this to me until it chose to stop, and there was nothing I could do about it.

It was dragging me across the kitchen floor. I didn't remember exactly how I'd gotten there. Then, with a power that felt like it was wrenching my arm out of my shoulder, it hauled me up and deposited me in the chair it had been in. The plate of cookies was in front of me. It patted my head gently.

"I'm a reasonable guy," it said. "And really, I think you'll see it's a pretty damn sweet deal I'm offering here. I don't have to go through the extra waiting time while they do all the paperwork. That's all I get. It's not much. And look at what you get in return. Your freedom. And Jayné gets to save her whole family. Her poor mommy. Her kid brother. Her daddy who's her uncle who's her daddy. You ever see *Chinatown*? Great fucking movie. And you want a bonus? I won't even kill her little playmates outside. Do you think she wouldn't choose to do that? I know Jayné Heller. She's a hero. She'd give her life in a heartbeat if it meant saving these people. You'd just be doing what she wanted."

It nodded. Paused. Looked at me, then up at the clock on the wall, then back at me. The wall it had beaten me against was caved in. There was blood on it. Ozzie was pacing back and forth in front of the doorway, her teeth bared and her eyes anxious.

"Okay," the Graveyard Child said. "You need to talk to me here. Communication's a two-way street."

Dad shifted. I could see him trying to move away, but he was bound too tightly to the chair. Mom's eyes were closed, her nostrils flaring and pinching thin as she hyperventilated. My body ached. Something deep in my belly shifted in a way I was pretty sure wasn't a good sign. My vision swam.

"I will not make this choice," the Black Sun said through me.

"You're gonna leave it to the meat? I like your style, kid. That's classy. Okay. Bring the meat girl up and let's have a little talk. Jayné? You in there? Hey. I don't know if you've been following all this . . ."

I tried to speak, but all I could manage was to shift my jaw a little. I tried to sit up and the pain left me gasping. The Graveyard Child helped me sit forward. I coughed, and the phlegm came up bloody.

"Ooh," the rider said. "That's gotta hurt. You're the kind of girl who really plays it rough, aren't you? No curb too high for a rental car. That's what I always say. So what do you think? Kill all your family or let 'em live. No pressure. Totally your call."

I gathered the strength I could. We were doomed. There was no way I could beat this thing in a fight. Chogyi Jake had warned me once—a long time ago, it seemed. Things work until they don't. Guns. Hordes of the possessed. Supernatural serial killers. I'd taken them all. This time I didn't stand a chance. I could save them all, and all it would mean was giving my soul to this thing. I looked over at Curt. My little brother, Curtis, who hadn't even hit Senior Prom yet. How could I take that away from him?

Okay, I thought. Fine. Take me. Just leave my family alone.

"Get him!" The voice wasn't mine. I thought for a moment that it was the Black Sun, but it had been a man's voice.

Ex's.

The front door burst open, and then half a second later the back one. The report of the shotgun was louder than I remembered. The Graveyard Child reared up, its arms spread wide.

"Oh, come on," it shouted, and there were storms in its voice. A depth like the deepest canyon. "I was almost done here."

Chogyi Jake stood by the back door and racked another round. And then another man stepped in behind him. Not Ex. A thicker man, older, whose dark skin made the tattoos on his face only a little less legible. Eduardo Martinez lifted his palms toward us, and I felt the blow of his will. The Graveyard Child stumbled back, its vast eyes going wide.

"By your name I bind you," a woman said from the front door. Idéa Smith, with Ex standing behind her. "Puer Mórtuus, I bind you."

"Well, this is fucked," the Graveyard Child said, and Jonathan Rhodes stepped through the door to the dining room. The power of his will laced with the others, pushing and pressing, fashioning a cage of information, meaning, and intent so powerful, it was almost visible. The Graveyard Child writhed back, twisting at the waist and clawing at Rhodes. The thin young man didn't even seem to notice the attack.

"By your name I bind you," he said, and the resonance of his voice made the walls themselves seem to sing and crack. "Abraxiel Unas, I bind you."

"You know," the Graveyard Child shouted, "there are other ways we could address this. God, you cocksuckers are—"

It dropped to its knees, and for a moment its skin seemed to run. I saw Jay, kneeling as if in prayer, his hands before him and his eyes pressed closed.

Yes, I thought. Fight it. Come back to us, Jay. You can do this.

"By your name I bind you," Martinez said. "Graveyard Child, by your name I bind you."

The house went silent. I could hear the tick-tick-tick of the clock. The soft hushing of the wind. Snow swirled in through the doorways, and the furnace clicked, hummed, and came to life. I tried to stand up but my knees wouldn't support me. Ex limped over to me and took my hand.

"Hey," he said. "Look what I found outside. Pretty cool, huh?"

I smiled. Jay lay on the floor in a fetal position. His eyes were closed. He could almost have been sleeping. Waves ran along under his skin. I couldn't imagine what it was to be him just then. Worse than being trapped in the cage with the monster, he *was* the cage.

"Exorcism," I said. "You have to get Jay back."

"I will," Ex said. "It may take a while, but it will happen."

Chogyi Jake and Idéa Smith were to my right, lifting my still-bound father back to where he could sit up. There was blood running down past his ear and his breathing was hard and labored. But he wasn't dead. He probably wasn't even badly hurt. Rhodes came toward me, grinning. His teeth were ornately carved, and there were black tattoos on his gums, and despite all that, he looked like a kid who'd just gotten his first bicycle.

"How did this happen?" I asked.

"We followed you," Rhodes said. "Nothing personal, but we weren't entirely sure our conversation back at my hotel wasn't a trick. When you left, we started surveillance. And when we got here, and you went in . . . well, that was kind of the acid test."

"I told them it would be okay with you," Ex said. "I didn't think you'd mind."

"You get a raise," I said.

Chogyi Jake had untied my father's hands and moved on to Curtis. Dad wasn't looking at me or anyone else in particular. His gaze was fixed on the middle of the table, his jaw set and angry. I tried to imagine how this all looked and felt to him. This was his home. The one place he'd always been able to assert control. And now look at it. Filled with freaks, demons, and unholy magicians. His eldest son caught in the grips of Satan and his disgraced daughter and her friends wandering through the place as if it were theirs. He was humiliated, broken, and embarrassed, and I didn't even know how to make it better for him. I got to my feet, still unsteady, and didn't look at him. Pretending not to notice was all I had to offer him now. Mom was being untied, her freed hands fluttering around her like pigeons on strings, frantic and pointless.

"We're going to need a space for the exorcism," Ex was saying. "My guess is that thing had its claws pretty deep in your brother. It may take some time to do this right. I was thinking that if your dad's garage—"

"Not here," I said. "It needs to be done, and so we'll do it, but not here."

Ex raised his eyebrows and shrugged.

"Whatever you say. You want me to start looking for decent ritual spaces? It could be kind of hard to find a place, with the holidays and all, but I can't see leaving him like that until January."

Jay, on the floor, twitched and shifted, his face distorting in something like a scream, only silent. His hands clenched and unclenched.

"No, you're right," I said. "We'll find something. Maybe the church. Would that be all right?"

"Sure," Ex said. "I can do nondenominational, if that's what we're working with. Just as long as you don't have any amateurs who want to get in on it. I don't have time or patience for that crap."

"I'm sure we can work something out," I said. "If nothing else, I'll rent a warehouse and you can consecrate it."

"Okay," he said, and sat on the table with a sigh. "You know, I'm really looking forward to not having my foot hurt."

"You caught a shotgun blast from one of the most powerful and dangerous riders I've ever heard of," I said. "I figure you're going to be faking a limp for decades."

"Me? Never," he said. "Years tops. Not decades."

I walked to the living room. Ozzie was sitting on the rug, panting. Her tongue hung out of her mouth and her eyes were wide and distressed. I squatted beside her, scratching her with bent fingers.

"Hey, girl," I said. "It's okay. That was freaky, I know. But it's over. Good guys won."

Ozzie looked at me and then past me to the kitchen door. Her mouth closed and she growled. I rubbed her ears. They were soft and fuzzy, just the way dogs ears should be.

"You did a fine job," I said. "You're a good, good—"

It came like a detonation. There was no sound, no physical movement, no sign or signal apart from the overwhelming sense of vast power released. I stumbled, trying to get to my feet. I got to the kitchen too late. The Graveyard Child stood in the room's center, Eduardo Martinez in its grip. In a fraction of a second I was in the small space behind my eyes, my body exploding forward. I dove, leading with my left elbow, and the impact actually made the thing lose its grip and stumble back. Eduardo lay on the kitchen floor, motionless. I couldn't even tell if he was breathing. My mother huddled back against the stove, her hands up over her ears, her eyes closed. Curtis knelt in front of her, his fists at the ready like a boxer on his knees. Dad was in the TV room, turning away. Idéa Smith and Rhodes were running toward the rider. I kicked twice, hard. The first one connected, but the second time it caught my ankle and twisted. Something in my knee tore, and I fell to the linoleum. Chogyi Jake was over me, one foot on either side of my chest. The shotgun went off three times in fast succession and the rider let go of me, batting Chogyi Jake away and rushing down the steps and into the TV room, where he lay still.

"By your name I bind you," Idéa Smith shouted, and I felt her will trying to take hold, trying to find some purchase on the implacable wall that was the Graveyard Child. "Puer Mórtuus, I bind you."

The Graveyard Child shrugged, picked up the chair my father had been tied to, and swung it against Idéa hard enough that the oak splintered. Rhodes paused. I saw him begin to breathe in, gathering his will, preparing the Oath of the Abyss. The Graveyard Child ran to him, moving so fast it was like watching a film with a few frames missing. It drove its knee up into the man's crotch, grabbed his head as he crumpled over, and casually ripped off an ear. Rhodes fell to his knees, his eyes open but unseeing. Ozzie was barking again, her yellow teeth flashing in threat. She could as easily not have been there.

The Graveyard Child tossed the ear to the floor, put its hands on its hips, and grinned.

"Well, that was something, wasn't it? I mean, *goddamn*, right?" Its eyes fixed on me, the irises contracting as the pupils dilated. "They almost had me fucked. You have got to respect that effort."

With a shout, my little brother grabbed a carving knife from the counter and flung it at the Graveyard Child. The blade sunk into its arm. The rider smacked its lips, plucked the blade back out, and with a perversely reflective expression dropped the knife to the floor.

"All right. Where was I?" it said. And then raised a single finger. "Oh. I remember. The *hard* way."

CHAPTER TWENTY-TWO

I fought my way to my feet. My knee felt loose, limp. I was afraid to put my weight on it.

"Face me," I said. "You wanted the body in exchange for them. Face me and take it."

"Jayné!" Ex shouted from behind me. "No!"

It shrugged, smiled at me mildly, and brought a foot down on Eduardo Martinez's throat. I wasn't trapped behind my eyes anymore, but I wasn't alone either. Together, the Black Sun and I pushed forward on my good leg, rising up through the air, then striking out hard with my heel. I felt the Graveyard

Child's nose break, and it stepped back. I landed on my good leg and both hands, going still as stone as soon as I touched the floor. I'd pushed the rider back a step. Martinez groaned. Not dead, then. I was good with not dead.

"You will leave this house, Satan!" my father roared, and three rapid pistol reports came with the words. I took a look back toward the TV room. Dad and Ex were both there. My father held the pistol in both hands, steadying it. As I watched, the muzzle flared again, and I heard the hiss of air after the bullet passed by my ear. Ex had Chogyi Jake's shotgun in hand, but he wasn't shooting. "You will leave my house and my family. In the name of Christ Jesus, I command you begone. Begone!" He fired again.

The Graveyard Child clapped a hand over its chest and stumbled backward. Its eyes went wide. Dark blood spilled over its wide fingers and it blinked in confusion.

"Dad?" it said in Jay's voice. "Dad, you . . . you shot me."

My father's face was a mask of horror, shock, and regret. He lurched up the steps toward the Graveyard Child, and the rider slapped him across the face hard enough to knock him against the wall.

"Just joshin'," the Graveyard Child said, then turned to me. "Honestly, sis, I don't think anyone understands this family but us. And *us* pretty much means *just me*."

It turned toward Curt and Mom with a sigh.

"Stop!" I screamed, but it only moved them gently aside and ripped the stove out from the wall, tossing it on the prone body of Idéa Smith. Ex came up the steps to stand beside me. My father was crawling on his hands and knees. Blood streamed down the side of his head, falling to the floor with a steady drip, drip, drip. I heard a hissing sound that I didn't understand until I smelled rotting eggs.

"Seriously," it said. "There are some conversations that I just won't be able to have with anybody once you're gone. I mean, except for Carla. But I think she just agrees with me to make me happy, don't you?"

Ex racked the shotgun. The Graveyard Child looked at him incredulously.

"How many times have you tried shooting me with that thing? It hasn't actually done anything yet, and you just keep going. You're *adorable*!"

"Ex," I said. "Get them out of here."

"Ex," it said, imitating me. "Die in a fire."

The Graveyard Child lifted its hands, and blue flame whooshed through the room. Curtis screamed and tried to pull Mom out of the kitchen. I didn't have time. I rushed at the rider, trying to push it back into the flames. It shrieked with laughter and pulled me close in a bear hug. It was small but terribly solid. It wrapped its arms around me and squeezed, shaking while it did like a terrier worrying a rat twice its own size. The heat of the fire was intense. Bright yellow flames were crawling up the wall, fanning out across the ceiling with ripples like the surface of a lake from below. I tried to get my hands up around the thing's throat. It had been Jay. It had been my brother. I didn't think about that, only the need for air and to get the others out. It twisted and I lost my balance, tried to catch myself on my wounded knee, and crashed to the floor. It writhed against me, its gums bared with effort, and I felt my ribs creaking from the strain. It was going to crush me like a grape, shatter me. Craning my neck, I saw Rhodes and Chogyi Jake helping each other out the front door. A fire alarm was sounding from somewhere close by. I didn't remember it starting. My mother was still lying on the floor, Curtis beside her, weeping and plucking at her.

Get out, I thought. Everyone get out.

I tried to center myself, tried to pull my qi together into a force I could use. I imagined the thin blue ball at my heart and I tried to push it out, expanding, but the Graveyard Child pressed in, compressing me with an invisible force that felt like nausea and despair. My breath grew shorter and shorter. The rider's hatred and rage battered at me, but for the moment the others were forgotten. It wanted my death enough to be distracted by it. I didn't need to live. I just needed to not die long enough for the others to get out. The gas that

had fed the stove was torn at the floorboards, and a
plume of flame billowed from it. I could smell my
hair burning. The pain from the heat was powerful,
but the Graveyard Child ignored it. Its wide mouth
came close to my ear, whispering obscenities and
threats. Even the veneer of humor was gone, and all
that was left was raw, vicious evil.

I looked up again. Ex was pulling Curtis away.
The flames were in the living room now. The Christmas tree would go up like fireworks, I thought.
Another argument in favor of Hanukkah. A few
candles, but no kindling. I was aware vaguely that
I'd blacked out for a moment. That I was dying. Ex
got Curt out. I smiled.

I win, I thought. Curt's safe. It's okay if I die now.

Only there was my mother, still on the floor.
Still with her hands clasped to her ears, her eyes
squeezed closed.

"Mother," I called, but it hardly came out as
a groan. Help me, I thought. Help me this one
last time. And the Black Sun, exhausted as I was,
brought its will to bear. I took a breath, the super-
heated air searing my lips and throat.

"Mother!" I shouted. *We* shouted. "*Mother!*"

And my mother moved, shifted. Her head turned
and she opened her eyes, weeping, staring. The eyes
of a trapped animal. She closed them again, shaking
her head. Her lips were moving in prayer.

"MOTHER!" we screamed for the last time.

My mother opened her eyes once more.

They were black as the desert night. I felt a wave of cool air wash over me. The Graveyard Child, lost in its killing fury, noticed nothing, but I could breathe again. The fire was all around us, consuming the walls. I could see it spreading up the stairs toward the bedrooms. The whole house would be engulfed in minutes if it wasn't already. But I was not burning. My mother stood, looking at the conflagration as if it were something surprising and mildly distasteful. She was clearly my own mother, the woman who had packed my lunch box in the mornings and who said my prayers with me at night, only proud now. Sure of herself and her power. When she unfurled her massive black-feathered wings, she was beautiful.

"Abraxiel," she whispered, and it carried over the roar of the flames.

The Graveyard Child looked up, its face a mask of shock and dismay. It looked around the kitchen as if seeing it for the first time. I rolled away, my ribs bruised and aching. I smelled the bright chemical smell of the smoke. The linoleum I lay on was curling up now, the flames traveling along it. At the sink, the bottle of dish soap was melting, the soap pushing the fire around like napalm. I sat up and my clothes were on fire, the cloth of my jeans searing and falling away in black clumps. The leather in my overcoat getting hard and black as armor. I felt the cool air of the desert against my skin.

"Sonnenrad," the Graveyard Child said.

"What have you done to my children?" our mothers asked with a single voice.

"You can't stop me," it said. "I've beaten you before. You aren't stronger than me."

She stepped forward and the flames retreated from her. I rose to my feet and she put her hand out, resting it on my shoulder. I had a sense of massive affection, of boundless love colored by regret and even jealousy. It was a complex and wordless emotion, and it made sense to me in a way I couldn't fit in language. With our mother behind us, we turned to look at the Graveyard Child. It stood in the heart of the flames now, like a comic-book Satan. Its wide hands were balled in fists, and its mouth twisted with rage.

"I beat you!" it screamed. "*I beat you!*"

"There was a time you deceived me," our mother said. "It will not happen again."

With a shout of despair, it launched itself at her, its arms outstretched. I stepped into the attack. My body felt whole and perfect, and I plucked it out of the air and slammed it down to the kitchen floor, which was also the wind-paved stones of the desert. *My* desert.

A black ichor dripped from the Graveyard Child's mouth. It struggled to its feet, slipping a little. It opened its mouth too wide for any human anatomy and shouted. The world seemed to lose its coherence for a moment. A deep and nameless dread welled up in me, but my mother's hand on my shoulder steadied me.

"You made a mistake," she said. "You transgressed against me. I can forgive that. But you have transgressed against the ones I love, and *that* I will not forgive you."

"Oh, really? 'Don't cross Mama Bear'? That's the best you've got?"

It leaped, again and again. I caught it and threw it to the ground and it bounced up at once, shrieking like a mad animal. Its attack was constant, vicious, and unrelenting, and I stood before it calmly, my arms and legs moving swift and sure and perfectly. In the house, something burst, a bloom of fire jetting out from under the sink. In the desert, everything was still. The two didn't contradict, and that was what we were, all three of us.

And the moment I understood that, I saw him. Jay. My brother. His fear and his misery. The loneliness at his core and his fear of a God and a father who did not approve of him. I saw him as a boy and as a man, grown empty.

And beneath him: Eric. For a moment he was alive again. He smiled and winked. I hadn't remembered him as being such a handsome man, but he was here before me as he had been. And more than he'd been. I saw the love in him, the joy, the certainty that he was special, and the desperation that filled him when he wasn't. Everything he'd done—to my mother, to Aubrey and Kim, to me, to Jay—became explicable in an instant. Not forgivable. Never that. But I knew him, and I saw how he had become evil. I saw the hurt at its base, and the blight that had come from it, and then he was gone too.

For a space of time that lasted years or seconds, I saw them before me. Men and women. I saw their narcissism and felt their need, their fears and hurts and irrational angers. The pain of a lost love or a lost child or an assault that betrayed the deepest trust. None of them were healed. All of them were degraded and debased and made less than they should have been. And all dead now. Gone past redemption.

I stood witness, neither passing judgment nor offering comfort, until the last one—a woman with a round face and wide blue eyes whose name I never knew—revealed her pride and rage and faded away. Like ripping a book apart page by page until nothing was left, the Graveyard Child was gone. The desert empty except for us.

I turned to our mother then. She looked down at me with black eyes as bright as wet stone. There were two of her as there were of me. The first and greater was the Black Sun. Not the child that lived and grew with and within me, but the vast mother in the fullness of her power, vast and inhuman and terrible. But with her was my own mother, and I saw her as I had seen the others. Margaret Fournier, who'd loved her father and resented her mother. Who'd married Gary Heller because she was in love and because she was afraid not to. I saw the irrationality of her faith and the depth of her guilt, her pride in her children and her jealousy of them. I saw all that she could have been and wasn't. And would never be. And I saw that the remnant of her—the twisted and unhealthy woman that she had become—was also beautiful in her way. Was also capable of moments of transcendence and grace.

I saw her looking at me, I saw her reacting to what she found there, but she did not say what it was.

"The time's come," we said, the Black Sun's daughter and I.

The desert faded but it did not vanish. I was aware of a vast fire all around me. The heat like a furnace, held away only by the will of our mothers. I stooped down and gathered the still form of my brother, cradling him in my arms. He felt as light as a child. Or a memory. Together, we walked, and the fire grew less. I felt other things. Wind. A biting coldness. A vast and angry weight of clouds and an invisible sun beyond them that radiated heat and light instead of purification. I heard sirens and a dog barking furiously, frantically, and filled with delight.

And then we were there, standing on the icy front lawn in a snowstorm while my childhood home went up like a torch. I staggered under Jay's sudden weight, and Ex appeared at my side, helping me lower the weeping, scorched man to the ground. Ozzie forced her way up to me, licking my face and barking like a puppy. I put my arm around her. She stank of smoke and wet dog. Chogyi Jake came to me too.

"We thought you were dead," he said.

"It was the safe bet," I said. "Did we all get out?"

"For some definitions of *out*," Ex said. "The Smith woman got a decent burn along one arm, and she's not focusing very well. Martinez is alive and breathing, but I'd bet you a week's paycheck he's concussed. Rhodes is getting them out before the officers of the law show up."

"Dad and Curt?" I asked.

"Well, their central nervous systems are fine," Ex said. "Some nasty scrapes and bruises. Nothing compared to the no doubt intense psychological trauma."

"Yeah," I said. "Well. That's not just this. That's the world."

"Your coat looks like it got broiled. What was it like in there?"

"Weird," I said. "Effective, though."

"Graveyard Child's banished?"

"More than that," I said. "I'm pretty sure we killed it."

"Good," Ex said.

To my left, my mother stood looking at the

burning house. Her spine was straight and her expression beatific. She'd had her angel again. I knew it wouldn't last. Nothing we'd done would change who she was. Or what any of us were. I didn't know whether that was wonderful or depressing. Dad came up to her and put his arm around her, offering protection and comfort just in the way he stood. A few seconds later she noticed him. The sirens were getting closer.

Jay coughed and his eyes swam, trying to focus. His face had the too-pink look of a burn. I took his hand.

"Jayné?" he said, and tears filled his eyes.

"Hey, big brother."

"I think . . ." he began, then stopped. "I think I may have done something very bad."

"You did," I said. "But there were some extenuating circumstances. And I still love you regardless."

"I think I did something bad to Carla?"

My mother put her hand on my shoulder and pulled me gently away, taking my place at Jay's side.

"You had an angel in you, didn't you? The glory of it can overwhelm. You can do things that you never imagined that you would. I understand. I know."

"Mom," Jay said, taking her hand. "I don't . . . I didn't . . . An angel? Was it an angel?"

I felt a flush of rage. The Graveyard Child was no more an angel than a wild dog was a good babysitter. But there was no point making the argument. They were going to have to make whatever sense of all this they could. What I had to offer wasn't going to be particularly more comforting or useful just because it was true.

I turned away and walked to the SUV. I needed to get someplace warm. And then I needed some new clothes. And then I didn't know what I needed. Ozzie trotted along beside me. A fire truck pulled up to the curb, and men in fire suits started making everyone get back to a safe distance. Chogyi Jake and Ex guided my mother back from Jay and the fire while paramedics descended on my big brother. While my father talked to the firemen, pointing angrily to the flames, Curt walked over to me, shivering. I opened the front passenger's door and let him in.

"Hey," I said.

"Hey." He swallowed, sighed. Something collapsed on the second floor of the house and a roll of flames poured out of the windows where my room used to be. Curt was crying. I took his hand.

"You gonna be okay?" I asked.

"I don't know," he said. And then a few seconds later: "This family is *seriously* messed up."

"You know," I said, "it really is."

CHAPTER TWENTY-THREE

Whatever I thought about the rest of the church, I had to agree that they were great in a crisis. My family's house burned to the foundation, the flames shrugging off water and snow and burning with a heat that surprised and confused the fire department. The family albums were destroyed. The Bible with the names of my ancestors turned to ash. All Mom's dresses, all Dad's suits. The site of almost all my memories of childhood was just gone. And then Pastor Michael put out the word, and from all around the city, help just *came*. Curtis went to

stay with his best friend, Billy Taft, since they went
to the same school and played the same console
games. Mom and Dad went to Jay's new house, and
the director at the church day care center dropped
off a foldout couch that Jay could keep. Food came
in, and sympathy. One of the parishioners was a
lawyer and stepped in to help Dad hash things out
with the insurance company.

It was like watching a massive family rise up
out of nowhere, and I would have been amazed if I
hadn't already known it worked that way. We were
an imperfect, broken family made from imperfect,
broken people, and our place in the community was
the same as everyone else's. They took care of their
own without complaint or debating whether they
should have to. It was a good thing to see, and I
would have liked to be part of it.

"Your father was very clear about it," Pastor Michael said. "I can't take your money."

"I have a lot of it. I won't miss it."

"That isn't the issue," he said. In his full-on wedding suit, he looked like a kindly lawyer. "Your father made a decision, and I've agreed to it. I know
you want to help him, but maybe you can find another way to do that."

Down the hallway, Carla leaned out of the dressing room and gestured frantically to me. I held up
my hand in a just-a-minute gesture.

"Do you have a suggestion?" I asked.

"You can pray for him," Pastor Michael said.

"I'm a lot better at cutting checks."

"Then praying for him is probably what you should do for yourself too. Don't you think?"

He put a hand on my shoulder, then headed off to the chapel. I rolled my eyes and trotted back to the dressing room.

New Year's had come and gone, and now even the most tenacious of the holiday decor had been put back in its boxes for next year. The wedding had come upon us. I still could barely bring myself to believe they were going through with it, but as Jay pointed out, it wasn't just a question of the two of them. It was like my father had taken up residence in Jay's brain, which, in context, was even creepier. And to make it all just that much more awkward, Carla had insisted that I be maid of honor, and I hadn't had the presence of mind to say no.

"How do I look?" she asked when I came in the room.

Pregnant, I thought.

"You look great, Carla. That's an amazing dress."

"I can't find the shoes. Have you seen them? The ones with the pearls?"

I glanced at the floor and then up, catching myself in the mirror. My black eyes were almost healed up, and the makeup covered the majority of what was left. I told myself that someone who didn't know wouldn't see it at all. And then, less charitably, that they wouldn't be looking at me anyway. Carla was starting to get a panicky look around her eyes.

"Hold on," I said, and dug through the tiny little accessory purse for my phone. Chogyi Jake picked up on the first ring. "Have you seen Carla's pearl shoes?"

"They're in the car," he said. "Would you like me to bring them?"

I gave Carla the thumbs-up. "That would be great," I said, and let the connection drop.

She sagged against the table, putting her hand to her belly. A week ago my brother had taken her shoes and her purse so she couldn't leave the house. Now she was getting ready to marry him. Granted, he'd been through some pretty big changes in between, but no transformation is ever complete. In her position I'd have been looking for my walking shoes, not the pearl heels.

"You know," I said, "I've got a car and enough money to get you a ticket anywhere you want to go. You get cold feet, I can get you out of here right now, and no one'll know it before you're in the air."

She laughed like I was joking. I hadn't really expected anything else.

"Thank you for doing all this," she said. "You're going to be the best sister-in-law God could have sent me."

"You're welcome," I said with a smile as her sister, Maria, pushed into the room.

"Carla! Where are your shoes!"

"They're coming," Carla said. "Come here, let me fix your makeup."

"My makeup's fine."

I snuck out to the hallway and took myself down to the drinking fountain even though I wasn't thirsty. Outside, the sun filled the sky and set the snow glowing. Even with the ice and snow, it looked warm. Nothing that bright could be cold. I watched Chogyi Jake walk briskly across the parking lot with an ash-gray shoe box in his hand. He looked great in a tuxedo. I'd seen Ex earlier. In deference to Pastor Michael, he'd skipped the clerical collar, but he'd kept the black shirt with his suit. With his hair down, he was looking more angelic than usual. And he was smiling more.

Truth was, I was feeling a little lighter about the shoulders too. For years I'd been hurrying from place to place, trying to answer questions I barely knew how to ask. I'd been a believer and a doubter, a refugee from my own home, a college coed, a college dropout, a demon hunter, a businesswoman, a victim, a heroine, and probably about a hundred other things that I'd forgotten about. I'd had everything I knew about myself blown up at least twice. My heart had been broken by loss and it had been broken by guilt. I'd done things I will regret to the day I die, and things I'm proud of, sometimes in the same moment.

Chogyi Jake pushed the door open and, seeing me, lifted the shoe box.

"Thank you," I said, stepping forward to take it from him.

"How is it going?"

"It's a friendly, upbeat kind of travesty," I said. "But there's always divorce."

He smiled.

"There are very few decisions we can make that will keep us from remaking ourselves again later," he said.

"Yeah," I said. "That's absolutely what I meant. I wasn't being catty at all."

He grinned and made a small bow to me.

"And anyway," I said, "it might all work out. Maybe this will turn out to have been the best thing ever for both of them."

"It's possible," he agreed, and we both left it there. Optimism and hope. Just another service we'd provide.

THE CEREMONY was long and earnest and more about Christ and faith and the importance of the church than Jay or Carla. They exchanged their vows and their rings, and they kissed for the first time as husband and wife. And for all my misgivings, it was still weirdly nice.

The reception was in the church's meeting rooms, catered by Subway and with a DJ who gleefully mixed Casting Crowns with Nirvana's "Smells Like Teen Spirit." I'd changed into jeans and a sweater the minute after I got out of the chapel, and I was sitting now with my sandwich and a bottle of water, watching people dance in the same room where I'd had it explained by a furiously blushing Sunday school teacher that Jesus didn't like it when girls touched themselves down there. The cognitive dissonance had a warm, nostalgic feel.

Jay and Carla were at a table near the double doors that lead to the hallway, shaking hands and hugging people and generally being happy. And I was happy for them. They were making a place for themselves, and if I'd have chewed my own arm off rather than trade places, it didn't matter. This was their screwed-up, shaky, uncertain life. I had one of my own.

When the music turned to "(I've Had) The Time of My Life" for the second time, I went to them.

"Are you going?" Carla said in mid-hug.

"I think so," I said. "It's late, and I'm pretty worn-out."

Jay took me in his arms, and I folded myself against him. He felt thinner than I expected. Slighter. I wondered if it had anything to do with the Graveyard Child. Ex and I had talked to him a little in the days after the fire. We'd told him about the rider and qliphoth and the Pleroma. At a guess, a tenth of it had actually sunk in. It would have to be enough.

"Thank you," he said. "I can't tell you how glad I am you came back when you did."

"Glad I could help," I said.

And then it was over. I walked out along the halls I'd been down a million times a decade ago, past the church offices, and out the door. Curtis was already gone, and we'd be texting each other later anyway. My mother and father were sharing a table with Carla's parents and didn't want to see me. I tested myself to see if I felt bad about that, and I did, but only a little.

Ex and Chogyi Jake were sitting on the steps of the church with Ozzie when I walked out.

"Hey," I said. "You guys ready to roll?"

"Anytime you are," Ex said, standing up. "We were just talking about Eric. How would you feel about having a little memorial for him?"

"We can," I said with a shrug. "Is there a reason why we should?"

"Because now we've put him to rest," Chogyi Jake said.

"Let me think about that," I said.

The night sky was beautiful. The moon was just about at its halfway mark, the darkness and the light almost equal, with maybe just a little more light. I let myself enjoy the cold for a few seconds and then walked toward the SUV, my other family ambling along behind me.

For all the darkness and pain in my life, I knew I

was lucky. Part of that was inheriting a vast fortune built up over generations by an evil spirit that I'd help destroy. Part of it was that I had a network of friends who had become family. And part of it— maybe the largest part—was that I was getting the hell out of Wichita. Again.

I opened the driver's door, slid up behind the wheel, and cued up some Pink Martini to get the taste of the DJ out of my metaphorical mouth. Joyful violins attacked the first notes of "Let's Never Stop Falling in Love," and I felt my spine relax. Behind me, Ozzie clambered up into her seat with a little help from Ex. Chogyi Jake belted himself into the front passenger's seat. I started the engine.

"So," Chogyi Jake said, "I think we have some options. We never did finish cataloging all of Eric's properties. Or there are the archives in Denver to look through if you'd prefer."

Wordless, I felt the rider within me paying attention, waiting. I remembered her in the desert where all masks failed, saying *I will outgrow you* and *I'm frightened*. I pulled out into traffic, heading south.

I wasn't frightened.

"Jayné?" Ex said. "What do you think? What's our next move?"

"Always the question, ain't it?"

Acknowledgments

I would like to thank all the people whose support and professionalism have made the Black Sun's Daughter series possible: the New Mexico Critical Mass group, who were there from the beginning; my agents, Shawna McCarthy and Danny Baror; my editors, Jennifer Heddle and Adam Wilson; and the whole brilliant crew at Pocket Books. Special thanks are due to Carrie Vaughn for years of conversation, analysis, and first reads. Without her, none of this would have even begun.

All failures and infelicities are, of course, my own.

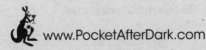

More bestselling
URBAN FANTASY
from Pocket Books!

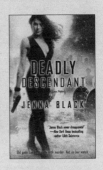

Available wherever books and eBooks are sold.
www.PocketAfterDark.com

POCKET BOOKS
A Division of Simon & Schuster
A CBS COMPANY

30213